G000075277

BLOOD REDEMPTION

Blood Destiny Series, Book 9

Connie Suttle

SubtleDemon Publishing, LLC

To Walter, Joe, Larry, Lee, Dianne, Sarah and Mark.
Thank you.

Acknowledgements

As always, this book is the result of collaboration. If it weren't for the support of my editor, my cover artist and my beta readers, it would be less than it is. All mistakes, as usual, are mine and no other's.

About the Author:

Connie Suttle lives in Oklahoma with her husband and a conglomerate of cats. They have finally banded together to make their demands, which has proven disconcerting to all humans involved.

You may find Connie in the following ways:
Facebook: Connie Suttle Author
Twitter: @subtledemon
Website and Blog: subtledemon.com

Other books by Connie Suttle:

Blood Destiny Series:
Blood Wager
Blood Passage
Blood Sense
Blood Domination
Blood Royal
Blood Queen
Blood Rebellion
Blood War
Blood Redemption

Blood Redemption

Blood Reunion
* * *

Legend of the Ir'Indicti Series:
Bumble
Shadowed
Target
Vendetta
Destroyer
* * *

High Demon Series:
Demon Lost
Demon Revealed
Demon's King
Demon's Quest
Demon's Revenge
Demon's Dream
* * *

God Wars Series:
Blood Double
Blood Trouble
Blood Revolution
Blood Love
Blood Finale
* * *

Saa Thalarr Series:
Hope and Vengeance
Wyvern and Company
Observe and Protect*
* * *

First Ordinance Series:

Finder
Keeper
BlackWing
SpellBreaker
WhiteWing
* * *

R-D Series:
Cloud Dust
Cloud Invasion
Cloud Rebel
* * *

Latter Day Demons Series:
Hot Demon in the City
A Demon's Work is Never Done
A Demon's Due
* * *

Seattle Elementals Series:
Your Money's Worth
Worth Your While*
* * *

BlackWing Pirates Series
MindSighted
MindMage
MindRogue*
* * *

Black Rose Sorceress Series
The Rose Mark
Rose and Thorn*

Other Titles from SubtleDemon Publishing:

Blood Redemption

Malefactor
Transgressor*
by Joe Scholes

*Forthcoming

Chapter 1

A vendor

"Where are you going?" Rabis blinked at the one who stood before him.

"I have to go fishing," the Mighty Hand replied. "Somebody has to reel her in." He disappeared in a brief flash of light.

* * *

Lissa

There is a difference between *Looking* for information and *Looking* into the future. Connegar and I had a talk, once, about *Looking* into the future. "It is never wise to *Look* too far into the future," he'd cautioned. "And it is particularly unwise to *Look* into one's own future, or that of those closest to us, lest we see what will come and precipitate its arrival when we seek to avoid it."

Blood Redemption

True words. Griffin had succumbed to that siren's call, who knows how many times.

"Your father lacks faith," Belen said to me, shortly after I'd come back to myself on Kifirin and found my way back to Earth.

Three hundred years had passed since Griffin had taken me away, and I'd found myself on a planet I barely recognized. I hadn't really considered Belen's words—not until now.

Belen was right, though; Griffin could only feel assured of an outcome if he pulled the strings himself. He couldn't conceive that things might turn out right at the end if he wasn't involved in some way. The fact that Belen had blinded Griffin to Wyatt's future meant one thing to me—that something in Wyatt's future might convince Griffin to interfere again.

Looking is a strange talent to begin with. You can't use it to see everything all at once; you must cast it toward a specific person, event or bit of information. Trying to get everything at once is like using a nuclear bomb to hammer a nail. It's too much, and you can fry your brain that way.

Even then, *Looking* into the future of an event or person is tricky business; you must sort through all possible paths the chosen event or individual might take. Kiarra calls those paths *Possibilities* and *Absolutes*.

Absolutes are a given—something that is locked in and will not change. Those, however, become fewer the farther into the future you *Look*. Otherwise, you deal with *Possibilities*, simply because of all the people and circumstances involved. All of those things might hold sway on something or someone, sending everything in another (and often unexpected) direction.

Chapter 1

Griffin is likely the most adept of the Saa Thalarr at *Looking*, considering the gift of foresight he had from his Elemaiyan mother. Obviously, he is not infallible. Larentii, who also hold the talent, generally find an outcome interesting but they have no desire to interfere. They will observe until the end of time, perhaps mark an event in their minds or record it for their archives, but they will not interfere. I think perhaps something in their past might have brought that lesson home.

Personally, I find *Looking* to be a frightening concept. Why *Look* to see if something terrible is coming when you are sworn not to interfere? You either drive yourself insane with worry or begin to think of ways to skirt the interference rules.

When I am humanoid, my emotions play a part in that. When I am corporeal, I am allowed to protect myself and those around me—with the skills I have. Unless one of The Mighty comes and directs my actions, that is.

So far, I'd only met one of them, and the power he holds is frightening. The Mighty Hand prefers to direct those beneath him, rather than expend a great deal of power himself. I hope I learn the reason for that, someday.

I am thankful too, that Connegar taught me how to form shields early in our relationship. I can do that while I am corporeal, by pulling a portion of the power I hold to create protection—not just for me but for those around me.

The rules of noninterference bind me when I am energy, and I stand to lose everything I have gained if I go too far and affect the timeline. When I am corporeal, I will use everything at my disposal to protect myself and those I care for. Shields are now just another weapon in my arsenal.

Blood Redemption

I considered remaining energy, too, after the debacle at Conclave. How much easier would it be if I allowed my body to die? Why become corporeal again, choosing to slip into a solid body filled to the brim with emotions and pain?

When I began thinking those thoughts, that's when The Mighty Hand showed up.

Again.

* * *

Gryphon Hall, Earth

Lissa

Franklin's soft snore welcomed me back to my body. Yeah, what a thing to come back to, I know. It had taken some nudging from The Mighty Hand (and then yelling, followed by astonishingly creative cursing) but I'd been convinced to come back.

Franklin snored again. It wasn't a loud snore, even by vampire standards. When my eyes unglued enough so I could open them, I found myself staring at the ceiling. Not a familiar ceiling, either. I couldn't recall being in this particular room, before.

The other thing I noticed was the IV line in my hand and a bag of blood hooked up to feed me. Frank (still snoring softly) was sleeping on a chair in a corner.

"Frank, honey, why don't you go to bed?" I tried to keep my voice soft, but it sounded like sandpaper used one time too many on a particularly rough piece of wood.

Three weeks—that's how long my spirit had been separated from my body. I knew that in just a few more days, if I hadn't come back, Kifirin had plans to pull the plug on corporeal Lissa. That would leave only spirit Lissa.

Chapter 1

As much as I might think that would be an improvement at times, I still had some things to do before I left this body behind.

The Mighty Hand reminded me of that when he'd found me flying through the universes. I ignored him at first. That's when he started yelling. After telling him to keep his pants on (that was a joke, we were both energy) he managed to convince me that I was being selfish.

Frank jerked awake at the sound of my voice, and he was at my elbow in a blink.

"Honey, you need to slow down; it's not an emergency," I told him. My voice was slightly better, that time.

Frank has Merrill's piercing blue eyes and jet-black hair, now, just like his fraternal twin, Jeff. They're both healers for the Saa Thalarr, although Franklin has an Engineering degree this time around. His bright-blue eyes were staring at me in surprise as he ran his hands over me, checking for anything that might still be wrong.

"Sometimes I miss how the old Franklin looked," I tried to pat his hand with mine, but it held the IV and the transfusion lines, so Frank just smiled and put my hand back on the bed.

"I know," he told me. "But I have Dad's genes this time, not someone else's," he said. "How are you feeling?"

"Hungry. Does anybody have potato chips?" My request made him laugh. It was night, I knew that much without *Looking*—I don't think you'll ever catch a vampire not knowing whether it's day or night. "Where am I?" That question was the one I really wanted answered.

"Gryphon Hall, little sister," Frank brushed hair away from my forehead. "Adam's ancestral manor. You don't recognize it because you've never seen any of the guest rooms." He ducked his head and a sigh escaped his lips. "We were just about to lose hope."

"I thought about not coming back," I told him truthfully.

"Lissa, don't make my heart stop," Franklin said, frowning at me. "I still have flashbacks of seeing your blackened body floating in a bathtub. I know how I felt then and I didn't like it. Life hasn't treated you well at all, little girl, but something has been squeezing my heart for three weeks now, and it's finally beating at a normal rhythm because you're awake and talking."

"I have a question for you," I reached for his hand and captured it, this time. I squeezed his fingers lightly, too.

"What's that?" he smiled again.

"Why wouldn't you and Greg let Merrill turn you? You know—before?"

"Ah. That." Franklin sighed and looked at the wall for a moment.

"It was Griffin, wasn't it?" I already knew the answer; I just wanted him to say it.

"Yeah, it was Griffin. I knew he saw things," Frank turned his gaze back to me. "I asked him once what he thought I should do. It took a few minutes to get a reply because his eyes lost focus, just as they do when he's *Looking* into the future or something. 'You can allow the turn,' he studied me with those hazel eyes of his, 'and you'll be a vampire. It won't be too bad, but you have a choice to make, Franklin. You can take the easy way and be a vampire and lead an okay life. Or, you can take the hard path, live out this life and die as you normally would—you and Greg both, and wait for the better life to come. It's your choice, young one. But if you could see what I see at the end of the second path,

Chapter 1

that is the way you'd go, I think.' He was right, as it turns out."

"It was a hard path, though, wasn't it?" I watched his face. He looked so much like Merrill it was frightening. I didn't see much of Kiarra there at all.

"It was the hardest path, and I almost caved in when Greg died," Franklin muttered, ducking his head again.

"I wish I'd been there," I sighed. "When can I get these tubes out of me?"

"When Karzac says," I saw a shadow of a smile come back to Franklin's face.

"Well, me and my IV stand may take a little trip to the kitchen, then," I grumped.

"That may not be a good idea," Frank attempted to talk me out of my kitchen-raiding plans.

"Uh-huh," I nodded. "Want me to mist you in there with me?"

"You want me to get in trouble with Karzac, don't you?"

"Well, he'll know you didn't have anything to do with it." I was trying to sit up in bed so I would be partly vertical before taking off.

"Lissa, your body has been practically inert for three weeks—you'll need to build up your strength again," Franklin cautioned. "We've been exercising your arms and legs and turning you during your out-of-body experience, but that's not the same thing."

"You sure know how to take the fun out of everything," I grumped. He was right, though—my arms and elbows were shaking, just from trying to sit up. "Damn," I muttered. "And I wanted something to eat and drink."

"I'll see if I can find something for you," Franklin said, trying to get me back down in the bed.

Blood Redemption

"Why did they put me here? In Gryphon Hall? Isn't there enough room in my overly large palace, somewhere?"

"Well, we need to tell you about that some other time." Franklin was putting me off, I could tell.

"They haven't turned my palace into a casino, have they?" I was just about to come off the bed anyway.

"I think Kifirin would murder everybody if that happened," Franklin replied, fluffing my pillow. "Now, will you sit still while I round up something for you to eat, or do I have to wake someone to watch you while I go to the kitchen?"

"I'll sit still." I wasn't happy, but I didn't want everybody in the house forced out of bed because I wanted a sandwich and a glass of juice.

Frank even had something to eat with me, then threatened to put me in a healing sleep afterward when I told him I wanted to brush my teeth. "Do it with power," he grumped, his arms crossed over his chest.

I cleaned my teeth with a bit of power, and he made sure I hadn't dislodged any of my tubes. Yeah, I hate those things in my hand and arm. Franklin stubbornly sat on his chair, although I tried to get him to go to bed. I even offered to scoot over so he could have the side of my bed. He refused and out-stubborned me to sleep.

* * *

"Liiisssa."

"Huh?" My eyes were refusing to open, like always. My mouth always works first. I'm sure most people I know would prefer things to be just the opposite.

"Thank goodness. We were worried Frank had imagined this." Drake held me against his chest, and Drew was

8

Chapter 1

impatiently waiting for his brother to scoot out of the way when my eyes eventually cooperated.

"Hi, honey," I lifted a hand and stroked Drake's cheek.

"Karzac's on his way," Drew hissed, so Drake handed me over. The stupid tubes were still attached, and I sure hoped Karzac would take the damn things out. Drew leaned down and kissed me while I got babied in his arms. Yeah, I like my Falchani. They put me back in bed just before Karzac walked into the room.

"Lissa is awake and do you send mindspeech?" Karzac could find something to grumble about in any situation, I think.

"Honey, I think I'll buy you a planet," I said.

"Lissa, do we need a psychiatric evaluation?" Karzac had an eyebrow lifted as he came to stand at my bedside.

"Now see, you just proved to me that you can find the flaw in any situation," I pointed a finger at him. Drake and Drew were doing their best not to snicker. "And it's nice to see you, too," I added. "Can I get in the hot tub now?"

"Lissa, please do not force me to slap my forehead. I have watched over your unconscious body for weeks now, and the first things out of your mouth are buying a planet and soaking in a hot tub?" Karzac was shaking his head in disbelief.

"I feel cold," I grumped.

"Then say that, instead of asking to get in the hot tub."

"Damn, no hot tub," I muttered. "Can I get a kiss, at least?" That I got, several times over, with a little mindspeech, too, telling me not to worry him like that again. I also got a big, thick quilt over my bed and the tubes pulled out.

Blood Redemption

"You may get up with assistance for dinner, if you feel well enough. Lunch will be brought in—I'm sure your other mates will come calling." Karzac was sending the IV stand somewhere and getting rid of the used blood bag with a thought. I never asked him what he did with that stuff.

"You could get in bed with me," I mumbled softly.

"Do not tempt me, Lissa," Karzac was very close to shaking a finger, I think. Instead, he sat on the edge of my bed, took my face in his hands and bumped his forehead against mine. "Promise you will not leave me," he whispered. "Promise me."

"If I go, I'll take you with me," I whispered back.

"As long as we talk it over, first," he replied and kissed me again before walking out of the room.

Of course, that left both sides of my bed open, so I was warmed nicely by two well-muscled Falchani. I slept like a lazy lizard in the sun between them.

* * *

Grey Planet

"Dad, I don't like this, and I have no idea what it will do to Lissa." Shadow raked a hand through dark hair as he stared angrily at his father, Raffian Grey, and his grandfather, Glendes, Eldest of Grey House.

"There is nothing to prevent you from having another mate, and Melida of Belancour will give you children," Glendes pointed out. "I have already had a rather lengthy discussion with my daughters—Kyler and Cleo worry about Lissa, too, but she's a vampire, Shadow. She can't help you pass on your talent to future generations of Greys. That's why this is so important."

"Grampa, I don't want any part of this," Shadow huffed.

10

Chapter 1

"This is a viable offer, Shadow, and one I don't want lose," Glendes snapped. "Marid says that other clans are interested, if we don't move in the next few days. Melida's spouse was killed in a raid on Cloudsong—he'd been hired by the King to act as bodyguard and was caught in the ambush that killed the crown prince. Melida lost their child over the stress of that, and now her father is looking to place her with a family who might care for her."

"You act as if I ought to just jump right in bed with her," Shadow cursed expertly after his statement. "Just dump Lissa for somebody who can get pregnant."

"We're not telling you to dump Lissa," Raffian swore briefly to illustrate his point. "Son, you and I both know that Lissa almost left you behind. That she almost left all her mates behind. You can't say she won't do the same thing in the future, either. You need another wife—one who can have children. You have a strong gift and it should be passed to another generation."

"Well, Dad, nobody is guaranteed a continued existence. Besides, what would you do if Mom couldn't have babies? Kick her out of bed in favor of somebody who could?" Shadow didn't want anyone to interfere in his relationships, and it was troubling enough that Lissa had nearly walked away from him and the others.

"That's not what I'm suggesting," Raffian sighed. "We both signed the contract with Grey House to provide heirs. If Shannon couldn't conceive, well," Raffian didn't finish.

Shadow growled in frustration. He'd signed the contract, just as his father pointed out. He was regretting it, now. "What will Melida expect?" he snapped. "I don't love her. I haven't even met her, for the sky's sake. Will she think she's just a brood mare? That's what it sounds like to me."

Blood Redemption

"Son, marriages are arranged between wizard clans all the time, and those usually have no love involved. It's to maintain or strengthen the wizard's gifts. Melida's first marriage was a love match—her father allowed it, although Findal wasn't as wealthy or as talented as others Melida might have married. Marid's stipulation was that Findal join the Belancours instead of staying with his family and bringing Melida to them. I think Melida knows how things stand, now—she's a widow; she has no place with Findal's family and she wants children, though her father says she has no desire to replace Findal in her heart."

"Fine, Dad, why don't you take her, then, and pass on more of those genes you're so proud of?" Shadow snapped. "Because when or if Melida gets pregnant, it will upset Lissa. It's not her fault she can't have children. I've talked with Drake and Drew. I know what her reaction was when she learned Grace was pregnant with Kevis. She demanded that Karzac stay with Grace and raise the baby. She doesn't expect him to visit and she never asks for any of his time. This will drive a wedge between Lissa and me. Why can't either of you see that?"

"You will stop this now," Glendes thundered. The Eldest of Grey House was finally weighing in. "You need to father children, Shadow. It's in the contract you signed with me and with Grey House. Melida is the best offer we've had—she already knows you have one mate and doesn't seem to mind. Anyone else would demand to be your only spouse, and if she didn't, she certainly wouldn't consent to be eclipsed by a Vampire Queen. I suggest you accept this offer within the next three days." Glendes flipped his black robes and folded out of Shadow's workshop.

Chapter 1

"Dad, right now I think I hate you and Grampa both," Shadow growled at Raffian before folding away.

* * *

Queen's Palace, Le-Ath Veronis

Radomir handled the meeting, because Gavin wanted to kill Norian Keef. Norian sat inside Gavin's office at the palace, nervously tapping a foot. That in itself irritated Gavin to the point of red-eyed, lengthy-fanged murder.

Radomir worked to calm Norian while Gavin looked on, mentally considering the many, painful ways Norian might meet his end.

This meeting was only taking place because every ruling member of an Alliance world was given an assignment at the end of each Conclave. Ildevar Wyyld, Founder of the Alliance, along with the twenty members of the Grand Alliance Council, handed out these assignments.

Normally, it was committee assignments. Lissa had been handed the position of Liaison for the Alliance Security Detail—the equivalent of the FBI, CIA and NSA combined on Earth. All Alliance spies and special tactics operatives worked for the ASD and they had been moved, lock, stock and overstuffed barrel, straight to Le-Ath Veronis once the assignment was announced.

The ASD's Director, Norian Keef, thought Lissa was recuperating from wounds received from a battle with several Ra'Ak, after Alliance regulars had failed to take the giant serpents down at the Five Year Conclave.

As he was forced to consult with her before engaging in sensitive missions, Norian expected daily reports on Lissa's status. He was also demanding a meeting with her as early as possible.

Blood Redemption

Lissa had been taken initially to Le-Ath Veronis, but upon the arrival of Norian Keef and the ASD, she'd been secretly moved to Gryphon Hall. Gavin had only received word that Lissa had wakened—he and Lissa's other mates were more than worried that she might not return to her body. Kifirin indicated at the beginning that the final choice was hers.

"While I realize the Alliance voted to allow each member planet to approve their own religions, it is in our best interests to investigate the new ones anyway. We do not need Solar Red or any number of other unhealthy factions to gain a legitimate toehold on any world. Surely you understand this," Norian Keef fumed as he paced in front of Radomir. "I cannot proceed with this covert operation until I have Queen Lissa's permission."

Gavin sat in a corner, wishing he had Gardevik's talent for showing displeasure by blowing smoke from his nostrils. They were all inside the office Gavin shared with Tony, and appointments had been canceled and comesuli chased away from their work just so Norian Keef could vent his frustration.

"Mr. Keef, we are in complete agreement with you regarding this matter. We will not prevent you or your staff from investigating these religions. Lissa will certainly agree with the purpose and intent of this operation, I assure you."

Radomir was becoming impatient with Norian, and that never happened with him. The ASD Director had a way of transferring his restless energy to anyone around him, causing things to remain in a constant state of unease. "Will you not accept our assurances and proceed with your investigations?"

Chapter 1

"But I am bound by law to receive her permission personally, before I can act," Norian was back to pacing. "I cannot accept anyone else's permission; it must be hers and recorded."

Gavin wasn't sure he appreciated the *recorded* part of Norian's words, but didn't voice his concerns aloud. Of the five hundred eighty-six members of the Alliance, forty-eight now had some new religion that needed to be secretly investigated—according to Norian, anyway.

There was also a long list of other Alliance members, all of whom wanted the ASD to investigate the new religions making application to establish themselves on those worlds.

"We will schedule an audience with the Queen for you as quickly as possible," Radomir's face bore the usual, vampiric non-expression. "In the meantime, has everything been done as far as research is concerned? Surely you can proceed with that before approaching the Queen."

"We are reaching the end of our resources where remote research is concerned—we need to have our feet upon the worlds in question," Norian grumbled. "I must meet with the Queen within two days. Please see that this is accomplished." The Director of the ASD all but stomped out of Lissa's study.

"Is there any way we can get her here—for a short meeting?" Radomir turned to Gavin.

"Karzac says she's as weak as a newborn lamb, although she won't admit it," Gavin grumbled. "She could do a short meeting, but short meetings with Norian tend to turn into longer meetings, and that habit he has of unsettling everyone may not be good for Lissa right now."

"Glendes and Raffian are asking for a meeting as well," Radomir stared at his hands. He knew what that meeting was about—Devin and Grace had told him. They'd heard the news from Shannon and Kyler; Grey House couldn't hold that information back. While that information would deliver a blow to Lissa at the best of times, delivering it now would be a hundred times worse. He had no idea why Glendes and Raffian were forcing the issue—surely it could have waited.

Other bad news waited for Lissa as well—Giff still hadn't budged on her desire to keep Yoff away. Rolfe had been unable to convince Giff to change her mind. She had an unnatural fear of bringing her child near Lissa since Toff, Roff's youngest child and Giff's brother, had been abducted while in Lissa's care. Giff didn't want her son anywhere near the Queen. Radomir sighed.

"How will we convince Lissa that coming back to us was a good idea?" Radomir spoke his worries aloud.

"No idea," Gavin muttered and rose from his chair.

* * *

"Child, Lissa had no part in Toff's kidnapping," Roff attempted to convince Giff, who was feeding Yoff tiny pieces of roast chicken while her parent spoke. Roff recognized the open mouth, waiting to be fed like a baby bird. He'd seen it twice with his own children. Yoff's minuscule hands were waving as he fed—he liked chicken already.

"Father, Yoff will not be taken anywhere near the Queen. She will not mean harm, but that does not guarantee it will not happen. Toff's taking was bad enough. My child will be kept as safe as I can keep him," Giff was adamant.

"You are giving up your position with the Queen permanently?"

"The Queen should have replaced me already," Giff snapped. "It is her fault if she has not done so."

"You are placing blame on the wrong one," Roff sighed.

16

Chapter 1

"No, I blame those others just as much—Rolfe has taken me several times to watch Toff from a distance—I did not wish to go among those heathen Fae if I could help it. I saw them eyeing my baby pouch while I stood outside their village." Giff's face held anger as well as pain.

"They are not used to humanoids reproducing as we do—it was curiosity, nothing more."

"I don't care what it was. They're not coming near Yoff, either. They've stolen one member of our family already. They won't get another."

"Do you think the Queen doesn't love you?" Roff's voice was gentle.

It was Giff's turn to sigh, and she hung her head. "Father, I cannot fault her in that respect. She loves us, I know, and even though I have not given her any effort, my wages still come, and she has sent me generous allowances for clothing and anything else I want or need. You should tell her to stop—Rolfe takes care of me, now."

"And what does Rolfe say about this?"

"He says I am overreacting," Giff turned away from her father. "I can't help the way I feel, though. I don't want anything to happen to Yoff."

"I was overprotective of you as well," Roff agreed. "You were my first and will always be my first. It is my hope that when Toff comes to adulthood, he will realize who he is and how he came to be where he is, and then make decisions accordingly. That is what keeps me going—hope."

"Then I will hope as well, father, but do not blame me if my hope is not as strong as yours. I believe that Toff is lost to us for all time."

"What do you think this will do to the Queen, when she learns you will never allow her to see Yoff?"

Blood Redemption

"She will hate me. And that is for the best, Father."

* * *

Gryphon Hall

"Could this not wait?" Karzac eyed Raffian, who looked guilty. Glendes had no expression. "She is very weak, in the physical sense. I have no idea what her mental state is, and she won't let any of us get close enough to find out."

"We have to take an answer to Melida's father tomorrow. I did not wish to convey our acceptance without giving the information to Lissa, first. Shadow isn't speaking to either of us at the moment, so we couldn't ask him to come and tell her."

"Then perhaps this isn't in the best interest of either of them—have you thought about that?" Karzac barked. "All you are doing is pointing out the glaring fault—as you see it, anyway—in Lissa. She is more than aware that she cannot have children. It did a great deal of damage when she learned that Grace was pregnant with Kevis. Now, you want to bring in a replacement for her."

"We're not trying to replace her," Raffian replied after cursing under his breath for a moment. "We are trying to make sure Grey House continues with the level of talent that we currently have. Melida is from a strong family of wizards. We have to take this opportunity while we have it."

"Lissa does not ask me to come to her. Or do anything for her. She also does not come to me—for any reason," Karzac sighed. He was regretting his refusal to climb into bed with her when she asked after waking. It was the first time she'd made a request since learning Grace was pregnant.

Lissa hadn't asked again, and Karzac had not failed to notice. He'd been the one to make the overture—every time.

Chapter 1

"If you think this will not drive a wedge between Lissa and Shadow," Karzac continued, "then you need to think again."

"That is not our intention, but we have no control over the emotions of others," Glendes spoke for the first time.

"You think not? Drop this now and Lissa will remain with Shadow. Bring this to her and see how things turn out." Karzac whirled and strode off angrily.

* * *

Lissa

"Lissa, Glendes and Raffian are here to see you." Kiarra had come into my borrowed bedroom at Gryphon Hall while I was dressing. I'd gotten cleaned up by myself, though Karzac had told me to wait for him to help.

I was still shaky and weak, but it was only because my body hadn't done anything while I'd traveled as energy across the universes. I knew that if I dropped my body right then and there, I'd feel strong again. I had to shove that thought aside—there were things out there waiting for me—things that I could deal with only in a solid body.

"Is something wrong? Is Shadow all right?" My heart stuttered into a gallop at the thought.

"Shadow is fine, I believe; they only wish to talk to you," Kiarra replied, ducking her head. Well, if somebody isn't looking you in the eye, that means something is wrong. I was afraid to *Look*, now, to see what that something might be.

"Do you need help getting to the kitchen?" Kiarra asked. "Adam and Merrill are both here, or I can call someone else."

"I'll get myself there," I muttered. I did, although my legs felt like rubber when I arrived in Kiarra's beautiful kitchen. Adam kept it updated for her; I recognized his work.

Glendes and Raffian were already there, having a cup of tea while they waited on me. Neither one was smiling as I entered. Kiarra was walking as close to me as she could without putting hands directly on me. Well, this didn't look good. Not good at all.

"Glendes, Raffian," I nodded to them, sliding onto one of the many barstools positioned around the kitchen island. Glendes and Raffian sat adjacent to me as Kiarra offered me something to drink. I declined. She took the stool next to mine and sat down with me.

"What's this about?" I said, right off. "Where is Shadow?"

"Shadow is working," Raffian replied. "We left him in his workshop this morning."

"Lissa, I want to preface our news with this—we do not wish to harm your relationship with Shadow in any way," Glendes said. "But it is in the best interest of Grey House for all our Master Wizards to have children, to ensure that Grey House remains as strong as it is. All our Master Wizards sign a contract with Grey House, when they are elevated to Master Wizard status. They are obligated to provide heirs who will carry on the Grey House tradition at the level of wizardry that is expected. We have received an offer from a neighboring wizard clan—and the match would be a good one for Shadow to have children. That is our goal in all this— for there to be children from this proposed union."

Honestly, I might have taken a direct punch in the face better than this. So many things raced through my brain at that moment, and all of them scattered, much like a flock of crows might before I could get a decent grip on any one of them.

"And how did you think this wouldn't damage our relationship?" I asked as calmly as I could when my breath

Chapter 1

came back. "And how will the other party react? Does she know that Shadow and I have been together?"

"She knows. She has no expectations," Raffian replied.

"No expectations?" That had to be a bald-faced lie. How could any woman approach a union, arranged or otherwise, with no expectations?

"You expect her to play second fiddle in all this? She's the one who'll provide the heirs. Doesn't that imply expectations?" I was standing now, and breathing with difficulty. "And how do you think Shadow's children are going to react, when they see how their mother is treated in all this? You are both fools if you think they won't resent that."

I was struggling to pull rings off my right index finger—Shadow's was in the middle. I finally got to it and slapped it down on the island in front of Glendes and Raffian. "There," I snapped, as strongly as I could muster breath to do it. "Shadow is free. He can do whatever he damn well pleases." I misted away.

* * *

"She's right, you know," Kiarra said, standing up. "About the children's feelings and the expectations. I have no idea if you planned this, Raffian Grey, but I have to tell you that I was right, all those years ago, to break the M'Fiyah between us. I wasn't guaranteed children then, either. And let me tell you, I would have kicked your ass before leaving, if you'd dumped this on me." Kiarra folded away.

Raffian reached out and drew the ring toward him with a finger. Shadow had crafted it himself, of gold and Tiralian crystal. It held a protection jewel—tuned to Lissa. No other would be able to wear it. "Dad, we've fucked this up pretty good," he sighed. "We just destroyed the relationship between Shadow and his mate."

"That wasn't our intention—we told her that at the beginning," Glendes tried to defend himself, although he was now realizing that this might have been handled differently.

Lira, his wife, had told him before he left Grey House that Lissa was fragile and he shouldn't be handling this. He should be allowing Shadow to approach Lissa at a more appropriate time. Now, he and Raffian were going to have to explain how they'd managed to destroy Shadow's union with the Queen of Le-Ath Veronis.

Chapter 2

Harifa Edus
    Lissa

"Lara'Kayan, they did not intend to hurt you. Not like this." Thurlow could find me. *Fuck*. I was sitting on a rocky outcropping overlooking a river on the northern continent of Harifa Edus.

My perch was far from the werewolf settlements—they wouldn't know I was there and sobbing my heart out. Thurlow, well, he didn't know when to leave well enough alone. I was shivering, too, although Harifa Edus was in early summer.

Thurlow wasn't touching me—he'd held back, much of the time. We had history, he and I, and he was waiting for forgiveness. I didn't know if it would ever come.

Blood Redemption

"Thurlow, not in the mood for company," I sobbed, hugging myself as hard as I could in an attempt to stop the shivering.

"But you are cold, love. And shaking because your body is weak. Allow me to help you, somehow." He was begging, but I wasn't in any mood to accept his comfort.

"F-fine," I stuttered. "F-find me an engineer for Le-Ath Veronis. We have a v-vacancy," I forced out. That had been Shadow's job. Until now.

"Lissa, I meant with you. Here and now."

"I kn-know what you meant," I muttered, wiping my face with a shaking hand.

* * *

Grey Planet

"Son, we just got back from seeing Lissa," Raffian was almost afraid to approach Shadow; he was pounding on a vise with a hammer, when he could have easily bent the thing back into alignment with power. Shadow gave the metal vise one last ringing blow with his hammer before looking up at his father.

"Well?" Shadow's growl would have made any vampire proud. He didn't want any part of this, but he'd signed the agreement with his Grandfather, just as all the other Master Wizards had. Glendes held the reins on this.

Raffian drew the ring from his pocket and held it out to Shadow on the palm of his hand. "Thanks, Dad," Shadow looked ready to crumble. "Thanks for fucking this up beyond repair." Shadow folded away, leaving his father standing in his workshop, his hand still extended.

* * *

Chapter 2

"Is this what you wanted?" Lira was as angry as she'd ever been with Glendes. "You wanted to break them up over this?" Lira's voice nearly cracked, she was so upset.

"No, I did not want to break them up," Glendes wanted to tug his hair out by the roots. "I have a responsibility to Grey House, Lira."

"And if I hadn't been capable of bearing children, Glendes? Would you have rubbed that in my face like this?"

"Lira, I would expect you to understand—you are from a wizard clan. I wouldn't have cared as much for any other— you know that. We have the linking, you and I. I doubt that it can be recreated with any other."

"Well, you have just sentenced your grandson to life without that. Haven't you? He won't love Melida. Not as he loves Lissa. Lissa is stepping aside for Melida's children. Surely even you can see that, Glendes. And now, if Shadow has children with Melida—he'll see them as the reason he doesn't have Lissa. How do you think that will make them feel? That he resents them?"

"They will have other family," Glendes grumbled.

"Not like their father. You think they won't feel that absence, Glendes? When he's right there in front of them, and still remote?" Lira turned away from her mate. "I'm going shopping. And you'll be sleeping alone for a while." Lira folded away.

* * *

Harifa Edus
Lissa
Thurlow knew to leave the moment Kifirin appeared. Smoke was already pouring from his nostrils, so Thurlow folded away as quickly as he could. I was still shivering and crying, and my chest hurt.

Blood Redemption

"Avilepha, they had no right to do this to you." Kifirin sat beside me and drew me into his arms. His body was hotter than normal—he was doing that for me. His hand went to my chest, too, and heat flooded in. I couldn't hold back the painful sob that came. "Hush, now." I was enveloped in Kifirin's embrace.

* * *

Queen's Palace, Le-Ath Veronis

"Kifirin is with her," Thurlow walked into an impromptu meeting of Lissa's mates. Rigo had found his way inside as well, though Lissa had still not accepted him. Karzac had arrived with Drake and Drew, bearing the news of what Grey House had done.

"You cannot blame Shadow—he didn't want this," Drake said. "All Master Wizards are required to sign a binding oath with Glendes, for the protection of Grey House and to produce heirs, if they are able. Shadow is able; therefore, Glendes and Raffian chose to take this opportunity, if you can call it that. They didn't want this to turn out the way it did, either, but it would have come as a blow to Lissa anytime it was put forward. They just chose the worst possible time. She is very weak right now, in a physical sense."

"She gave his ring back? Then it is over, as far as Lissa is concerned." Gavin knew her. He also knew about Aryn. He'd figured it out quickly, actually. Tony knew as well, but they were keeping the secret for the moment.

He suspected that Lissa also knew. She was not making any advances, although Aryn's eyes followed her whenever she was near. Rigo also wanted her so badly he was about to go crazy. And this thing with Shadow—he was worried now that Lissa might turn them all out.

Chapter 2

Erland and Garde listened while the others talked. Gardevik was angry—extremely so. The Grey House Wizards were fools—they could have found a surrogate—there were plenty of options open to them. Shadow could provide sperm and a donor egg could be manipulated with some of Lissa's DNA to produce a child. In fact, he'd been considering it himself, as had Erland. That way, the child would have some of Lissa's genes, in addition to his or any other of Lissa's mates who chose to pursue that option.

A child could be had, if Lissa wanted. Grey House refused to consider it, however, preferring in the long term to upset Lissa and force Shadow to take a mate he didn't want. If it were the wizard's talent they hoped for, what did they think Lissa's talents might do? She was a quarter Karathian witch and a quarter Bright Elemaiya. Glendes was shortsighted in the extreme. Smoke curled from Garde's nostrils.

"I know what you're thinking, my friend, and I am in total agreement," Erland said softly. "Wylend was prepared to go in that direction before he learned his son was alive, and then Wyatt was born shortly after. If that had not happened, Wylend would still have obtained an heir."

"We will make Lissa the mother she wishes to be, if she consents," Garde agreed.

"Wylend wants a great-grandson from Lissa very much," Erland nodded. "He wishes to see how powerful he might be." Erland was smiling—few knew how powerful Erland was. Wylend knew. Combine that with Lissa's talents and the result could be amazing.

"Shall we search for two surrogates, instead of one?" A mischievous glint appeared in Gardevik's eyes.

Blood Redemption

"We could get both at the same time." Erland was becoming excited at the prospect. All they had to do was convince Lissa.

* * *

"My love," Kifirin kissed me carefully. The tears had finally stopped, but it had taken some time. I was convincing myself that I would find a way to live without Shadow. My heart still hurt, and there would be more tears. I had to get past that. Shadow's children deserved the best they could get, as did the mother who bore them.

"Lissa," Kifirin brought my attention back to him.

"Honey?" I realized he had something to say to me. Blinking away tears, I gazed into his dark eyes. This was one of those times when they were filled with stars. I could lose myself in those eyes, if I let myself go.

"Gardevik Rath and Erland Morphis will come to you with a proposal very soon. Say yes, avilepha."

"What are they going to ask for?" I didn't want to say yes if I didn't know what I was agreeing with.

"You will learn of it soon enough. Now, you should come with me to Le-Ath Veronis. Much work waits for you there."

"Yeah. I was afraid of that," I muttered with only a hint of sarcasm in my voice. Kifirin had been feeding me energy the entire time he'd held me. I wasn't nearly as weak as I'd been before. I just had to find a way to deal with my life—living without my wizard. I wanted to cry again, just thinking about it.

"They will regret their decision one day," Kifirin nuzzled my temple, before placing warm lips against it. "While you may not have kept track of all who have mistreated you, I will not be so generous."

Chapter 2

Surprisingly, Kifirin folded me to Casino City. We walked down one of the main thoroughfares, taking in the sights. I hadn't been in this part before—I'd only been to the landing station, where the shuttles delivered tourists and gamblers from the space station. And then inside the Chessman, Adam's casino, for a party honoring his and Kiarra's anniversary. Actually, the Chessman was three blocks away from the street where Kifirin and I walked. My hand was tucked in the crook of Kifirin's elbow as I stared around me.

"Honey, this makes me want ice cream," I said as we strolled brick-lined streets amid exclusive little shops and boutiques. "Or a cookie," I added. It did. Either of those things sounded good.

"There are no shops offering either," Kifirin smiled down at me and patted my arm. "You could open them, love. That would be a ready income for you, to use any way you pleased."

"It would, wouldn't it?" I agreed with him. I still had the funds that had been turned over to me—money that had originally come from Sergio Velenci, which Merrill had invested. A tidy sum in the beginning, it had grown exponentially since then and had been recently moved to a bank on Le-Ath Veronis.

I was running through this in my mind—I could open sweet shops and sell fresh baked cookies and ice cream made onsite. Maybe brownies or other goodies. Visitors flocked to Casino City; they'd buy, I think.

"I'm going to do this," I breathed. "I just need to find someone to run all this for me."

"Many would leap at the chance," Kifirin agreed. "They will come to you, avilepha. I know they will."

Blood Redemption

* * *

Kifirin and I sneaked into my study later and pored over a map of Casino City with Grant and Heathe, both of whom gave me a big hug when I arrived. I knew Kifirin was distracting me from the Shadow debacle, but it was working for the moment. I just wasn't looking forward to the time when Kifirin left, as he invariably did. I'd have to face my other mates, then.

How had things come to this? How? Glendes and Raffian had known what I was when Shadow made his proposal in the beginning. They were throwing a wrench into the works now, instead of at the start of our relationship. I didn't understand this at all.

"Avilepha, you are wandering away from me," Kifirin touched my face gently and drew me back to the map. I sighed as I examined available spaces in the shopping districts of Casino City.

"This one," Grant pointed out a shop that had recently come up for sale—it was a jewelry and souvenir shop—one of many on the same street, and couldn't compete with its neighbors. It was large enough, too, to house a bakery in the back, plus ice cream machines.

"Grant, can you and Heathe get on that for me? Ask the sellers to quote a price, and make sure they're not gouging. That looks like the perfect spot to open our first business." I looked at both my assistants—Heathe was grinning—he was excited about this, I could tell.

And, since both of them could now eat normal food if they wanted, well, so much the better. Grant was already planning this out in his head—I recognized the signs of turning wheels.

Chapter 2

"I think you should name it Niff's; that is what Gardevik and the others were calling you when you woke among the High Demons," Kifirin teased me gently.

"Yeah, that's better than Queenie's any day," I agreed. "And we can use my cookie recipes."

"If you sell apple pie, you'll have people lined up at the door," Grant sighed. He loved apple pie.

"We'll sell apple pie and you can eat what we don't sell," I gave him a hug. We settled on half interest for me and a quarter interest each for Grant and Heathe. It made me miss Davan—I think he would have loved to be a part of this.

"Lissa, I must go," Kifirin leaned in to kiss me. "I will return in a few days and I will spend the night." He bumped his forehead against mine. Nights with Kifirin were sporadic at best, so I wasn't about to tell him no, even though I wasn't in the mood to have anybody else in my bed at the moment.

Karzac would have a screaming fit anyway, I think, if I considered sex with anybody until he said otherwise. I just nodded, gave Kifirin a kiss back and stared at the space he'd occupied when he disappeared.

"What is this? You come back and do not inform us?" Gavin, Tony, Garde, Winkler, Drake and Drew all folded in. It made me wonder where Erland and Roff were, but then Roff was probably at the winery.

I hadn't seen my Larentii, either, but I didn't question what kept them—probably big Larentii secrets or something. Rigo and Thurlow appeared moments later, while Gavin stared at me, his arms crossed over his chest.

"Honey, things haven't gone well since I woke up," I muttered, hanging my head. If Kifirin hadn't come to get me on Harifa Edus and fed me his energy, I might not have made it off the planet. He'd helped with my misery, too, but it had only been tabled for the moment. I expected it to come calling again very soon, when I had time for it to catch up with me again.

"We heard about Shadow." Drake and Drew didn't sound happy about that, but they'd been friends with Shadow before I came along.

"I'm not going to interfere with your friendship," I muttered.

"We know that, but you ought to talk to him—he's really upset," Drew told me. "Baby, he had a meltdown when Raffian took your ring back. Now he won't speak to anyone from Grey House."

"Uh-huh. What am I supposed to do about that? Good old Dad and Granddad saw fit to tell me, in the nicest way possible, that I wasn't a fit mate, so they had to bring in reinforcements. All while saying they'll treat the reinforcement like crap just so they can get heirs out of the whole thing. That really made my day." I was just about to walk away from the rest of my mates, right then and there. Honestly—how did they think I was going to feel about all this?

"Lissy, they didn't handle this very well. If they were going to do this, they should have done it at the beginning, instead of blind-siding you with it two years later." That was Tony talking, and he was voicing my concern over the whole thing. Why wouldn't they say something right away? I didn't understand at all.

"You have a lot to discuss with your, uh, mates," Grant rolled up the map we'd spread across my desk. "Heathe and I will get to work on this project, and report back to you later."

Grant and Heathe sidled out the door, which allowed someone else to walk in—someone I didn't recognize. Gavin

Chapter 2

rubbed the space between his eyebrows—his signal that this wasn't in the plans.

"There you are," the new arrival announced. "I have been waiting weeks and had assurances that I would be notified as soon as you were up and around, yet here you are, holding a meeting and I come across it by accident." His fists were on his hips in angry indignation.

I stared at him, most likely openmouthed. Nervous energy radiated off him, otherwise he might be quite pleasant. He was around five-ten or so, with medium-brown hair, green eyes and a nice nose. Actually, his nose was his nicest feature. That didn't mean I knew a single thing about him, including his name.

"I'm sorry, have we been introduced?" I asked, as politely as I could.

"No! We have not been introduced. In fact, I've been informed that your health was not sufficient for you to meet with me. Please explain the miraculous recovery."

"You expect me to explain myself to you?" I'd been leaning against my desk, but that brought me upright in a hurry. Garde was already blowing smoke and scowling at the new guy.

"Look, I really don't have time for explanations," new guy growled. "All I know is that Solar Red is disguising itself as a legitimate religion on Twylec and people are dying. Since their Queen was killed on Nemizan by those monsters, her cousin has been trying to run that world, but word is he's dying, too. That doesn't include the rumors that Satris and the former Queen accepted money to allow Solar Red to set up shop, or any number of other things that have come to my attention. And that is only the barest tip of that mountain. There are dozens of other reports, and I have to sit here, with

33

my staff and my agents, waiting for you to get off your ass and give permission for me to do something about it." New guy wasn't mincing words. I wasn't about to mince anything, either, except for a few Solar Red, maybe.

"You say Solar Red is on Twylec?" I'd expected as much, but then I hadn't been conscious since the Conclave, except for the past two days, that is. "Come on, then." I misted to him, grabbed his arm and folded him straight to Twylec. If Kifirin hadn't given me some of his strength, I'd never have been able to do what I did.

New guy got tossed onto the floor of Solar Red's huge new temple in the capital city of Rolanthis, and then he watched while I went to mist and blew the whole thing up around him, allowing huge blocks of marble, brick, stone and other building materials to rain down on four hundred Solar Red priests.

Sure, they tried to run, but the building collapsed too fast. It was such a tragedy that the murderous assholes were all crushed to death.

When I was satisfied the priests were dead, I destroyed the floor surrounding new guy. He found himself standing on a small island of tile near the center, with the dungeons beneath the temple exposed.

New guy wobbled to keep his balance as he stared into the dark depths of Solar Red's torture chambers. As usual, their victims were imprisoned there. I gathered new guy into my mist and we pulled all the victims into my mist as well, delivering them to the nearest medical facility afterward.

Doctors and other personnel were running and shouting as thirty former prisoners were dropped off in their emergency department. New guy was then folded back to Le-Ath Veronis; I landed him in the same spot where he'd stood only minutes before. I'd just used up everything that Kifirin had given me and almost dropped in the floor when I rematerialized.

"There, you stupid schmuck. I hope that's all you wanted to do today, because my energy just ran out," I breathed. I must have fainted after that, because I don't remember anything past that statement.

* * *

"If you did not represent the Alliance, I would have you locked in a cell downstairs." Gavin gripped Norian Keef's shirtfront tightly and hissed the threat in Norian's face.

"I didn't expect her to do anything like that," Norian's voice was only a whisper, but it held a reverence that even he didn't recognize.

"She doesn't have the strength to go haring about, yet," Karzac appeared, causing Norian's eyebrows to rise even further than they had already. "If Kifirin hadn't transferred some of his energy to her, she wouldn't have been able to stand upright. Yet you guilt her into going after Solar Red priests before her body is capable of doing so. You disgust me," Karzac growled.

"I didn't know how weak she was," Norian was having trouble breathing—Gavin's grip was quite strong.

Drake and Drew had Lissa—well, Drake held Lissa and Drew was trying to bring her back to consciousness while the others crowded around. Thurlow was doing his best to get to her, for some reason.

"Gavin, you'll strangle him if you don't let go." Winkler attempted to get Gavin's attention. It worked—once Norian began to turn a deep shade of blue. Norian gasped for breath and struggled to draw air into his lungs the moment Gavin released him.

"Maybe you ought to go to the kitchens and get a cup of tea, or a stiff brandy," Winkler suggested, baring his teeth and growling. The werewolf was threatening and Winkler was about to give Norian a head start before turning.

Norian nodded, straightened his clothing and walked out of Lissa's study with as much dignity as he could muster.

"Let's take Lissa to her suite," Karzac ordered, and someone folded them away.

* * *

"What happened?" Roff was frightened when he saw the knot of people surrounding Lissa's bed.

"I believe she went to Twylec and blew up the Solar Red temple," Thurlow said softly. He and Rigo were still on the perimeter of the large group of males surrounding Lissa's bed. "It took all the energy she had, and she wouldn't have had that if Kifirin hadn't given it to her. She was upset earlier over the thing with the Grey House Wizards, and now this. She wasn't in any shape to do this. Not now, anyway."

"What happened with Grey House?" Roff hadn't heard.

"Nothing good—for Lissa, anyway," Rigo muttered. He thought the entire episode was cruel and thoughtless.

"Perhaps you should tell me." Roff led both of them to the hall outside Lissa's suite.

* * *

Grey Planet

"Shannon, what are you doing?" Raffian watched as Shannon threw clothing into a trunk. She was angry and Raffian knew it.

"Packing, Raffian Grey. When did you stop using common sense? You can see well enough what I'm doing." Shannon tossed an armload of clothing into the trunk, not even bothering to fold any of it.

Chapter 2

"And just where are you going?"

"To the beach house. Jeff and the others are waiting for me. Shadow is our son, Raffian. If you had any sense at all, you'd realize that Shadow and Lissa both needed to be introduced to anybody you wanted to include in their relationship, and both would have to approve before you did this. You treated them like misbehaving children instead, handing out orders because your father said so." Shannon slammed the lid of her trunk angrily.

"When are you coming back?"

"Maybe never." Shannon leveled a gaze at Raffian. "I never thought I'd say this about you or your father, but you're both idiots." Shannon blew a stray strand of hair away from her face and folded away right in front of Raffian, her trunk disappearing simultaneously.

* * *

"The contract has already been signed with the Belancour Clan; I don't care what anyone else thinks." Glendes had been backed into a corner, and he wasn't about to admit any error or give up easily. "Melida will be here by the end of the week. Her father is coming and he expects to see a union of some sort."

"I was hoping Lissa would be here to welcome her," Raffian grumbled. "How were we to know she was so damned sensitive about not being able to have babies? Have you gone over the contract completely? Is there anything in there that we should be concerned about?"

"It's just the usual—she agrees to provide heirs and gives up any rights to them if she chooses to leave after they're born. We take on any of her outstanding debts, but there's nothing there to speak of. They're not providing a dowry; Marid, Melida's father, held back on that, since

Shadow is mated already. I said it didn't matter; that's not what we were after, anyway."

"We only want the children. I just hope Shadow is able to do his duty," Raffian grumbled.

"Melida's pretty enough," Glendes sighed. "Still, it may take a while."

"Shannon's gone," Raffian said.

"She'll come back."

"I hope you're right."

* * *

King's Palace, Karathia

"I was planning to ask Poradina," Wylend looked across his desk at Erland while he sipped his morning tea. "She is more than willing, and the money would not go amiss, either. Both her children are grown, and Zellar left her with nothing, as you know."

"I still don't understand how he could abandon her like that and clean out her banking account when he did it." Erland was shaking his head. "And we both know he has broken our laws—many times."

"I would hold him accountable, if we could find him," Wylend grumbled. Zellar hadn't been seen for two hundred years. Poradina had been forced to work for others, doing menial tasks and low-level spells to support herself. If she agreed to act as surrogate to Erland and Lissa, the funds to reestablish herself would be provided.

"I want to approach Lissa's Larentii, to see if they will assist. I would like for this child to have as much of Lissa as we can provide in the egg."

"They would be capable, I'm sure, but the question is how willing they will be to help." Wylend set his cup on its saucer.

Chapter 2

"I intend to find out," Erland said.

"You have my blessings, either way," Wylend said. "I will be most interested in how strong and talented a child of this union might be." Wylend smiled at the thought.

* * *

Palace Kitchen, Le-Ath Veronis

"Cheedas, tell me about your Queen." Norian hadn't thought to ask one of the comesuli before, but he was correcting that mistake now.

Norian had gone to the kitchen as instructed, and the cook and several of his assistants put a plate of food together for the Director of the ASD. Norian had eaten while reflecting on what he'd seen earlier.

Queen Lissa had gotten him to Twylec in less than a blink. She then proceeded to destroy the Solar Red temple somehow, in addition to all its priests, and then hauled torture victims to a hospital for medical care.

She'd collapsed after bringing him back—she didn't have the strength to do what she did. He knew that, now; she was still recovering.

"What do you wish to know?" Cheedas, head chef in the Queen's kitchens, sat on a stool at the wide, granite island with a cup of tea as he scrutinized Norian Keef. Cheedas also held a position in Lissa's Second Circle; he proudly wore the silver Claw Crown ring she'd given him.

"I have seen her do things that I might have said were impossible, before."

Cheedas snorted softly at Norian's words. "I'm sure you have barely touched the surface of that ocean," he replied. "Few know exactly what our Queen is, or what she means to us. I watched those proceedings at the Conclave. I saw how my Queen was mistreated. Ungrateful *difiks*."

Blood Redemption

"Yes. I am in agreement with that." Norian had been on Le-Ath Veronis long enough to know what difik meant. "Do you know how long it will take for her to recover? I really need her help, I think."

"Ask her healer mate. He will know," Cheedas sipped his tea.

"What is his name?" Norian hadn't seen that particular mate until earlier that evening.

"Karzac. He was Refizani, once," Cheedas said. "We had no idea how little medical knowledge we had until he and a few others came to teach us. I have become friends with Orliff, who is chief physician for the comesuli. He is grateful for the teaching he has received since we came to Le-Ath Veronis. He works at the main hospital on the light side of the planet and is doing very well."

"I haven't been there, yet," Norian observed.

"You should go—it is quite beautiful. I have a sunlamp in my quarters but it is not the same. I sometimes go to the ocean on my off-days; the Queen allows anyone who works in the palace to use her beach house, there. It is quite peaceful. I think she would allow you to stay there as well, if you asked."

"I'm not sure about that," Norian stared into his teacup. "If nothing else, I think her mates might object."

"That is why you need to ask the Queen yourself. Let her decide. Her mates will only be thinking about her and no others."

"I heard one of them wasn't thinking about her."

"That was not him, but his father and grandfather," Cheedas grumped. "Shadow loves the Queen. His father and grandfather are thinking of other things. This will turn out

Chapter 2

badly for them, I think, but that is only an old cook talking." Cheedas slipped off his stool. "Do you wish for dessert?"

"No, thank you. I am quite satisfied," Norian nodded to Cheedas.

"Leave your plate, then; my assistants will take care of it." Cheedas handed his cup to one of those assistants and walked out of the kitchen.

* * *

Lissa

"Lissa? Thank goodness. She's waking."

Those were the words I woke to—and I was completely disoriented when I did wake. I barely recognized Winkler's voice; he appeared to be talking to someone else. I was attempting to sort out the scents.

"Lissa, wake and eat, love, or I will be forced to administer another transfusion." Karzac spoke now, and my eyes popped open in pure self-defense. "Ah, I knew that would bring her around if nothing else would."

I blinked, bringing Winkler and Karzac into focus. Gavin, Garde, Erland and the others were standing behind those two. Except Shadow. My wizard wasn't there, and wasn't likely to ever be there. Not anymore. I wanted to cry.

"Lissa, you must put that out of your mind and come to the kitchens. We need to get your body back in condition. While a vampire will recover faster than anyone else, this will still take a few days, I think." Karzac moved Winkler away and sat on the side of my bed. He lifted my hand and kissed it.

"Honey, you haven't been here all this time, have you?" I didn't want to take any of Karzac's time away from little Kevis. He was six months old, now. As was Wyatt. Yeah, I had a little brother I'd barely seen. I wondered if I were behaving badly over that.

"Lissa, it matters not how long I've been here. Grace and Kevis are not being mistreated. They are with Mack and Justin at the Strawberry Farm. I spent most of the night there, with them. Now are you satisfied?" Karzac was lifting an eyebrow—my signal that he was done with the discussion.

The Strawberry Farm was on the light half of Le-Ath Veronis—we'd moved one of Kiarra and Adam's old homes there before it was knocked down in Fresno roughly two hundred years in the past. It was the home their son, Justin, had grown up in and he and some of the others frequented it.

They often came to the palace for meals when they were visiting, too. Even Kiarra, Adam, Merrill and Pheligar came every few weeks. It had turned into a good decision to move the house, the garages and the guesthouse to Le-Ath Veronis from Fresno's past.

"Then let's go to the Strawberry Farm for breakfast," I suggested. "Unless you don't think that's a good idea." I didn't want to barge in on Grace and the others.

"Lissa, you would be most welcome there, but we have to get you up and dressed, first," Karzac leaned in to give me an arm so I could pull myself up. I still felt shaky, and everybody was going to see *that*.

"I will help her shower." Roff elbowed his way past the others, which surprised me. Roff was now a stronger, more confident Roff, since becoming vampire. His wings were tucked tightly against his body—Tony had informed me that Roff was able to use them as weapons at times—he and Gavin had started teaching Roff fighting skills.

Chapter 2

"Honey, I'm glad to see you." I held out my arms and Karzac moved aside quickly so I could get a hug from my former comesula.

"Not as glad as I to see you," Roff mumbled into my hair while he gave me a series of kisses wherever his mouth wandered.

Flavio was giving him more and more freedom, I'd noticed. Roff still spent nights at Flavio's manor, but he spent much of his waking hours at the winery or with Giff, his brother Markoff and his nephew Dariff.

I wanted to ask him about Giff, but held off for the moment. Instead, Roff lifted me and carried me toward my walk-in shower.

Chapter 3

Strawberry Farm, Le-Ath Veronis
Lissa

I was having breakfast with my mate posse plus Grace, Kevis, Justin and Mack when the news update appeared on the vid screen. We'd been watching the local news—not much new on that front, until this.

"We have been unable to determine by any means available, just what has caused so much devastation on Twylec."

The journalist was standing in front of the Solar Red temple I'd destroyed. "While the former Queen received payment from Solar Red to set up this temple under a false name, many local residents were not deceived."

"My brother was tortured—he's in the hospital now," a teary-faced young woman spoke to the camera. "We all knew what this was the minute they set up and people began to disappear. They were protected by the crown."

"Tamaritha made a mistake," Satris, the newly crowned king of Twylec declared to another journalist. "But the religion was so firmly entrenched when I came to the throne that I knew it would be next to impossible to rid ourselves of it. I received death threats from them if I didn't cooperate, as did many of my staff."

"Did you notify the Alliance Security Detail?" The journalist asked. Satris went into a coughing fit, and his assistant waved the camera off. The feed cut back to the original journalist standing outside the remains of the temple.

"The locals are preparing a low-key celebration over the demise of Solar Red and the legitimate religions are assisting in this. They also continue to search for any records concerning the hundreds of citizens who have been reported missing since Solar Red came to Twylec. This is Jandel Santiz, reporting for news twenty-two."

"I hope they have someone ready to take Satris's place when he croaks," Mack growled, his dark eyes expressing anger. He was Martin Walters' son, through and through. Not just in looks, but temperament, too. He wanted fair treatment for everyone, just as his father did.

"Have you seen the news, Lissa?" Jeral folded in with Aurelius. They'd become very good friends and spent a lot of time together, when they weren't on assignment. Jeral had taken quickly to dispensing justice for the Saa Thalarr. Aurelius, too, was helping him through Davan's death.

I wanted to sigh as Davan's image appeared in my mind. I missed him terribly. "Uncle Jeral, how are you?" I asked

Chapter 3

instead. He came to stand beside me, bending slightly to give me a peck on the cheek.

Aurelius did the same, and he offered a smile with the kiss. "And I just saw the news, if you mean the whole thing with Twylec."

"I did. I understand all the security cameras became fuzzy when my niece went a little crazy." Jeral grinned widely—a very unusual display of emotion for him.

"I can't have them seeing *that*. They'll all be on my doorstep tomorrow, wanting something similar or calling for my head, depending on how you look at all this," I teased. "The only good thing about Solar Red or Red Hand is that all the criminals congregate together, so I can kill them all at once."

"Nice of them to do that," Drew hugged me—I'd sat between him and Drake to eat my breakfast. Gavin was giving me looks, though. I think he wanted to haul me out of there as quickly as he could. Maybe he'd settle for a stint in the hot tub—I still felt cold.

"And we'll all settle for a little time in the hot tub, I think." Drake grinned at me and then at his brother. He'd read my thoughts—I hadn't shielded them.

"No sex for a week," Karzac laid down the law.

"Honey, you enjoy that, don't you?" I wanted to throw an uneaten piece of toast at my Refizani physician mate. Karzac threw the term sex around as if it didn't embarrass me in the least. With as many mates as I had, I suppose it shouldn't embarrass me. It did.

"I do not wish to be forced to heal the debilitating headache afterward," Karzac grumbled at me. "And you do not wish to have the headache either—be honest."

Blood Redemption

"Fine," I huffed. If I were honest, as Karzac said, I was still feeling shaky.

* * *

The hot tub was where Rigo and Thurlow found me later, only seconds after my posse and I had gotten into it (all naked, of course). Then new guy showed up, just as Rigo and Thurlow were shucking clothes to get in, too. I slapped a hand over my face.

"I am sorry I didn't introduce myself earlier; I am Norian Keef, Director of the ASD," new guy said and started shucking his clothes, too. Well, he might fit in, after all. He slipped into the water on the other side of Thurlow. "This is nice," he said. "Why didn't I know about this before?"

"Uh, Lissa, your new assignment for the Alliance is working with the ASD Director, here," Tony jerked his head toward Norian Keef.

"ASD—Alliance Security Detail?" I asked, my voice almost a squeak. "How the hell did that happen?"

"The Founder and twenty members of the Grand Alliance Council always choose who works as Liaison, and the Liaison's world always houses the ASD for a period of thirty years," Norian cracked a smile, as if his current circumstances pleased him in some way.

At least he was calm and relaxed today. Not only was he relaxed, he was naked, sitting in hot water up to his nipples and smiling. *Nice.* "Don't worry," Norian held out a hand, "we're paid by the Alliance, and our housing costs are reimbursed. I've already worked that out with Kyler—I understand she's your niece?"

"Yes." I wasn't thrilled with her father at the moment, however. I still wanted to slap Glendes and Raffian through a wall. "The Founder and Twenty Charter members decided?"

Chapter 3

My question was flat and resigned. It was one of those things—you don't show up for the meeting, you get the assignment. Didn't matter that I'd been separated—body and spirit—at the time.

The assignment and Norian's words brought worries and suspicions to my mind, but I shoved them aside before any of my mates picked up on them. This was my concern, and I didn't want to trouble the others with it. I'd just wait and see how it all played out.

"They haven't lost sight of what happened on Refizan three centuries ago, even if the others haven't studied their Alliance history," Norian said, leaning his head back and closing his eyes.

"The Governor of the Realm on Refizan hasn't forgotten," Karzac muttered.

"I have copies of that footage, now. I didn't know what they were talking about—wasn't sure it was possible, even. I know differently, now." Norian lifted his head and stared at me.

"Don't make me place compulsion not to spread that around," I grumbled.

"Don't worry," Norian held out a hand. "I'm just looking forward to the next time. I sent out my agents this morning. I'll be getting information within days."

"Lissa will not be going out again for at least two weeks, and that may be pushing it," Karzac glared at Norian.

"Calm down, I was planning to ask when she might be able to help out," Norian replied. "And I'll depend on you to give me status reports in the future, if our Queen isn't up to these activities. I wasn't looking forward to this when I was notified of the assignment to Le-Ath Veronis. After yesterday, my heart rate and my stress level dropped dramatically. Not that they won't rise again," he offered a brief, roguish grin, "but for now, things are so much better."

"You might ask *me* if I'm prepared to go off with you," I huffed. "Difik." I misted right out of the hot tub and into my suite.

* * *

"Not a good idea to press those buttons," Drake and Drew said together. Norian's eyebrows lifted in surprise. These twins were identical, except for the color of ink on their dragon tattoos.

"She called me an idiot, didn't she?" Norian grinned.

"That is the closest you can get to a direct translation," Garde agreed. He lifted a hand from the hot water—his fingers were wrinkled. "I'll go check on Lissa," he said and skipped away.

* * *

Lissa

I was standing in my closet, wrapped in a towel when fifteen males, all in various stages of dress, trooped into my bedroom. I don't know how Norian thought he rated just walking in with the rest of my mates plus Rigo and Thurlow, but he was there, too. I'm not sure they'd even noticed he'd followed them.

"Lissa, tell me what you intend to do," Karzac spoke first.

"I was going to see Cheedas," I muttered. I was tired and wanted a nap right after I got something to drink. And I wanted to ask Cheedas to find somebody who could take Giff's place. I'd gone *Looking* while I searched for something to wear. I knew how things stood on that front, now. Giff's permanent defection was one more blow in a long line of others.

Chapter 3

"What did you want to see Cheedas for?" Roff was working his way through the others.

"Honey," I was wiping my face, now, "I know Giff doesn't want to come back and I know she doesn't ever want me to see the baby. I was going to ask Cheedas if he knew somebody who could take her place."

"*Fuck*," I heard Tony whisper off to the side. Roff stopped three feet away from me, a stricken expression on his face.

"I'm not mad at you," I stifled the sob that came. "I just need to see Cheedas." Right then, I might have had thoughts of just dropping to the floor and sobbing. I didn't have my wizard and I didn't have Giff—and I wasn't going to get to see her baby.

Ever.

My life since waking had been nothing but crap. I jerked a shirt and jeans off hangers and slammed the bathroom door behind me. I did my best to straighten myself up while I dressed, and then stomped out while fifteen males watched.

Rolfe was standing guard outside the door to my suite, so I made a huge production of slamming that door, too, before anybody had a chance to come out behind me.

I think I heard the thick wood crack as I ran down the hall. That meant I was breathing heavily when I made my way into the kitchen, my breaths coming in gasps and sobs. Cheedas stood patiently while I rushed toward him, threw myself into his arms and wept.

If I'd thought to worry whether Cheedas might be uncomfortable while I cried, then my worries would have been unfounded. Honestly, I was wishing we didn't have an audience right then. Cheedas was doing his best to stop my tears, but that was easier said than done.

Blood Redemption

He murmured nonsense to me and rubbed my back while everybody else watched silently. I was shaking by the time Cheedas sat on a barstool and pulled me onto his lap. A glass of juice was handed over and he helped me drink.

When I got myself under control after a while, I wiped my face with unsteady fingers and looked up at Cheedas. "I need somebody to take Giff's place."

"I know this," he sighed. "There are two who would fit well and I think you should hire both."

"Where are they? I think I should talk to them soon." I scrubbed my face with a shaking hand.

"I will have them here tomorrow morning. I do not think you should worry about this for the rest of the day. Have one of your mates take you to your room, Raona. You should rest. I will fix something good for your lunch and someone will bring it to you."

"Cara, come with me." I buried my head against Gavin's neck when he lifted me away from Cheedas. Gavin didn't use his new folding skills very often, but he used them now. I was back inside my suite in a blink. My clothing was pulled off and I was dressed quickly in warm fleece instead—Gavin saw to that.

"Let us lie here and talk," Gavin settled my head on his shoulder—we had a dozen pillows piled around us on the bed, making a comfortable nest.

"Why did they do this to me, Gavin? What did I do to them?" I watched his dark brown eyes as I asked the question, hoping for an answer in their depths. He kissed my forehead carefully before offering a reply.

"Shhh, cara, you did nothing wrong. There is no good purpose behind any of this. Shadow still loves you—he is being mistreated, just as you are. This could well have

Chapter 3

waited, or another method could have been found. I find this senseless, my love. Giff's fears are irrational. Giff is a new parent and is frightened for her child because Toff's taking was such a blow. It is my hope that this will work itself out. Rolfe holds this hope as well, because he finds it difficult to choose between two that he loves."

"He needs to stay with Giff. If we need to find another guard, then we'll find another guard." I sniffled—Rolfe was like the North Star for me—always at his post unless his position as Spawn Hunter for the Saa Thalarr called him away.

"No, cara," Gavin whispered against my hair. "Rolfe will not stand for that and even Giff knows not to ask. Giff needs to think this through rationally one day and she will discover that without you, she would not enjoy the life that she does. Rolfe would have been kept from her, if you had not come to rule Le-Ath Veronis."

"I don't want anything from her if she's not willing to give it," I said. Yeah, I was wallowing in self-pity.

"Cara, try to let this go for now. These are undeserved blows and it grieves me to see them aimed at you."

"What am I supposed to do, instead?" I watched Gavin's face—a muscle worked in his jaw—an emotional response he seldom displayed. His eyes weren't full of stars, either, as Kifirin's often were, but there was love and concern there. For me.

"Do you know why I was so worried about your walking into the sun, so long ago, cara? Why Aurelius was drawn into a trap so easily, when Xenides' whelp lied to him, telling him that one of his was injured by walking into the sun?"

I blinked up at Gavin. I'd wondered about that—many times, in fact. It had seemed so incongruous, at the time—

Blood Redemption

Gavin had been sent by the Council to eliminate me, but he'd begged me not to kill myself by walking into sunlight. I'd never figured that out.

"Tell me," I sighed.

"Aurelius made a female vampire, two centuries after René and I were turned. Her name was Lucia." I blinked at Gavin in shock and wondered if anyone else had heard this story.

"We were all a little in love with her, I think," Gavin went on. "Lucia was barely nineteen and left for dead by travelers who'd been attacked by bandits. Aurelius attempted the turn and like a miracle, it worked. I think she must have had Elemaiyan blood, just as you do, cara. Else she would probably have died her final death. She lived with us for seventy years before giving herself to the sun." He shook his head sadly at remembered pain.

"Aurelius was inconsolable afterward. He barely kept himself alive. René and I were also devastated, but we forced ourselves to bring donors to Aurelius so he would feed, otherwise he might have wasted away. This went on for nearly twenty years, before my vampire sire finally pulled himself together. Then, that information was used against him—many knew how much he cared for his children. Aurelius died, or we were led to believe that he did. Therefore, René and I were reluctant to speak of it again—it was much too painful for us." I lifted a hand and traced Gavin's jaw—this was the first time he'd opened up to me regarding his past, and certainly the first time he'd displayed this much emotion.

"René went on to turn several and he loved them very much," Gavin continued. "I was unable to make any turns, because I did not believe I could deal with the pain of a

Chapter 3

child's death should it come to that. But you, cara, if I could turn back the clock and know of you and where you were, I would have been there a moment before Sergio could snatch you away. I would have turned you, just to make you mine. Wlodek would have been notified immediately. You would not have suffered, cara mia. Not at my hands."

"What happened to Devlin's posse?" I'd been pulled away by Griffin after Devlin and some of Xenides' get had been captured at the Council's Annual Meeting. Devlin had handed information to Xenides, because he was jealous of Tony after René turned him. Devlin died that night, but his many followers still had to be dealt with.

"I wish you could have been at that Council meeting, love. Seven of Devlin's conspirators stood before Wlodek for judgment that night. We'd learned of your death only days earlier, and many of us were half-mad with grief. This was before we were made to forget you and it was not a good time for the vampire race as a whole. Wlodek asked me if I wanted to draw out any of their deaths. Sebastian was always the one who'd done that before. I thought about it. Considered it. In the end, I did their beheadings as swiftly as I'd done all the others. They did not suffer, though they deserved the suffering."

"Do you think Devlin felt any remorse for causing René's death?"

"He blamed others for that and not himself," Gavin grumbled.

"What about Cecil and Nestor?"

"Nestor was killed by one of the humans who hunted us years later. While going through his and Cecil's records after their deaths, we found that they had collaborated with Saxom many times and brought wealth to themselves through his machinations. Cecil tried to kill Flavio after he took Wlodek's position. Kyler killed Cecil, I believe, when he attempted to eliminate Flavio, who was newly mated to her. Cecil had become more than wealthy through the centuries by selling weapons to terrorists. He also had his eye on the Honored One's place in the Council, and made careful plans to take it. Cecil gathered vampires sympathetic to his efforts in the attempted coup, in exchange for seats on the Council. Earth's vampires owe Kyler for eliminating that threat."

"I tried to tell Merrill there was something wrong with him," I pointed out.

"And we all should have paid attention. We did not know, cara. We failed to realize that you would not say something like that unless it was important. We know better, now. Did you know that Fox foresaw what you did to the Elemaiya? Merrill told me this, not long ago after Anthony and I were given the abilities by Kiarra."

"I haven't heard that before," I mumbled and snuggled closer against Gavin.

"Fox it was who snatched the Khos'Mirai away from the Ra'Ak in the beginning, to ransom her father and brother, whom the Bright Elemaiya had kidnapped. When she brought the Khos-Mirai back to them, she learned they'd allowed her father to die while they held him and her brother captive. Fox pronounced their doom at that moment. She told them that one day the most unlikely one of all would stand before them and bring justice."

"Yeah, too bad they didn't pay attention. They just went right out and signed up with their Dark cousins. And the Ra'Ak, too."

"I know." Gavin leaned in to give me a kiss. A really good kiss.

Chapter 3

"Honey, you've always tasted as good as you smell to me," I stroked his cheek.

"I remember the first time I kissed you—I couldn't stop myself from biting. I am sorry for the compulsion after—very sorry, cara."

"Kiss me again and we won't talk about that," I said. Gavin complied.

* * *

"Here is a list of available surrogates." Erland set a microcomputer in front of Garde. "Poradina has two friends on this list, so it wouldn't be a bad thing if they were together in this. The money would be well spent, too. I've already spoken with Poradina—she's willing to have in-vitro fertilization. I just need to track those Larentii down."

"You may stop searching; we are here and we know what you want," Connegar folded in with Reemagar. "The Wise Ones called us in and they support this decision completely. Therefore, we will willingly redesign the donor eggs with integrated DNA from Lissa. The egg will be hers in all respects when we finish."

"I think you just made my millennia," Erland smiled.

"Graegar says to choose this one," Reemagar pointed out a name on the list that Garde was staring at on the microcomputer.

"Evaline? That's one of Poradina's friends," Erland remarked, looking over Garde's shoulder.

"Yes, Graegar was quite positive about that," Reemagar nodded. "We want this to go as smoothly as possible for Lissa, as well as the surrogates. The choice you made, Lord Morphis, along with her friend, yields the best possible outcome."

Blood Redemption

"Now all we have to do is approach Lissa with this and hope she likes the idea. I certainly don't want to upset her. These will be her babies, in every respect. She just won't carry them."

Erland had already sent mindspeech to Wylend. Wylend had agreed to put up the fees for both surrogates, as a gift to his granddaughter, Lissa. He and Erland would be ready with the detachment spell, too, if it were needed.

Erland didn't think it would be—both women knew the child would not be theirs and they had readily volunteered when they learned Lissa was unable to bear children of her own. Poradina had two grown children; Evaline had one.

"We will come with you and explain that the donated eggs will become hers," Connegar said. "I hope she will like this from the start—I do not wish to be forced to convince her it is a good idea. The Wise Ones think this is very important."

"I think it's important too, but everything depends on Lissa liking it," Garde observed. "When do we go to her?"

"We will come in two days—she will feel better then and the marriage between Shadow Grey and Melida of Belancour will be complete." Reemagar didn't look as if he appreciated that fact. Not even a little.

"You know something." Erland stared up at the eight-foot Larentii. Reemagar was tall, but Connegar towered over Reemagar by a foot and a half.

"The Wise Ones say we may not interfere. Therefore, we will not. Things will progress as they will, no matter our feelings in this."

* * *

Lissa

58

Chapter 3

Cheedas brought in both candidates he'd selected to take Giff's place. Winkler came with me—he was good at interviewing, so we met in my study. Norian was lurking outside when Winkler walked down the hall with me, a solicitous hand at my back.

"Norian Keef, do I get a moment to interview assistants, first?" I still felt grumpy at his high-handedness. I think I made a face at him, too. He deliberately ignored it.

"Of course. May I sit in?"

"Oh, sure. Do you intend to ask questions on how they intend to keep my closet updated, just to make sure it meets ASD guidelines?" My hands were on my hips as I bristled at Norian's intended interference.

"I'm not any good at that sort of thing," Norian grinned. "The ASD only has uniform guidelines. A Queen's garb has never been standard ASD issue."

Was he teasing? Where was that coming from? Gavin told me the man was a total bear until I'd hauled him off to Twylec. Now he was all smiles and sunlight. Go figure.

"But I would still like to sit in," he continued, his expression turning serious.

"Fine. Sit in," I snapped. Cheedas had a tray of tea, coffee and pastry sitting on my desk as we walked inside my study, and Heathe and Grant were already eating. Cheedas and the two candidates were sitting in guest chairs, waiting for my arrival.

"These two are vampires?" Norian nodded toward Grant and Heathe, who were grinning and eating cherry turnovers.

"Yes," I sighed. "I sure as hell hope you know how to keep secrets, Norian Keef."

"Oh, I know how to keep secrets," he agreed. "Very well." He helped himself to the turnovers and coffee. Winkler

59

and I just had coffee, although mine was mixed with cream and sugar.

"This is Taff, and this is Mora," Cheedas introduced the two comesuli. They were both shy—I don't think they'd been this close to me before. I didn't recognize their scents; I knew that much.

"So, you both want to wait on me, buy my clothes and keep up with my closet and my suite?" I asked.

"Oh, yes, Raona," Taff sounded breathless with anticipation. I did some *Looking*—they would both be female vampires one day. They were still very young, too—less than sixty. That was young for comesuli.

"Raona, I want this very much," Mora chimed in. "My parent would be so happy if I became an assistant to the Queen."

"Both have worked in the clothing shops in Casino City, but have not been treated well," Cheedas supplied. I blinked at my cook in alarm.

"Have those jerks who think they're fashion experts been mistreating my people?" I demanded.

"Only one or two," Cheedas replied with a shrug.

"Can you give me names? I'll have this investigated right away." Grant put his plate down and was poised to enter information into his handheld. "Grant, have Trevor look into this—those people signed contracts before they got here. If they haven't adhered to those contracts, I want to know and I want their butts in these seats as quickly as possible. They'll be off this planet before they can sneeze if they're fucking employees around." Grant nodded and entered the names Cheedas, Taff and Mora supplied.

"Already transmitted to Trevor's office," Grant nodded and set his handheld down.

Chapter 3

"Good. Keep me advised on that. Tell Trevor to let me know as soon as possible."

"Already done," Grant smiled.

"Perfect. Now, where were we?" I turned back to Taff and Mora.

"We know where all the good clothing can be found," Taff said. "Mora and I would go through the shops every week just to see what the others had. The good jewelry, too. Plus, we know where to order—we took care of that for our employer, who went out gambling every afternoon."

"That's another violation," I nodded to Grant. The shop owners weren't allowed to gamble; it was one of the few rules that had migrated from Campiaa. No casino employees of any kind, or shop owners or casino owners were allowed to gamble. There was too much opportunity for crime to enter the picture.

Winkler asked standard questions after that. He and I were both satisfied and we settled on duties, off-days and salary. I had two new assistants before midmorning.

Cheedas offered to take them to my suite so they could get started, so I turned to Norian. "What's the problem du jour?" I asked as sweetly as I could. He didn't understand the French phrase. Winkler explained it for him.

"We have information from Trell," Norian said. "We're having some trouble there—one of my investigators disappeared a while back. I need to find out what happened to him. I was hoping you might get me there quickly, when you're able," Norian held up a hand, holding off my questions.

"My agent was investigating an influx of money into the royal treasury and we want to know what that's about. Trell wasn't one of the worlds that wanted to approve their own religions without Alliance interference, but you can't ever tell about these things. Perhaps they only wanted to draw attention away from the fact that this is what they intended anyway."

"We can go next week," I said. "I think."

"That is what I was hoping for," Norian said, rising from his seat. "I'll be checking in with you occasionally."

"I'm sure you will," I muttered.

"Of course I will. I don't think I've ever enjoyed an assignment as much as this." Norian was smiling as he strutted out of my study.

"Raona, wait until you see what we've done," Grant and Heathe hauled out plans for Niff's Sweet Shop when Norian was out of hearing range. Not only had my assistants arranged for the shop to be purchased in Casino City, but another in Sun City, the version of Casino City located near the beach on the light half of Le-Ath Veronis.

"Not bad," Winkler went over the plans with me while Grant and Heathe talked excitedly about setting up the businesses.

"We're ordering ovens and ice-cream machines and setting things up to get the fruit, milk and other ingredients straight from the farms," Grant said. "I think we can open in three months."

"That sounds really good," I nodded at their assessment. "Get whatever you need from my personal account."

Winkler stayed with me while I signed papers, answered communications and did everything else that needed to be done. Garde, Aurelius and Aryn had taken over the Council meetings in my absence and they were still handling things.

Chapter 3

I only had a few things in front of me that had been tabled—they were waiting for me to get back to handle those things. Nothing urgent, actually, they just wanted my input.

"Do you feel like a field trip?" I asked Winkler after the last bit had been handled. I knew there was much more, but Heathe and Grant had been instructed not to tire me out.

"If you'll have lunch with me and take a nap afterward," Winkler agreed.

"Sounds good. Let's go visit the Green Fae." Winkler's black eyes looked at me carefully before he nodded. He was the one to fold us there, too.

He and I stood on the edge of the Green Fae village, beneath a large tree that had been a sapling a month or two before and watched as the Green Fae went about their business. We caught sight of Redbird once; she was carrying a basket of fruit while little Toff trotted along behind her. I sighed.

"Raona." Corent walked over and stood beside us.

"How are you, Corent?" I asked.

"Very well, as are the others. Toff is growing, as you saw." I could only nod; I didn't trust my voice to answer.

"We are all watching over him—that is the way of our people. He is talking a bit, now, as you might imagine. And learning to eat with utensils."

"That's good," I managed to say without choking up. "Does he need anything? Clothing or something?"

"We are well supplied; trade is going very well with the comesuli," Corent informed me. "We appreciate the gift of tools you sent." I was back to nodding again. Corent's hair was changing color, from light to dark blue as the leaves shifted and swayed over our heads in the mid-day breeze. Winkler put his arms around me. I leaned into his warmth.

Blood Redemption

"This is one of your mates?" Corent looked up at Winkler, who had a good eight inches on Corent.

"Yes, this is my wolf mate," I said.

"Werewolf?"

"Yes."

"I have never seen one before."

Winkler changed, right on the spot. He didn't have to disrobe any longer—with the abilities bestowed by the Saa Thalarr, it was no longer necessary. I ruffled the fur around Winkler's ears as he stood with me. Corent was quite surprised.

"He hunts on the full moon?" Le-Ath Veronis had only one moon. Harifa Edus had six. That's where Winkler and the other wolves of the Saa Thalarr usually went when they wanted a run. I had a feeling they watched as the werewolves there hunted, brought down game and challenged one another. It was the way things happened with werewolves.

"He usually goes to Harifa Edus. Do you know about that?"

"No. What is it?"

"Harifa Edus was the original werewolf planet, and it was uninhabited for a very long time. We have been working to repopulate it. Winkler visits at least once a month, during one of the six full moons."

"You did this—repopulating that world. Didn't you?"

"That was one of my goals, yes," I nodded.

"We thought we were taking from a selfish Karathian," Corent sighed. "A being who might deserve to have his child taken away. If we had known that the child we took was nothing of the kind," Corent didn't finish his statement.

"What's done is done," I couldn't stop the tears this time. I was embarrassed when one dripped onto my blouse

Chapter 3

before I could wipe it away. Winkler was back to himself quickly.

"Please excuse us," he nodded to Corent and folded me back to the palace.

* * *

"What did the Queen have to say?" Tiearan walked over to Corent.

"She wanted to see Toff, even from a distance. She was crying there at the end, so her werewolf mate took her away."

* * *

King's Palace, Cloudsong

Jenderlin, the newly elevated crown prince of Cloudsong, sat inside the crown prince's suite while his father paced incessantly. Jenderlin wanted to halt his father with a word, but he had no words. Nothing would assuage his father's guilt over sending his brother out to a waiting ambush. Nothing.

Jenderlin had always known that his father doted on Brandelin, his older brother. Jenderlin had always been the weaker of the two, in his father's eyes. Not even good enough to train in the military, although Jenderlin had read all the historical accounts of battles won and lost and had studied strategy, in addition to his other lessons.

Now, instead of advising his brother as his father planned when Brandelin took the throne, Jenderlin would take the high seat instead and he was frightened at the prospect. He had no desire to plot the course of Cloudsong's future. A welcome knock came on the door.

"Come," King Kenderlin growled. Kenderlin's master of the guard entered, hauling a prisoner along, his fist gripping the back of the captive's collar.

Blood Redemption

"I have news, albeit unwilling news," the master of the guard's growl eclipsed that of the king. "News that will explain your son's death." Kenderlin nearly gaped at the two who'd entered his study, but recovered his composure swiftly.

"Perhaps you should explain, then," Kenderlin sat behind Jenderlin's desk and glared at the prisoner.

Chapter 4

*G*rey Planet

"Melida, we are very pleased to have you here." Glendes nodded at the new arrival. "Marid, thank you for bringing her." Glendes gave another nod to Melida's father. Marid was Chief of the Belancour Wizards and quite powerful.

"We have everything arranged," Glendes continued, "The union will take place tonight before dinner, with the celebrations afterward."

"I wish to meet your grandson's other mate." Melida, dark-haired and pretty, looked about her as if she were weighing the worth of Glendes' study. Glendes looked slightly uncomfortable at Melida's question.

"That is not an option—Lissa has released Shadow from his union with her. You may be his only mate from this point on, unless he can convince her to return, somehow."

"I heard she was highly placed." Marid commented dryly.

"We were not at liberty to reveal that before, due to her position. It would have been improper of us at the time. Since she has released Shadow and we are no longer obligated to her or she to us, then I feel we can provide that information," Glendes replied smoothly.

"Who was she? Have I destroyed anything important?" Melida's question sounded insincere. Glendes wanted to release a sigh. As Eldest of Grey House, he was a good judge of character, having lived so long. Melida had a mercenary streak about her and Glendes didn't like it.

"A queen," Glendes shoved his thoughts aside and replied as smoothly as he could. "The Queen of Le-Ath Veronis. I will not lie to you—Shadow is most upset over this. Perhaps you may find a way to divert him from his anger and obsession."

Glendes hoped desperately that Melida's beauty and any charms she might possess would serve to distract Shadow. His work was off and he remained uncommunicative.

"You expect me to divert him?" Melida snorted. "That was never my intention and not what you led me to believe when we reviewed your offer. I was to provide heirs only. I have no desire to become close to anyone. Ever again."

"You say the union has been completely dissolved— between the Queen of Le-Ath Veronis and your grandson?" Marid's gaze was intent on Glendes' face. Glendes wondered why Marid seemed so interested in Shadow's union with Lissa.

"It was never bound by written contract—it was spoken only and the Queen severed the spoken contract when she

Chapter 4

returned Shadow's ring. There is no hold on her—by any of us. She was free to go if she chose and that is what she did."

Glendes attempted to read Marid's expression, but Marid was quite old and had learned long ago to hide his true intentions and interests behind a mask when it was prudent to do so.

Raffian had stood at his father's shoulder the entire time, listening. He, too, wondered why Marid was so interested in Lissa's contract—or lack of one—with Grey House. Glendes was handling this, however, so Raffian didn't ask.

"Come, Shadow and his grandmother are waiting in my suite," Glendes urged Marid and Melida from his study. "I'd like you to meet them."

* * *

Queen's Palace, Le-Ath Veronis
Lissa

Garde and Erland had called a meeting of the Inner Circle, so I had to be there. It would be the first time we met without Shadow. Well, there were plenty of firsts ahead of me if I measured them in that way.

We met in the library, as we usually did. Rigo, Thurlow and even Norian Keef grumbled when they discovered they weren't included. Norian Keef had moved into a suite at the palace and then proceeded to act as if he belonged there. Well, he was going to belong—for the next thirty years or so. I had to get used to that.

"We have a proposal." Erland was the one who spoke first. Garde sat beside him around the conference table. Even my two Larentii folded in at the last minute.

Roff was resting his wings, allowing them to droop over the arms of his chair, the tips of soft brown leather touching the floor. Karzac was sitting on Erland's other side and it looked as if he were in on this, too—whatever it was.

"What's the proposal?" I leaned back in my chair to watch my mates. Kifirin was the only one absent, but that was the case much of the time.

"We want you to have children," Karzac said. "And there is a way to do this, if you consent."

Well, if anybody wanted to get my attention, that might be the way to do it. "What are you talking about?" I asked.

"Surrogate mothers," Gardevik chimed in. "The Larentii here tell us that they can manipulate a donor egg with your DNA, making it your egg. Erland and I have already secured willing surrogates and their fees will be paid if you consent. We can put them up at the beach house during their pregnancy. The children will be yours and ours, avilepha."

I was stunned. Completely. "Are you sure?" I squeaked. "The babies will be mine, with my genes and everything? Not the surrogate's or the egg donor's?"

"They will be, little mate," Connegar said, smiling at me. Okay, those blue eyes smiling at me were something to see. "We will extract a bit of your DNA and place it in the egg—afterward, it will match yours completely. Ferrigar has approved this—he says it is deserved."

"You'll get two babies, fathered by Erland and Gardevik first," Karzac had already talked to the Larentii, I could tell. "Then, if you want others, the rest of us will be happy to find surrogates and donate sperm."

"Karzac, do not kid me about this," I was standing suddenly, feeling numb. Was this true? They could do this?

"We can and will do this, if you say yes," Reemagar was smiling now, too. Both my Larentii smiling at the same time? Wow.

Chapter 4

"Then I say yes. When can we do this?" I was so excited suddenly I was nearly vibrating.

"We will do this in two days—we will bring the surrogates then," Erland was considering coming across the table, I think, just so we could embrace. I misted to him instead.

"You're sure they don't mind?" I kissed Erland and asked questions in between.

"Love, they are very willing and the money will be well spent," Erland replied.

"Will they replace Toff in your heart?" Roff was now behind Erland.

"Honey," I started crying, then. "If I could get Toff back right this minute, I would. Nothing is ever going to fill that hole in my heart." I was kissing my winged vampire, then, and crying at the same time.

"I did not mean to upset you," I think Roff was crying with me. I could only hope that one day Toff would come back to us. I think we both clung to that hope.

"Honey, we have a right to be upset." I had my arms and my legs wrapped around Roff, and the others disappeared from the room like mist on a bright sunny day.

* * *

"Director, we have evidence that Black Mist may have scouted the planet." Vice Director Lendill Schaff had contacted Norian via comp-vid, and now they were discussing a new turn of events. "I know you wanted to investigate Trell first, but that can wait. This is more important."

Norian thought so, too. "We knew they would attempt to relocate eventually; I was hoping they'd head for Campiaa. Our spies there have been watching for them for months."

Blood Redemption

"Even those criminals wouldn't appreciate Black Mist living among them," Lendill Schaff replied. He and Norian had argued at length about placing spies on Campiaa. "Darthin is perfect for them—Black Mist prefers longer nights and shorter days for some reason. Campiaa is much too sunny."

"Do you think they intend to destroy the population on Darthin?"

"I have no idea, but they appear to be working their way through the capital city of Darthough. Murders and other crimes have certainly risen, and before this, Darthough had very little crime."

"Well, the Liaison will be available for travel in two days. We will attempt to join you there. I hope to find a reason for this and stop it before it is too late."

Norian broke the communication with Lendill and sat back in his chair. He liked his office very much—Lissa had given him a better one than the closet he'd originally had. The space was quite large and had original art on the walls and a nice rug on the floor. He could spend thirty years using this office with no trouble.

* * *

Lissa

"Lissa, why wouldn't you allow us in?" Thurlow actually sounded hurt. I didn't know what to do with that. Rigo looked crushed.

"Look, it was private, all right? Besides, it's not like you both couldn't hear what was going on anyway." I went to Rigo and brushed a lock of dark hair away from his face. "It'll work out. You'll see," I told him.

"Sit with me," he begged.

"All right. Where do you want to sit?"

72

Chapter 4

"Come to dinner with me at New Fangled," he suggested.

"You're saying you're hungry?" I asked. I think I was smiling foolishly at him. After Thurlow had done whatever it was he'd done for Rigo—he could eat just as I could, although he still drank blood substitute most of the time.

"I could eat." Rigo was smiling, too.

"You know I've only been there once," I said, taking his arm. "And I only had blood substitute. What do they have on the menu that's good?" I folded Rigo to New Fangled.

"I am still getting used to the fact that many of your mates can transport themselves in this manner," Rigo smiled and put his arm around me as we walked through New Fangled's doors.

* * *

"My heir was actually my brother's son—my nephew," Rigo told me later over a plate of spaghetti. "My queen died in childbirth and I had no other wife. A very old vampire came to me as I was aging and voiced his worries regarding Argovarnus' penchant for self-absorption. I agreed with him and he offered vampirism as a solution, so I might guide my nephew's steps. At first I refused, but as Argo continued in his excess and his mistreatment of the population, I had no choice."

Rigo sipped his glass of wine, smiled at me and when I remained silent, he continued. "I hid myself away after my turning, only giving suggestions wrapped in compulsion, to this one or that. Until Halimel came along. He welcomed my advice and ruled wisely. Hal was my first turn. Then Rondival came, Alrenardo after that, and finally Brinelodus and Yandiveri. We formed a vampire army, too—when it was necessary to repel several takeover attempts. We became the

73

Blood Redemption

Order of the Night Flower upon Hraede—my five vampire children and I. We often wished we could turn females, but after three failures, we no longer made the attempt. We became a living myth to the monarchs who had neither the ability nor the desire to rule wisely, and trusted advisors to the ones who had Hraede's best interests at heart. Over the years, too, we developed our poisons—the ones we used when there was no other way to eliminate evil."

I watched Rigo as he talked—he toyed with his wineglass while he told his story. "That's what happened to Satris, isn't it?" I asked.

"Tiessa, he would have been put to death here, had he not slipped through our grasp under the guise of diplomatic immunity. Therefore, two of your mates and I made sure that his sentence was carried out, by alternative means."

"I know. He took money from Solar Red and then refused to do or say anything when he knew those monsters were killing his people." I didn't add that he was responsible for Davan's death, in addition to the attempt on my life.

"Someone else will take his place in a few weeks. I hope they rule with a wiser head."

"I hope there's someone in line for the throne who *has* a wiser head," I grumped.

"Tiessa, that is not for you to worry about." Rigo lifted my chin in his fingers. He'd insisted we sit together in the small booth against the wall and he leaned down to kiss me. "Someday, love, you and I will be mated. I am content to wait, but do not shut me out again, I beg you," he whispered against my mouth.

* * *

"You mean you're going to lift the specimen away without going through the usual?" I couldn't bring myself to

Chapter 4

say masturbation out loud. Connegar, Reemagar, Karzac, Jeff, Joey, Franklin and Gilfraith were all there, to either help or observe.

"I will do this—we have the donated eggs already; we took DNA samples from you and the eggs have been prepared. Now we only need sperm from Erland and Gardevik," Connegar smiled.

Garde and Erland were both inside the master suite of the beach house on the light half. The two surrogates were in a bedroom down the hall—as soon as the sperm was obtained and the eggs fertilized, they would be placed with Larentii power and know-how into the wombs of the surrogates. Things were happening so fast, now.

I really didn't see anything—the specimens were taken amid blinding light, somehow combined with the eggs that Connegar *Pulled* in from somewhere and then Connegar and the healers folded into the bedroom next door for a few minutes. I didn't even have time to pace before they were all back. "We have a successful transfer and impregnation on both surrogates," Connegar was smiling.

"Wow, honey, that's spectacular," I said, giving him a hug.

"You might repay us by spending some time together," Connegar suggested.

"Right now, you can have anything you want," I smiled back at him.

We did spend some time together—about four hours—before Norian Keef came looking for me.

* * *

"We have trouble on Darthin—my agents believe the capital city of Darthough is being infiltrated by Black Mist.

75

Blood Redemption

This may be the vanguard for a complete takeover. That's how they took Phraxes years ago."

Norian had such hope in his eyes—hope that I'd take him and see what we could discover on Darthin. His fingers itched to clutch the throats of criminals, I just knew it. And, if he could corner Black Mist, he'd like it even better.

He'd mentioned Phraxes, too; it was now a dead world, located just outside the Alliance. Phraxes was a haunted world, filled with ghosts and little else. Somehow, Black Mist had managed to kill the entire planet before relocating. The ASD had struggled to track Black Mist ever since.

"Do I need to pack?" I asked, resignation plain in my voice. Norian was determined to drag me away from Le-Ath Veronis.

"Well, since we don't know what is going on, you probably should." Norian's green eyes searched my face.

"How much are you packing?" I'd been sitting with my Larentii near the pool—we'd had sun lamps installed in case anyone wanted to use them. Normal vampires stayed away from my pool and hot tub, but Connegar and Reemagar were happily soaking up artificial sun.

"At least a week's worth," Norian replied, doing his best to hurry me without being obvious about it. He had the nervous energy about him again, as if he wanted what he wanted, at least two weeks ago.

"Fine." I got up, kissed both my Larentii and followed Norian, who was talking while he led me toward my suite. I learned the name of his main operative and second-in-command—Lendill Schaff—who would meet us on Darthin.

Norian also filled me in on the numbers of murdered Darthinians, which now stood in the thousands in less than a month. I sent my mates mindspeech, telling them I might be

Chapter 4

gone for a few days. I heard quite a bit of grumbling as a result—apparently, Garde and Erland wanted to celebrate impending fatherhood. I told them we'd do it when I got back.

Norian was still talking while I threw clothes into a bag with the help of Taff, one of my new assistants. I packed mostly jeans—then braided my hair, tossed in shampoo and toiletries, closed my bag and asked Norian where his bag was. He was still blathering about something and hadn't realized I'd tuned him out long ago.

"Norian, do I have to put a hand over your mouth?" I stood before him with hands on my hips. He grinned. "My bag is in my office," he said. I folded us to his office, he picked up his bag and we were off to Darthin.

* * *

"This is the headquarters for the ASD on Darthin," Norian explained as we dropped our bags off in the cramped sleeping quarters. Four small, low-walled cubicles painted white with no doors lay before me, coupled with two undersized, tiled showers, a single toilet and two sinks.

A supply of extra towels, sheets and blankets were hidden inside a cramped closet, and all of it was fronted by a tiny kitchen area located behind an outer office with a desk. The building was hidden in a business complex, too, and had a fake sign out front. Go figure.

"I'm hungry. Feel like going out?" Norian hefted his bag onto the small bed inside his cubicle. "Go ahead; you get the one next door." With only a low wall separating each bed, there would be no privacy.

I wasn't sure I was up to seeing Norian in his undies, or letting him see me in my PJs. It shouldn't worry me, though; I'd already seen him naked once, when he'd climbed into the hot tub with everybody else. Norian was compact and muscular, no doubt about that.

"Have you been here before? Where are we going first? What do we have to investigate?" I dumped my bag on the bed next door. I could see Norian's head and shoulders easily over the low wall that separated our cubicles. Yep—no privacy. Or anything close, even.

"Lissa Beth, you'll just have to trust me."

"Honey, I don't trust many people, and nobody calls me Lissa Beth."

"Lissa Beth, we'll be eating local cuisine first. I'll let you know our next move after that. Get used to the name," Norian's eyes crinkled around the corners when he smiled.

"I can put you through a wall, I'll have you know."

"Yes. I know that about you. Come on, stop being a grump."

"I wasn't being a grump," I grumped as I followed him out the door.

* * *

"This is a type of hare that is raised here for meat," Norian ordered for both of us. We ended up with pocket sandwiches stuffed with spiced meat, lettuce and vegetables. The food was good, as long as I didn't think about little, fluffy bunnies while I ate.

Another man, carrying a plate of food, walked up and sat across from us at our outdoor table—it was late spring on Darthin, with perfect weather for dining outside.

"Well?" Norian asked.

"Got two leads—we can track tonight," the man said, lifting his sandwich and biting into it.

"Lissa Beth, this is Lendill Schaff, my second-in-command," Norian introduced us. I nodded to him,

Chapter 4

assuming he was more than aware of who I was even without Norian calling me Lissa Beth.

"The vids don't do you justice and I thought they looked pretty damn good," Lendill took another bite of his sandwich. I had no idea how to respond to that, so I didn't. Lendill had short, almost-blond hair, dark blue eyes, a slightly crooked nose (as if he'd broken it in a fight or two) and a nice mouth. He was taller than Norian, too—Lendill stood at six feet, even.

We followed Lendill away from the sandwich shop after our meal and hopped onto the public bus, which took us toward the downtown area. The buses all ran on a track and were computer operated—no drivers needed.

The workday was over so the bus wasn't crowded; it was only half-full, if that. We got off after a while and walked about twelve blocks until we came to a barricaded building. Lendill led us to the back of the squat, ugly brick structure, opening a door there with a key.

"Three city workers were murdered in this building," Lendill said, leading us inside. I knew that already, just by the scents. Those deaths had been bloody, too; I smelled the blood before we ever got to the room where they'd been killed.

Of course, the scents of the killers were now mixed with the scents of the local investigators and medical personnel who'd been called to the scene. I wouldn't be able to sort it all out unless I was introduced to each of the emergency responders, and that would be next to impossible.

A buzz and a blurring of images appeared whenever I attempted to *Look*, and that spelled power to me. Could be wizards, warlocks or a number of other possibilities.

Blood Redemption

"Was there any connection among the three? Did they work together, on the same shift or anything?"

"Sometimes—they worked maintenance; usually on the sewer and water lines." Lendill had done some legwork already.

"Did they work together on anything recently?" I continued my questioning.

"A busted water line below street level, located three blocks from city hall a few days ago," Lendill replied.

"Any fingerprints or other evidence at the scene?" Norian asked.

"Nothing, boss. The victims' throats were slashed; no weapons, footprints or fingerprints were found and we don't know how they got into the building to begin with—the doors were locked and the alarm was set. This is a city-owned facility and the workers can come here during breaks for lunch or to take a quick shower if they've been doing dirty work."

"Somehow, all three of them ended up here, at the same time. The door was shut and locked already—none of the three used their code to get in or set the alarm, and then all of them were killed. The killer managed to get in and out without setting off the alarm or using anyone's code—the employee who set the code last was here two days before the murders. He also has a solid alibi." Norian shook his head.

"Well, if a wizard or warlock is involved, or someone else with power, it would be easy," I said. Erland could circumvent electronics and surveillance equipment with half a thought. He could also transport several people at once—without blinking.

"That's a nasty thought—if Black Mist has managed to hire or coerce a wizard." Norian didn't sound happy. "We

Chapter 4

haven't had any evidence of this before, but then they might be desperate after a bunch of their top assassins were killed not long ago. We're still trying to figure that out."

I knew, but I wasn't about to let that slip—Erland and Wylend had sent out some of their own and Solar Red, Red Hand and Black Mist had all gotten hit. They didn't know that I knew, but I did.

They'd complained, too, that they hadn't been able to find Black Mist's or Solar Red's headquarters—they'd settled for temples on several worlds, and managed to find a few Black Mist operatives who'd moved in with Solar Red or Red Hand at those temples.

I hadn't told Erland, either, but I'd gone *Looking* for Black Mist myself, and what I'd found, or in this case *hadn't* found, worried me greatly. There was a blurring of information surrounding Black Mist, just as there was a buzz blocking information on the murders we were investigating. If Black Mist was able to block me from finding them, then somebody connected to the organization likely held a great deal of power. We'd have to track Black Mist by normal methods. I couldn't find them otherwise, and that was quite aggravating.

"Can we go to the last place the three victims worked together?" Norian asked, interrupting my thoughts.

"I'm ahead of you, boss—that's next on the list," Lendill said. We walked ten blocks or so and then Lendill attempted to manhandle the heavy, steel cover that concealed an entrance into the city's sewers. After watching him struggle for a while with the heavy weight, I moved him aside and lifted the cover off easily. Lendill quirked an eyebrow at me. Norian didn't even blink.

81

Blood Redemption

"They couldn't find a nicer smelling place to work?" I complained as we climbed down a narrow metal ladder and dropped into the round, brick-lined tunnel.

"Lissa Beth, are you going to complain the whole thirty years we work together?" Norian was back to smiling.

"More than likely," I replied. "If you don't like it, feel free to go to the Charter Members and demand another Liaison."

"That will not happen. They were quite insistent I work with you on this. I am stuck with you and you with me."

"Are you sure they said thirty years? That seems too long to me," I was back to being grumpy.

"I thought you were immortal—thirty years is no time at all," Norian pointed out as we followed Lendill.

"Is it part of your job description to be a thorn in my side and to continuously point out the obvious?" I wanted to poke Norian in the ribs.

"It is. In fact, I asked for that stipulation to be added to my contract shortly before I came to Le-Ath Veronis."

"So, tact and diplomacy aren't your strong suit?" I had to stop myself from elbowing Norian. As tight and muscular as his body was, he might not even feel it if I did.

"If I had either of those things, I'd be working as an ambassador for the Alliance." Norian was grinning again. Choosing to ignore Norian for a while, I turned my attention to our surroundings. Dim lights shone over our heads; otherwise, Lendill and Norian would have been walking blindly through the sewer. We branched off to the right after a while, until we came to the recent repair. New brick and mortar patched a hole large enough for a man to crawl inside on one wall. My skin itched. Something was wrong here and it had me worried.

Chapter 4

"Norian, I think you and Lendill should stand back," I said, and turning my arm to mist I reached through the wall, found what had been placed inside and drew it out. If we'd torn the brick out, a device would have been tripped and the bombers would be notified. Instead, I'd moved around that, pulling out the detonation device itself.

Lendill cursed and Norian had some choice words to offer as well. "Boss, what are we going to do with that?" Lendill asked when he ran out of expletives. I wanted to point out that neither one of them was holding the stupid bomb, but decided against it. For now, I was faced with handling a bomb. That was a new experience for me, and one I had no real desire to repeat.

While I'd attended Conclave, a deserted planet had been chosen to drop Alliance trash and refuse on—I decided to take the bomb there right away before any of us were blown to bits.

While Norian and Lendill casually discussed what we might do with the bomb, I folded away, placed the bomb carefully upon a tall mound of trash dumped on the deserted world of Tykl and folded back to Norian and Lendill.

"You may want to let the Alliance members know that the bomb is now on Tykl," I said, dusting myself off. Tykl wasn't a clean place—not with that much trash and debris dumped on it. Norian and Lendill shut up immediately and stared, blinking a time or two before shrugging their acceptance at my solution.

Lendill was the one who offered to make the communication. "Lissa Beth, I know you have a sensitive nose," Norian said instead. "Can you give us information on who was down here while the patch was placed?"

Blood Redemption

"Honey, it stinks so bad, I can't even sort out the scents of the three workers. If anybody knew that somebody might be looking for scents, they chose the perfect place to hide that bomb," I complained. It worried me, too—if they were concerned about scents, then they knew I might be one of the investigators.

"That bomb would have taken out half the city," Lendill observed dryly.

"Do you think that half the city is all they were aiming for, or is there another one of those things out there somewhere?" I asked, holding back a shiver.

"Lendill, can we get into the city records and find out where maintenance crews have been working in the sewers recently on the other side of town?" Norian asked.

"Sure. Let's go back to headquarters and we can pull up the information," Lendill nodded.

I wasn't willing to spend any longer in the sewer than I had to, so I misted the three of us to the opening, replaced the cover and then misted us to ASD headquarters.

"Why haven't we found somebody to do this for us before?" Lendill asked when I dropped him and Norian off inside the small office that doubled as sleeping quarters.

"Because nobody else can do this," Norian straightened his clothing absently. "Lissa Beth is the only one, aren't you, Lissa Beth?"

"How the hell should I know? And stop calling me Lissa Beth."

"But Lissa Beth, I like that name too much," Norian smiled. Yeah—looked like I was going to be stuck with thirty years of being called Lissa Beth. Lendill went to the wall opposite the sleeping cubicles, tapped a code into an alarm system keypad and a computer console slid out of the wall.

Chapter 4

"I think I saw this in a James Bond film once," I said, watching while Lendill sat at the console and began searching for information on sewer repairs.

"James Bond?" Now Norian was interested.

"A fictional spy character," I mumbled. "Around three hundred years ago."

"Maybe a little more than that," Norian was grinning again.

"Norian, have you been snooping around?" My hands were on my hips now and I was glaring at him.

"I have—I check out all my Liaisons. Information from Earth isn't easy to come by, but it can be had."

One of my claws slid out and I pointed it at him. "You'd better be able to keep your mouth shut, Norian Keef."

* * *

Norian watched Lissa carefully. He'd gotten the information, all right. The memoirs of the man who'd held the office of President when Lissa disappeared had been copied and placed carefully back in the archives before he was done, and then he'd placed a few well-planned questions here and there among the vampires who'd come to Le-Ath Veronis from Earth.

The windfall had come from her personal guard, who threatened Norian afterward. Norian now knew about Lissa's childhood; he'd gone to pull those records himself. He didn't blame Rolfe for making the threat—Lissa needed to be protected in that way. Norian was the only person inside the ASD who held all that information, and it would stay with him. He understood the devastation of a cruel childhood all too well.

* * *

Lissa

Blood Redemption

Norian was lost in thought for a few seconds and didn't seem concerned at all about the claw pointed in his direction. I let it slide back in. "Here we go, boss," Lendill had been working to get the required information, oblivious of what had passed between Norian and me.

Norian turned to see what Lendill had. We found records of seven repairs made in the sewers citywide, so we set out to check every stinking (in the literal sense) one of them.

Why is it that the thing you're looking for is always at the last place on your list? As if you have to put in the effort before the reward comes. We found a second bomb, but this time we also found something else.

This patch job was the biggest of all of them, so I misted inside and nearly gagged. Nine bodies, in addition to the bomb, lay inside a hastily excavated tomb. Bringing the bomb out first, I placed it beside its twin on Tykl before returning and misting the bloodied bodies out of their bricked-up hole. Norian and Lendill stared at one in particular.

"No way to know if he was in on this, or got too close and was killed as a result," Norian grumbled angrily as they glared at one of their missing agents, now deceased. Lendill nodded at Norian's assessment.

The other bodies were dressed in various ways—some looked like maintenance workers; the others could have been anyone. The nametags and ID hadn't been removed from the maintenance workers, though—three men and one woman still wore their city-issued identification. One of the nine was Norian's agent, so that left four others whom we couldn't identify.

Chapter 4

"Lissa, can you take these to the city morgue?" Norian asked me.

"Yeah, I can take them there. How are we going to explain this?"

"We have someone there," Norian replied enigmatically.

Lendill called somebody on his communicator and passed along information, then supplied directions. I gathered all the bodies as mist, then lifted Norian and Lendill. Someone met us on the loading dock behind the city morgue with nine body bags. Norian, Lendill and I helped get the bodies inside the bags then hauled them inside.

The agent who met us was barely five-four and nearly balding, with a round face. He looked to be the physician type to me. Norian then got on his communicator and I figured he was contacting somebody at Charter Headquarters.

If anybody ran the Alliance, it was the Founder and the Charter Members. They had their own staff, seldom came to Conclaves and cast their votes from remote locations. Must be nice to be them.

All of us were covered in blood and muck after the bodies had been stored in refrigerated boxes, so Norian finished filing his report quickly. We left the morgue employee behind and walked roughly two blocks before I turned to mist again, getting us back to ASD headquarters as swiftly as I could. The smell of rotting bodies clung to my clothes and skin and I wanted it gone.

"Go ahead and get a shower," Norian pointed Lendill and me toward the two shower cubicles. "I have a few more people to speak with."

I was happy to get into the shower as quickly as I could—the scent of death was making me gag.

Blood Redemption

At least the showers had doors that shut and afforded a little privacy. I came out after a while, clean, dressed in my PJs and a robe and combing out my hair. Norian was still waiting outside—I'd deliberately showered quickly so Norian could get his bath if he wanted. He nodded to me and went inside.

I'd brought a couple of books on comp-vid with me, so I settled down to read for a while. "I thought you'd be asleep," Lendill observed after stepping out of the shower wearing a bathrobe. At least he had some modesty—Norian didn't seem to own any.

"I will be before long," I answered his question while covering a yawn. Lendill nodded and went toward his cubicle—it was the last one, just past Norian's sleeping spot.

I tapped a bookmark in place between digital pages and snapped off the light above my bed. At least the beds were wide and comfortable—I couldn't fault the Alliance over that, even if they did need to learn a few things about privacy.

* * *

An unusual scent greeted my nostrils the following morning, and I was trying to puzzle it out in my mind before opening my eyes. I stretched beneath the covers—it's always a good idea to work the kinks out of muscles before rising.

The covers felt heavy for some reason—heavier than they had the night before. I managed to crack open my right eye and when I did, I found myself staring into the eyes of a huge snake resting on top of me.

If my scenting skills hadn't given me information there at the last second, I might have killed the snake before shrieking and misting off the bed, which would have been disastrous.

Chapter 5

*L*issa

My hands were shaking and I was trembling head to heels as I slid down the wall of my cubicle. It took several seconds to convince my voice to work as I watched the huge snake rise up in my bed and spread his hood, much like a cobra might. Only this hood appeared to be fringed with tiny, hair-like points.

This snake was at least twelve feet in length and nine inches in diameter at the widest point. "Norian Keef," I managed to gasp eventually, "change back this instant. I could have killed you, you stupid schmuck!"

Norian was giving me his widest grin yet as he materialized on my bed, completely naked. "Now see," he chuckled, "you're the first woman I've ever met who worried that she might kill me instead of the other way around."

Blood Redemption

"You couldn't discuss this over breakfast or something? You had to crawl into my bed? And what kind of snake is that, anyway?" I was still trying to catch my breath and keep my body from shivering.

"A lion snake," Norian replied casually, shrugging his shoulders indifferently. A lion snake. A fucking *lion snake*. Only the most poisonous snake in the known universes. He might have killed me while I slept.

"No, *breah-mul*, I would never do that," Norian must have seen the realization flash across my face. Well, it was all fine and good to say that. Another thing to actually do it, or in this case, *not* do it.

"I understand the trust issue; I have it myself," he went on when I didn't say anything. "My kind have our own form of compulsion and there are few who have discovered what I am that still remember. You are the one whom I cannot make to forget, so you will have to keep my secrets as well."

"Unless you decide to kill me," I struggled to my feet. "How many Liaisons have you killed, Norian Keef?" He looked hurt at my question.

"Not one, breah-mul," he snapped. "And the others never saw me as you have seen me."

"Norian, put some clothes on." His erection was distracting, to say the least. I wondered where Lendill was and if he knew.

"Lendill doesn't know—he's gone out to do some snooping. I couldn't help myself, little queen—I wanted to rest my head between your breasts. Just for a moment."

Norian rose and stalked off toward his own cubicle, as if he were the injured party. He'd called me breah-mul, too—in a few languages, it meant *my breath*.

90

Chapter 5

What was I supposed to do? Tell him it was okay to scare the bejeezus out of me and that one or the other of us could have ended up dead as a result? I slapped a hand over my face and we didn't talk to each other for the rest of the morning.

Lendill came back after a while with breakfast for Norian and me. We were both dressed by that time and ate little breakfast rolls stuffed with meat in an uncomfortable silence.

I won't give your secret away, I sent in grumpy mindspeech to Norian. The only indication he gave that he'd heard me was a brief widening of his eyes. He caught my arm later when we walked out to the streets, leaving Lendill behind at headquarters, working on the computer.

"Why didn't I know you could send mindspeech to anyone?" He hissed at me, shoving me against a wall in an alley.

"Maybe you didn't ask," I jerked my arm out of his grasp.

"Tell me you didn't scent something different about me," he had my arm in his grasp again. "Your scenting ability is legendary. Or is that a lie?"

"Not a lie," I muttered angrily. "But I've never scented one of your kind before. All races have a different scent. Trust me; if I run across another of your kind, I'll know it. And, if I happen to run across your parents or any of your relatives, I'll know that, too." That caused Norian to drop his hand and stare at me.

"You can tell who my parents are, just by smelling them?" His voice sounded hopeful and I had no idea why.

"Of course," I said. "Didn't all your records that you went to so much trouble to find say that?"

"No." His voice was clipped. He turned his head and cursed. "They must have thought the information was too sensitive to record."

"Yeah—those vampires, they're such a secretive bunch." I couldn't keep the sarcasm from my voice.

"We'll discuss this later—we've got places to go, first."

Those places turned out to be homes and apartments where the people we'd found the night before lived. Some of them had family or lovers, and they were all there, waiting for us when we arrived.

"He didn't tell me he had any new acquaintances," the first wife sobbed as she answered questions. "He worked as a clerk for the city. He scheduled the maintenance crews and made sure the equipment was delivered onsite. Why would anyone want to kill him?"

Norian managed to look sympathetic and shook his head, although he could have given a partial reason. We just couldn't tip our hand. Lendill was already checking on bank deposits and transfers—Darthin didn't use any kind of cash—it was credit chip only.

"Did he seem worried about anything? Uncomfortable maybe?"

"No, why would that make any difference?" I could tell by the woman's answer that Darthin wasn't used to murder.

"In case someone was threatening him," I replied tiredly. She blinked at me a few times, and then the light came on.

"Why would anyone threaten my Parett? He wasn't important and his job was boring."

"He would be extremely useful if somebody wanted to plant bombs in the sewers," I grumped, before placing

Chapter 5

compulsion for her not to remember my questions or that she'd seen me to begin with. Norian and I walked out.

"They're not used to anything like this, so they don't even have suspicions," Norian observed when we walked away from the apartment. It made me think of the animals found on the Galapagos Islands, when the archipelago was first explored. The animals hadn't known to be afraid of humans. Here, something was killing Darthinians indiscriminately and they didn't have a clue.

Thankfully, the next house was empty—a widowed maintenance worker had lived there. There weren't any scents inside the house that were fresh, indicating the man hadn't been taken from there.

The next one was the home of the female worker, and her husband and two young children answered the door. The children—two little girls—were gripping their father's pants legs and peering around him, looking frightened. He had to put them in their room to play before coming out to talk to us.

"She's really dead, isn't she?" The man looked haggard.

"I'm afraid so," Norian answered. "I'm sorry to be here asking questions so quickly, but if we are to catch the ones responsible, we need information now."

"I understand," the man nodded tiredly. Norian went through his list of questions and the answers were much the same as before, except that the man did say his wife had lunch with someone the day before she was killed.

"She didn't pack a lunch the next morning, because she said she didn't eat the one she'd taken the day before. I asked her why, and she said she had lunch with a friend, but never did say who it was and I knew all her friends at work."

Blood Redemption

Norian asked for the list of friends, thanked the man and we left. I didn't know how he was going to tell his daughters that their mother wasn't going to come home.

Lendill received the list of names Norian collected before we arrived at the next house. We didn't get any useful information the rest of the day.

"All the people on that list work for the city, except one," Lendill said when Norian and I dragged back to headquarters later. "I contacted all of them and they say they didn't have lunch with the dead woman. This one here says she saw a strange man walking away when she returned from lunch, though."

"Where did she see him?" Norian asked.

"Outside the Vintel Street maintenance building," Lendill replied.

"Let's go," Norian gripped my arm and pulled me toward the door.

* * *

A confusion of scents greeted us as we made our way to the Vintel Street maintenance building's front entrance. I couldn't get anything from it since I had no reference point.

"Is this where all the employees go in and out, or is there another door?" I asked. Norian and I walked the perimeter and found three more exits in the low, rectangular building. The one at the back made me draw in a breath, though. Honestly, I didn't know why I hadn't thought of it before.

"A vampire was here," I whispered. Norian stared at me in shock.

"How long ago?" he snapped.

"The scent isn't fresh, maybe two or three days," I admitted. "Was she a night worker? The woman who was

Chapter 5

killed? A vampire could have lured her away to get information, then placed compulsion after, so she'd think she had lunch with a friend. It would be easy."

"Two-thirds are, since the evenings are so long, here," Norian grumbled. "Do you think this is why Black Mist favors the worlds with lengthy nights?"

"There may be a deeper meaning to the name Black Mist," I offered. "If any of them are misters, then that's how they find it so easy to kill—they can get in anywhere by turning to mist."

"Do you think they're all vampires?"

"No, honey," I replied absently, trying to piece this together. "I don't think there are many who might have escaped Kifirin's attention. He was out looking for vampires, after all. These vampires, if they're working with a wizard or warlock, could be hiding that way, behind a shield of some kind."

I didn't add that the wizard or warlock had to be mighty powerful, to block my *Looking* skills. I was frightened enough about it. No sense scaring the scales off Norian Keef, especially since I had very little information to offer.

"Can you track this one? This vampire?" Norian asked.

I did track him for a while, until he got onto public transportation; that's where the scent became confused with other passengers' scents and I couldn't get past that. Everyone in the city used public transportation and there were six million living in Darthough.

"Here's my question," I flung out a hand as we walked inside our headquarters later. "Were they planning to stay in the city when they blew it up, or were they going to get the hell out of Dodge before they pressed the button? If that's the case, what do you think they'll do after they press the button and nothing happens?"

"All right," Norian held up a hand, "explain what hell and Dodge are. The rest are valid questions."

"They're all valid questions," I elbowed him in the ribs. I did have to explain both hell and Dodge before it was over, though.

"Yes, there was a place called Dodge City," I fell over on my bed in exhausted resignation. I was tired and hungry and hadn't gone to energy in several days. That wasn't a good thing.

"Breah-mul, I wish I had your talent for getting people around by unconventional means, but I do not. You'll have to lean on me while we walk to a restaurant," Norian murmured next to my ear.

I thought that leaning on Norian might give Lendill ideas, so I didn't. We walked seven blocks to a restaurant and I got something similar to roast chicken in a gravy sauce. The food was good and Lendill ate what I couldn't finish.

Later, I was nearly too tired to change into my PJs and brush my teeth when we got back, but I managed. I left my body behind the minute the light was out and stayed energy for almost four hours before returning. I wasn't the least surprised to find Norian's lion snake draped over and around my torso the following morning.

* * *

"Look, I'm not sure what the others would think if they found you in my bed like this," I muttered, stroking his large, triangular head carefully. Norian opened a slitted eye and stared pitifully at me, as if he were afraid I'd chase him off or something.

Chapter 5

In the Reth Alliance, there are three varieties of snakes that can blink their eyes. Lion snakes are one of those varieties. Norian continued to blink at me, and I didn't know whether he was trying to wake up or convince me to let him lie there a few minutes longer.

"Don't turn those sad, snake eyes on me," I lifted the part of him that was weighing me down and set it aside. "Come on," I patted his gray and black patterned scales, "don't we have work to do?"

Norian plopped onto the floor and crawled toward his cubicle, reappearing a few minutes later in humanoid form, dressed and ready to go. "Where would the vampires be, if they were in the city?" he asked as we left headquarters behind.

"They could be anywhere, as long as they were convinced they were safe and away from sunlight," I said. "We used to stay in hotels; we just had to make sure the staff wouldn't disturb us during the day. We'd stop breathing once we went into the rejuvenating sleep, and we had to make certain we wouldn't be in danger of exposure to sunlight."

Norian had his communicator out quickly, talking to someone just as fast and asking if any hotel guests had requested they not be disturbed during the short, Darthinian days.

We had a list of six hotels in very little time and were on our way to the nearest one in five minutes. Norian also had agents on their way to other hotels, vampire cuffs in hand.

Together, we hauled in eight unconscious vampires and ten humans. Norian wanted them all taken to an underground facility, so that's where we ended up. When night fell, I sent mindspeech to Gavin. He, Tony, Aryn and Rigo all showed up to question rogues.

Blood Redemption

The vampires didn't want to talk, but none of them were stronger or older than Rigo and Aryn. They were talking as soon as compulsion was laid and Norian had Lendill and several others recording all of it.

* * *

Cloudsong

"This is the contract your deceased son-in-law signed with us," Kenderlin, monarch of Cloudsong, pushed a copy of the contract across the table toward Marid. "As you well know, when the safety of a Cloudsong monarch is concerned, if there is evidence of treachery or treason on the part of the wizard's family, then the head of the family must offer his life in exchange, if the death of the ruling monarch or his heir occurs as a result of the treason. We require your life, Marid of Belancour. You signed this contract with us, as did your son-in-law, before he came to protect Brandelin. We have evidence that Findal, your daughter's husband, threw in his lot with Black Mist in order to kill my son and secure the throne for the opposition."

"Under normal circumstances, if your evidence holds up in court, you might have required my life. But since you are no longer in possession of all the facts, then your ignorance may be excused," Marid pushed the contract back toward Kenderlin.

"My daughter was recently taken to wed by Shadow Grey of Grey House, and all debts were signed over to them as part of the marriage contract. Glendes Grey is now considered the head of the family in question. Feel free to present your claim for the life of the head of household to Glendes Grey himself."

"Is this the truth?" King Kenderlin's Prime Minister and his legal counselor both stared at Marid.

Chapter 5

"Oh, yes. I can provide a copy of the marriage contract for you quickly, should you desire to pursue the matter."

"Was Grey House made aware that something of this nature might be presented to them?" Kenderlin thought to ask. Grey House was extremely powerful and they might not have been made aware of the circumstances.

"I was not even aware myself, so how could they be?" Marid huffed indignantly. "You will be forced to provide unquestionable evidence, before Grey House will submit to any demands."

"Send a copy of the marriage contract immediately," Kenderlin's legal counsel, an ancient and graying stork of a man, demanded. Marid nodded and stood, prepared to leave immediately.

"We cannot demand Glendes' life—Grey House had no part of this," Kenderlin's Prime Minister hissed as soon as Marid was out of hearing range.

"But we can demand payment, and that payment will be substantial," a slow smile spread across legal counsel's face.

* * *

Grey Planet

"This was just delivered by courier." Cleo dropped the box in front of her father, Glendes of Grey House. "It's addressed to you and Shadow, from Kenderlin of Cloudsong."

"What is it? Some of Findal's effects after the attack?" Glendes was busy putting the monthly accounts together at his desk and barely spared a glance at the package.

"That might be the logical thing to assume, but I don't think that's it, Daddy. I have a feeling you should open this right away."

"Are you going to stand there until I do?" Glendes looked up at the youngest of his twin daughters.

"I think I should, Daddy. Kyler said to."

"The same Kyler who refused to come to the last family dinner?"

"That's the one," Cleo nodded.

"Fine," Glendes grumbled and reached for the package.

* * *

Darthin

Lissa

"It's probably the sire-child bond—nobody can get past that," Tony attempted to explain to Norian why the information regarding the bombs and who'd ordered them set wasn't coming.

I watched Norian from my seat next to Rigo. He'd settled beside me after his bout of questioning vampires was over and now held my hand in his, refusing to let go.

"Tiessa, you should have brought me with you at the beginning; I could have helped with this," Rigo told me softly as Norian asked other questions that Tony was doing his best to answer.

"I know, honey," I replied, squeezing his fingers. All we'd gotten from the captured vampires was that the bombs were scheduled to be detonated in two days. I had no idea what the leader or leaders of Black Mist intended to do when their bombs didn't explode according to schedule. Alliance bomb squads had been dispatched to Tykl to disarm what I'd dropped off there already.

"If we notify the local authorities that Black Mist is attempting a takeover, it will cause widespread panic. If we don't notify them and an attack happens anyway, lives will be

Chapter 5

lost. This is the worst kind of mess," Norian raked hands through his hair in frustration.

"They need to know, boss," Lendill walked over to stand next to Norian.

"I suppose you're right," Norian sighed. "Get the Chancellor on the communicator—see if he can come down here himself." Lendill nodded and pulled out his communicator.

* * *

"It isn't just vampires—it's humanoids and possibly rogue wizards as well," Norian and Lendill were trying to get the Chancellor to calm down—he was about to condemn all vampires, even as he was surrounded by them at the moment. We weren't about to alert him to that fact. The Chancellor was still railing several minutes later when I tired of listening to his rant.

"It is in times like these that we learn what our leaders are made of," I barked at him. He was so shocked he shut up for a moment. "That's better," I said. "Now, this could have been any world under attack by Black Mist. They chose yours, for reasons known only to them. What do you intend to do about it? How are you going to keep your people safe? Now is the time to act, Chancellor. Yesterday is gone and tomorrow may be too late."

I watched as his mouth worked for several seconds—he wasn't bad looking or particularly old and I wondered what his qualifications had been for his election. Of course, none of that mattered now—it was what he did from this point forward that would define him and his rule.

"We will not succumb to these threats," he said finally. "I must tell my people that Black Mist wants our world and we must stand strong and refuse to let them take it."

Blood Redemption

"The Alliance already has three legions on the way, but you must have your security personnel ready to coordinate and get the population involved. We will invite the media in, too, and this story will be spread across the Alliance. All will know that Black Mist is attempting to take control of Darthin." Norian nodded with satisfaction.

Put all the Alliance worlds with long nights on alert, I sent to Norian, who nodded discreetly to acknowledge my sending. *And alert the other cities here—the ones we caught didn't have information on other attacks, but that doesn't mean there won't be any.*

"Already on it," Norian mumbled, knowing I would hear. That's how we ended up in two more cities later that evening; Norian's agents had found twelve more vampires and sixteen humans. They'd all been taken into custody before the sun set; the agents were waiting for Norian and the rest of us to arrive and question the vampires after nightfall.

We also found the bombs set in those city sewers; they were shipped offworld to the bomb squad on Tykl. Gavin and Tony began their questioning after I told them that the oldest of these vampires was barely two hundred. That had Norian raising an eyebrow and hauling me out of the questioning tank, Rigo right behind.

"Do not harm my Queen," Rigo eyed Norian's hand, which gripped my upper arm.

"Do you think I would?" Norian gave a snort but dropped his hand anyway. "You can tell the ages?" We were back to *that* again.

"Norian, I have no idea what you've learned about me or whether any of it is true. Maybe we should get together later

Chapter 5

and discuss it. In the meantime, you and Rigo should try to get along. You have some things in common, after all."

"And what would that be?" Norian snapped. He was about to get hissy, I figured, and that didn't need to happen with so many others close by.

"I think you could have a long conversation about poisons," I grumbled and attempted to move past Norian.

They were both staring at me now—Rigo and Norian—as if I'd let the most important cat out of the biggest bag ever. "Look," I said, "If both of you think you're going to end up in my bed, then all my mates need to know. Therefore, 'fess up."

"They have already guessed about me, after Satris," Rigo grumbled.

"You did that? Then you have my support and admiration," Norian clapped Rigo on the back. "I couldn't have done better myself."

"He almost killed my tiessa," Rigo defended his actions.

"You think I don't know that?" Norian displayed one of his famous grins. "I might have hunted him down myself. You saved me the trouble."

"See, you do have a lot to talk about. I need a drink." I moved away from them but they caught up almost immediately. Neither of them was satisfied with sitting on the opposite side of the booth at a nearby bar, so I was wedged between Rigo and Norian while I sipped a fruit drink.

Norian was quite impressed with Rigo and his story, and I had a feeling Norian would be studying up on his Hraedan history just as soon as possible. Rigo was Rigovarnus I. Six other Rigovarnuses had ruled Hraede after him, but none were good enough for the turn, according to Rigo.

Blood Redemption

I bumped his shoulder and teased him about it—he doesn't like the formal version of his name much. He leaned in to kiss me, which caused our server to raise eyebrows.

We had to take Rigo to a nearby ASD office later so Norian could make the turn and Rigo, after he recovered from the initial shock, asked Norian if he could have poison to work with.

Norian carries the poison glands all the time; they're just well-hidden while he's humanoid. He showed Rigo the sacs, located on the sides of his neck.

"I can extract some for you, but I have to release it," Norian explained. Rigo nodded—he had extensive knowledge and a healthy respect for all poisons.

Rigo and Norian were well on their way to a strong friendship when we got back to the others. The information regarding Black Mist's attempted takeover had already been distributed to the media across the Alliance, so we were watching the news reports as they were broadcast.

* * *

Black Mist Headquarters

"Do you see this?" Viregruz wanted to smash the vid screen with his fists, but he needed the information and another vid screen might be hard to come by at that time of night.

Viregruz looked sixteen of his thirty-six hundred years, and anyone who failed to respect him when they were looking to join Black Mist, died in the most painful way possible.

Viregruz's two Blood Captains nodded deferentially to Viregruz. They were talented as vampires—both could turn to mist, but neither held the complement of talents that

Chapter 5

Viregruz held. He not only had misting ability; he could mindspeak and shapeshift.

Viregruz became a falcon when he shifted, and while falcons were day flyers, Viregruz's alter ego could see as well as any vampire in darkness. He could take that shape in an instant, rather than waiting lengthy minutes to become mist.

Many were the times when he'd gotten into a closed room as mist to commit murder, and then shifted to falcon and sat in the rafters or some other out-of-the-way place while everyone went looking for a humanoid perpetrator.

"The Alliance is behind this—only they would notify the authorities and spread this across the Alliance worlds," Viregruz cursed again.

"The ASD," one of his Blood Captains ventured to speak.

"Of course the bloody ASD," Viregruz growled. "If it were that Queen Bitch Vampire, she'd have killed my operatives and kept it quiet."

"Do you want us to switch the vendetta?" Viregruz's second Blood Captain asked.

Viregruz had pulled back the reward on the Queen Vampire's head, announcing a vendetta against her instead. Viregruz's war with the queen had become personal when she'd managed to kill his brothers, who were his six best operatives. Black Mist would be eliminating her itself, and if Viregruz could do it single-handedly, so much the better.

"No, I want you to add that fucking director of the ASD to the list. Get them both. I demand satisfaction in this."

"Are we going to attempt a rescue?"

"And risk losing others? Besides, our operatives were my turns. No important information will be given out." Viregruz at least had that satisfaction. "The humans were merely slaves. They knew nothing; they were only there to be watchful during the days."

What irritated Viregruz most, even if he held it back from his captains, was that the Alliance now knew that Black Mist had vampires working for them. Perhaps they didn't realize yet that it was also run by vampires, but that supposition had to be there.

Too bad they didn't know about Viregruz's stable of rogue wizards and warlocks. That trump card was still well hidden and remained up Viregruz's sleeve. If anyone might be able to track the director of the ASD and the Queen Vampire when she was away from her world, his power-wielding members would.

"Bring Zellar to me, I have an assignment for him," Viregruz smiled grimly.

* * *

Grey Planet

"Have you been to bed with her?"

Shadow was offended at his grandfather's question. "No! And I bloody well don't intend to get in bed with her. She's rude to the servants, expects them to wait on her hand and foot and hasn't lifted a finger to do anything. You wanted Calebert to assess her talent—I suggest you ask him how that went!" Shadow wanted to throw something, there just wasn't anything on Glendes' usually cluttered desk to throw.

"Son, settle down." Raffian had come and was now sitting at a corner of Glendes' desk.

Shadow had already seen the demands from Kenderlin of Cloudsong when Glendes called him to his study and handed over the package. Glendes had already opened it and read the messages before giving it to Shadow.

Chapter 5

Shadow was more than angry—his father and grandfather had not only destroyed his relationship with Lissa, they'd brought trouble to Grey House in the form of Melida of Belancour.

"We'll attempt to get a writ of detachment," Glendes sighed. "Your father and I suspect that Marid and Melida both knew of this before shopping Melida around so quickly after Findal's death."

He lifted a pile of papers from a desk drawer and pushed them toward Shadow. "If we can't get the writ of detachment, things will go very badly for Grey House."

Shadow now wore a look of concern as he drew the papers toward him and began to read.

* * *

Le-Ath Veronis

Lissa

"Lissa, this worries me. You are considering taking a shapeshifter who becomes a lion snake as a mate?" Roff was pacing at the foot of my bed and rustling his wings.

"Honey, I don't get any bad vibes off him. Rigo and his Hraedan Order of the Night Flower concoct poisons all the time, yet you don't have any problem with him." I watched Roff pace. If he had a problem with Norian, what were the others going to say?

"But Rigo is a vampire and only wishes to protect you. How can we know about Norian Keef?"

"If Norian wanted me dead, I'd be dead already," I huffed. In the physical sense, anyway.

"Then give this some time. Surely, you can wait a few months before offering a ring. Do you love him, Lissa? Do you love him already?"

107

"Honey, I don't know what I feel," I told him honestly. "But there's a part of Norian that is vulnerable, and terrified of rejection. I'm worried about him."

"Then he can court you, as the others have. If you do not love him after six months, then you should reject him, no matter what the effect will be. You are taking in strays, my love. Do not allow the Grey House betrayal to affect your judgment in this."

"But you don't care if Rigo comes on board."

"No. In fact, the others have wondered why you have dithered so long over this."

"You've talked about this behind my back." I wasn't sure how I felt about that.

"Love, this affects all of us, so of course we have discussed it. If you are happy, then we are happy. Things have been off for a while, Lissa. You have not invited Karzac to your bed since Kevis was born. He loves you, and you are both upset. Do not make him feel guilt over having a child."

"Roff, what do you expect? Toff was stolen away after the worst kind of betrayal, and Kevis needs to know who his father is. I don't want Karzac to be forced to divide his attention—his child deserves as much of that as he can get."

"Lissa, a night or two during each month is not stealing time away from Kevis. That child gets more than enough attention from Radomir, Justin, Mack, Lisster and the others to smother any normal baby. You did not turn me out of your bed because you were worried that Toff wouldn't know who I was."

"No, but it was accomplished by other means," I sighed and fell back on my bed. "Roff, what are we going to do? I want that baby back so bad I can taste it, and now Erland and Garde have children on the way. Black Mist is out there,

Chapter 5

seething because I killed those six pet Ra'Ak of theirs, I'm not speaking to my father and he's refused to apologize. And Shadow hasn't even tried to talk to me."

"You sent his ring back; perhaps he doesn't feel welcome."

"What would you have done, Roff? Say okay, fine, go right ahead and rub it in a little more that I can't have babies?"

"Lissa," Roff sat beside me and stroked hair away from my forehead. "That wasn't Shadow talking. That was his father and grandfather talking, and they had no right to carry such news to you—not at any time and especially at the moment they did. You were ill, and while that would have been a blow at the best of times, it was particularly heavy then. My concern is that they have not approached you since then and tried to set things right."

"Roff, they were glad to get rid of me. I'm just a barren Vampire Queen who has nothing to offer Grey House. Admit it—they're happy I gave Shadow's ring back."

"My love, they cannot be anything of the kind. They have made Shadow miserable and they know this. I have spoken with your Falchani twins—they know Shadow well. Things are not going so well for Grey House at the moment." Roff leaned down to kiss me, preventing me from asking questions. After a while, the questions didn't matter anyway.

* * *

"Are you both well? Do you need anything?" Connegar and Reemagar had shown up after my unplanned nap with Roff and folded me to my beach house where Poradina and Evaline were. The two surrogates were smiling at me.

"She's worse than any new mother," Poradina laughed. "We're only a month along, stop fretting. We haven't even

109

felt sick yet, and this beach house is amazing. The comesuli bring us anything we want and if we don't gain forty pounds, then it will be the biggest surprise."

"You're handling this much better than I would," I said. Yeah, I was completely amazed.

"Because these are your children and not ours. You get to rise in the night to feed them and chase after them and listen to them whine over something they can't have," Evaline teased.

"I'm looking forward to it," I said.

"We know; that's why we're teasing you about it. Don't worry about us. We're living in luxury."

"We will bring an apprentice Larentii surrogate next week—this will be good training for Daragar," Connegar smiled brightly.

"What will a Larentii do for us?" Poradina asked. She was very curious, but wasn't rejecting the idea.

"He will help with the morning illness and will trill for you if it is needed," Reemagar replied.

"What is trilling?" Evaline wanted to know.

"Only the most restful sound in the universes," I answered her question. "If they do it for me, I fall asleep in no time."

"It is for the mothers, mostly, but it will soothe any female if it is needed," Connegar explained. "We love our mate and that is why we do it."

"That's so nice of you, honey," I reached up and hugged his waist.

"We will take our mate, now. Let the comesuli know if you require anything," Reemagar said before folding me away.

* * *

Chapter 5

Grey Planet

"First of all, I don't see how they could do this, and to name Lissa as part of this and attempt to extort money from her is preposterous!" Shadow was ready to take the workshop apart.

"Any legal counsel will attempt this—to get as many parties involved as possible. They're looking at not only how profitable Grey House is, but Le-Ath Veronis as well. If Marid and Melida were aware of Findal's perfidy, then they plotted this out well. I know you haven't been to bed with her—Shannon verified it for me," Raffian held up a hand to hold off Shadow's ready complaint. "But Melida got pregnant somehow. Who knows how that happened? This is so confusing," Raffian hissed angrily, pinching the bridge of his nose to stave off an impending headache.

"Mom says it had to happen sometime before Melida got here. They wanted insurance and they went to great lengths to get it," Shadow pointed out. "This is to keep Marid's head and body connected. We know that now, but what is Lissa going to do when she discovers she's been dragged into this?"

Shadow felt sick. Before the package had arrived from Cloudsong, he'd been toying with the idea of approaching Lissa and trying to apologize, just to see if he couldn't repair things in some way. Marid and Melida were going to destroy any chance he might have with Lissa.

"Son, if it makes you feel any better, we moved too quickly on this—your grandfather and I. I heard from Kyler that Lissa has two surrogates pregnant right now—her Larentii received permission to manipulate the DNA in two donor eggs and now Gardevik and Erland Morphis are going to be parents with Lissa. They might have done this for you, too. We've managed to fuck this up all the way around and now that Cloudsong is attempting to get judgment against us and Lissa as well, I think you know what the outcome is likely to be where Lissa is concerned."

"Yeah, Dad. That has already crossed my mind."

Chapter 6

*L*e-Ath Veronis
　　　　Lissa
　　　"What is this?" Rigo was almost afraid to take the small box I held out to him.

"Something you have waited for," Thurlow was there in a flash of light. It's a good thing he doesn't feel jealousy. I'd called Rigo to my study and asked Grant and Heathe to leave us alone for a little while. Too bad Thurlow can go anywhere he likes, being what he is and all.

"You were approved by the others," I said, as Rigo opened the box. The gold signet ring bearing the claw crown crest nestled inside. I'd had to *Look* to get it made in the proper size.

I'd had a second ring made, too—in Norian's size. My mind was turning to him more and more often, lately. He'd wiggled his way into my heart, and not in any traditional manner. I was going to give it a while, as Roff suggested, but I didn't know how long I could hold out.

I'd already warned the inner circle and the palace guards and comesuli not to harm any lion snake they might come across—lion snakes weren't native to Le-Ath Veronis. Somehow, Norian had heard of it and came to dinner grinning hugely.

"Tiessa, is this real?" Rigo was having trouble breathing, I think.

"Honey, it's real," I said.

"I want you to place it on my finger."

"All right. This is for my love," I took his left hand and slid the ring onto his finger.

"And this is for mine," Rigo leaned down and kissed me. Thurlow disappeared just as suddenly as he'd shown up and Rigo was too eager, even, to allow me to fold us to my suite.

It's a good thing the sofa in my study is long and comfortable. Rigo wasn't satisfied until he'd touched every part of me. I gave him permission to bite and he was so gentle I didn't even feel it. We were both nearly asleep when I managed to fold us to my suite.

* * *

Several kinds of news waited for me when Rigo and I arrived for dinner. I expected Drake and Drew to snicker and tease me, but that didn't happen.

All the news I got was bad. I wondered why Raffian, Shadow, Glendes, Kyler and Cleo had come to dinner—I hadn't invited them and honestly, three out of that five weren't particularly welcome on Le-Ath Veronis at the moment. Erland and Wylend folded in as I was sitting down, as did Merrill, Kiarra, Adam and Wlodek.

Chapter 6

"We know an apology won't be appreciated or accepted right now," Glendes began as the first course was laid before us. I had to hold a snort back—right then they were imposing on my good graces by being at my table uninvited. I watched Shadow—I couldn't help it—but he was staring at his plate and not eating.

"We never expected anything like this to happen; it is completely unprecedented," Raffian went on. "At no other time have we or any other wizard clan dealt with something like this."

"Then maybe you should stop beating around the bush and just tell me," I said, setting my fork down. They were destroying what should have been a good day for Rigo and me.

Gavin was frowning deeply from his seat next to Rigo, and I think Norian would have given anything at that moment to be able to send mindspeech. Wylend looked like a thundercloud and Erland was ready with the thunder and lightning. Garde must have gotten mindspeech from somebody, because he skipped in late for dinner.

"This begins with Findal, Melida's wizard mate and the contract he signed with Kenderlin of Cloudsong to protect Brandelin, the royal heir," Glendes said. "Cloudsong is one of the few worlds which require this sort of contract—in fact, it is this that kept them out of the Alliance forty years ago. They weren't willing to give up the rights, if you can call them that."

"What he means, Lissa, is that where the safety and well-being of Cloudsong's crown or its heirs are concerned, they make sure that the ones they contract with only have the best interests of the crown at heart," Merrill took up the explanation. "Cloudsong requires that the wizard and the wizard's head of household, if there is one, sign the contract. If the wizard willfully fails in his duty to protect or perform, then their life is forfeit, as well as the life of the head of their household. This is their way of making sure the lives of the crown are protected."

"So? What does this have to do with me?" I asked. I hadn't signed a contract with Cloudsong, and I wasn't the head of any household involved.

"It has to do with Findal, Melida's deceased spouse," Glendes said.

"Melida being the one who can have babies." I didn't hold the snort back that time.

"Yes. That is indeed the one," Glendes nodded. "King Kenderlin of Cloudsong learned recently that Findal joined Black Mist to take down the crown Prince. Both Brandelin and Findal died in the ambush, when Findal gave away their location. Kenderlin demanded the blood price against Marid, Melida's father, as head of household for the Belancour Wizards. Unfortunately, Melida had already come to Shadow and the marriage had taken place. In the contract Grey House signed with Marid of Belancour, I am not only Melida's new head of household, but we agreed to take on any debts that Melida and Findal incurred. At the time of my signing, the debts were insignificant."

"So those fuckers are now after your head?" I was about to come out of my seat. Rigo placed a careful hand over mine to hold me down.

"The communication we received from Cloudsong's legal counsel informs us that they are being generous, as they realize we had nothing to do with Brandelin's death—they are merely demanding all proceeds from our work for the

Chapter 6

next fifty years and all profits from Le-Ath Veronis for the same amount of time."

"And how are they connecting my mate to all this?" Kifirin was suddenly in the dining room, blowing smoke and ready to go Thifilathi, I think. Everybody needed to get the hell out if that happened.

"They learned of Shadow and Lissa, most likely from Marid," Raffian replied carefully. "Since Shadow still wears Lissa's ring, Cloudsong intends to reap as much profit from this as they can. They are demanding their price from anyone involved and they feel this includes Lissa, as Shadow's mate. Shadow is also listed as Melida's mate of record. Melida managed to get herself pregnant before she came to us, so she'd have an ironclad reason to stay mated to Shadow. The child isn't his, but Cloudsong doesn't recognize DNA evidence or anything of the sort. Any male is responsible for their female mate's child, according to their laws."

"They thought this out well, didn't they, and then they threw the bait your way and reeled you right in." I threw my napkin on the table. "Do they expect me to take this lying down? Because I can assure you, I will not. If you'll get miss pregnant pants in front of me in the next five minutes, we'll find out whose baby it is."

"Lissa, we can't do that; when we mentioned it to her before in an attempt to discover who fathered her child, she went into hysterics and Selkirk had to place her in a healing sleep. She seems terrified of vampires."

"She may have reason to be," Gavin growled.

"Gavin, you and Anthony gave an oath when you were brought in as auxiliary Spawn Hunters," Kiarra said. "You are not allowed to confront these—it is not a direct attack against your mate." Well, I was learning something new, I think. I didn't know there were oaths attached to their signing up with the Saa Thalarr.

"Lissa, we should have explained this a little better," Merrill said.

"Uh-huh," I stood, then—even Rigo couldn't hold me down.

"Not all her mates are held to those standards," Rigo stood beside me.

"Lissa should take care of this herself—the hearing is scheduled in six days." Thurlow showed up by folding into the dining hall. If anybody wasn't already aware that he wasn't just an official from the Alliance, they knew now.

"Oh, my God." Kiarra was now standing and staring at Thurlow. She knew if nobody else did. "Lissa, do you know who this is?" I'd never seen Kiarra so upset, I don't think.

"Yes, I know exactly who it is," I replied, looking at Thurlow, who used to be Thorsten. "At least he says he loves me, which is more than my father says nowadays." I'd had enough of this, so I folded away.

* * *

Norian settled back in his chair, unsure whether he should be amused at all the commotion, or upset on Lissa's behalf. He felt both emotions—Lissa was obviously upset and he understood that. It was amusing, too, watching Adam and Merrill try to get to Thurlow, before a blinding light appeared and someone named Belen called them back, explaining that Thurlow, who'd been someone named Thorsten long ago, had paid his debts, except what he owed to Lissa. Now he was trying to make up for a great mistake he made where she was concerned.

The fact that Thurlow was acting as an agent for the Alliance concerned Norian not at all. Norian wished he could

Chapter 6

find Lissa—he would tend to her if the others wouldn't. They seemed content to argue with Belen, Thurlow, Glendes of Grey House and his son and grandson. Norian settled in to watch the entire debacle—it was more amusing that Alliance vid-vision.

* * *

Harifa Edus
Lissa

If my life wasn't fucked up in one way, it was fucked up in another. I was held responsible for the screw up on Cloudsong, though I hadn't signed anything and had no part in any of it? That was priceless, and not in any good way.

Did I need legal counsel? Cloudsong obviously had some fucked up rules. Once again, I'd chosen Harifa Edus as my place to hide. Too bad the planet was still in its second infancy—there weren't any tall buildings to sit on to ponder life's little problems.

* * *

Le-Ath Veronis

"We were trying to find a good time to tell her," Tony muttered to Wlodek. He still felt as if he were under obligation to the former Head of the Vampire Council.

"You should know how much she hates the withholding of information," Wlodek reminded Tony. Gavin stood nearby, not offering any excuse. "There must be a way out of this, without employing vampires to threaten the crown of Cloudsong, although they have no right to harm Lissa in any way." Wlodek raked a hand through thick, black hair. "I will speak to the others, including Dragon and Crane, to see if they have suggestions."

"They will not harm my Lissa," Gavin was back to growling.

"They're not threatening physical harm," Wlodek pointed out.

"It is emotional harm—how is that not physical in the long term?" Tony demanded.

"That is true, but there is still a fine line—you can't interfere," Wlodek added.

* * *

"Cloudsong is a world of light; you cannot destroy it, especially since they are not making a physical threat against your mate," Belen pointed out to Kifirin, who stood and glowered at his Light Brother and counterpart.

Kifirin was still actively blowing smoke, but that presented no threat to Belen. Belen knew that Kifirin was angry—dangerously so. Still, Belen could not be harmed. "Lissa will have to deal with this—when she was made, she was given the ability to traverse both sides of the universes. The ones above us wanted this."

"You know as well as I, Brother, that there is much she cannot do so long as she holds to this corporeal body. And she will not willingly release it for a very long time."

"I know this, but there is still much she can accomplish. We must leave this in her hands. We cannot come rushing to her defense every time there is a problem." Belen crossed arms over his chest—a humanoid gesture he liked very much.

"When have we ever rushed to her defense, Belen? When?" Kifirin demanded.

"Well, perhaps it is the other way around," Belen admitted. "If she had not acted, we would have all gone back to the beginning. We have done small things, here and there, but Lissa mostly takes care of herself and the others."

Chapter 6

"Yes—Lissa takes care of the others, generally before she thinks of herself. When can we think about her, Belen? Do you dislike her?"

"You ask such a question?"

"I merely wish to learn that you mean her no harm."

Belen watched his dark brother for the space of a few humanoid breaths. "Would you like to come with me, Brother, and rectify a wrong?" he asked.

"Which wrong do you mean? There are so many of them."

"Come and see." Belen folded Kifirin away.

"Where is this?" Belen had dropped Kifirin inside a very dark and cluttered space. Belen allowed his light to shine dimly, illuminating the place. It was a cellar on Earth, more than three hundred years past.

"No," Kifirin muttered at the slight form, which had been carelessly dumped onto a bare space on the cold floor. Lissa's limbs were tangled; she'd been dropped with disregard onto the rough surface and abandoned. Sergio and Edward didn't care if she woke at all, no matter her discomfort if she did happen to wake.

"She will wake in a few minutes," Belen murmured.

"Avilepha, how could they leave you like this?" Kifirin was crooning and turning Lissa onto her back, arranging her limbs in a more comfortable position. "What wrong are we making right?" Kifirin looked at Belen.

"This." Belen held out his hand and a paper square appeared in it. He carefully settled the napkin on the corner of a nearby desk. "Edward and Sergio did not leave their agreement in this cellar, Brother, and without it, Lissa might not have been afraid enough to leave this place. Do you still think I do not care for her? That I might wish her harm?

121

Neither of those things is true. You chose her as your mate. I will not interfere with that. She belongs to all of us, though. Surely you know this."

"I will search for her and hold her. Do you think she does not need that?"

"Of course she needs that. As long as she retains this body, she will need that." Belen knelt, reaching out to touch Lissa's cheek. "We will meet again soon, little one. I am sorry to leave you now." Belen folded Kifirin away.

* * *

Harifa Edus
Lissa

"Avilepha, what are you thinking?" Kifirin found me again. At least I wasn't shaking and crying this time. Truthfully, I felt angry and hurt. Glendes, Raffian and Shadow had come to dump their problem in my lap, with no offer to help get me out of it. It infuriated me that they'd placed me in this position to begin with.

"I was thinking about all the greedy people in the universes," I muttered. I still couldn't understand how Cloudsong felt I was obligated because somebody I'd never met had signed up with Black Mist and managed to die with the prince he was supposed to protect.

"My love, you must find a way out of this."

"How am I going to explain to my Council that somebody we didn't even know about now wants our profits for the next fifty years?" I snapped. "How can you expect a fair hearing on the planet that wants to rape and extort in the first place? Is this payment for my getting children after all?"

"Avilepha, your children are not in exchange for this," Kifirin sighed. "Your children are a gift to you, as any child is. A weak wizard who could not fight Black Mist put this in

Chapter 6

motion. Then, his daughter, with full knowledge of what her husband had done, acted in the only way she could to keep herself and her father alive. She is angry, avilepha, and guilty. She knew what was happening and did not attempt to stop it."

"She knew about her husband's alliance with Black Mist." I shook my head at the complexity of the situation.

"Yes," Kifirin confirmed. "She wished to form a new clan with her husband and willingly agreed to the amount offered by Black Mist. Of course, the money never materialized and her husband then paid for the treachery with his life. Now, she cannot tell her father that part of the story, because she would have competed against her own family for the same business. Additionally, the fact that Black Mist was involved would warrant a death sentence at her father's own hand. Therefore, her reasons for becoming pregnant were twofold. It was to save her life and to obligate Grey House at one and the same time. Her family will not execute a mother."

"What kind of mother do you think she's going to be to her child?" I asked.

"I do not know, love."

"Kifirin?"

"What is it, Lissa?"

"What am I going to do?"

"My love, I do not know. Even Belen says you must find a way out of this."

"What am I supposed to do about Shadow and Grey House? Right now, I want to slap Glendes and Raffian through a wall and before, I liked them. How did things turn out so badly?"

"I don't think they meant to harm you. Not as they did, and they certainly had no knowledge of this. They should have done more investigation, however, before taking Melida as quickly as they did. I feel Marid was to blame for that—he made it appear as if there were more offers for his daughter than there were. He knew, somehow, that Shadow was without an heir and unlikely to get one with his current mate."

"So everything is fucked up, now. I don't know what to do about Shadow and me," I sighed.

"You must decide whether you love him or not. Then decide whether that love is sufficient to weather this. And if you decide to stay with Shadow, you must find a way to deal with his father and grandfather."

"That sounds like so much fun."

* * *

"Thank the skies," Norian muttered when I appeared inside his office after folding away from Kifirin.

"Tell me why you sounded hopeful when I told you I'd know your parents if I met them, Norian," I sat on one of the chairs placed before his desk. Norian looked shocked at my words and didn't speak for a while, settling for watching me instead.

"Because I don't know who they are," he said angrily. "I was taken away from them—stolen and thrown into a cage, because my kind aren't supposed to make poison until they turn nine. I was four, Lissa Beth, and somebody wanted to add a lion snake shapeshifter to his menagerie. They had to capture a child, because the adults were too dangerous. The starship I was hauled away on was boarded by Alliance Security. I was too young to tell them where I was from, and with very little information available, they couldn't return me to my parents." He shook his head.

Chapter 6

"Understandably, those of my kind remain hidden," he continued. "My disappearance may have been reported locally on the planet of my birth, but there was no reason to believe I might be transported away—children can be stolen anywhere, but the expense of shipping them offworld is usually too much to consider. Unless the child is very special, that is, and my parents would probably not reveal that information. Child abductions are generally not handled by the ASD."

"Norian, this sounds like a tragedy in the making," I sighed.

"It was—on the first full moon, the Alliance officers discovered what I was and I know they discussed killing me. They did not, so I was raised in a laboratory, almost. There were a few I cared for as I grew up, but not many. They were frightened of me, breah-mul. Frightened of what I became. It affected their treatment of me. Yes, I realize it is unusual for me to be working for them now, but one of the Charter Members approached me after I was old enough to apply for ASD officer training, and suggested it might be a good fit. That is why I am here, now. And hopeful, now, too, that you may run across my parents one day. We live a long life, Lissa Beth. I am one hundred sixteen and I expect to live for centuries unless I am killed."

"Are you afraid of me?" I asked.

"Lissa Beth, I am only afraid that you will reject me and turn me out of your palace."

"What about that temper of yours, Nori? Will you be angry enough to sink those fangs of yours into me someday?"

Norian rose from his chair, walked around his desk and sank to a knee beside my chair. "Lissa Beth, you hurt me to even suggest that. Yes, I anger quickly—I think it is part of what I am. I have never killed anyone except criminals. They died swiftly, breah-mul. Much like those you kill."

He lifted one of my hands and kissed it, setting it on the arm of my chair before turning before my eyes, his clothing dropping away from his snake form. I sat there as he tilted forward until his head lay on my shoulder, and when I didn't object, he slid slowly around the back of my neck, his head coming to rest on my breast on the opposite side.

I reached up and stroked his head gently—his scales were smooth and cool under my hand. He closed his eyes under my touch—it must have been so hard for him as a child, knowing that none of those who raised him would touch him like this.

"Norian, we have work to do," I breathed. "And I haven't eaten, yet. Dinner sort of got ruined for me."

"So I have to get dressed again?" Norian was back to humanoid, and he cursed softly under his breath while he reached for his clothes.

"You can come with me as lion snake," I offered. "I just don't know how the kitchen staff might feel about that when we show up to raid the fridge."

"Will you feed me? I didn't get much to eat earlier either—I was too busy listening to the debate. What does Saa Thalarr mean?"

"You heard that?" Norian still hadn't made any effort to put clothes on and he wasn't trying to hide anything from me. I'll be honest; my eyes kept straying to certain parts of his anatomy. Finally, I slapped a hand over my eyes. "Norian, either get dressed or turn. I can't keep myself from staring and that's not polite."

Norian laughed, lifted my hand away from my eyes, gave me a quick kiss and turned to his twelve-foot alter ego.

Chapter 6

His head came up to my waist as he slithered along the marble hall toward the kitchens. If any of my guards thought to question, they kept the words behind their teeth.

Norian ate an entire roasted chicken as a snake. Yeah, just worked his flexible lower jaw somehow and swallowed the whole carcass. "Are you trying to freak me out?" I asked as I ate a drumstick I'd wrestled away from him at the last minute. "If you are, remember you're talking to the woman who can and does drink blood for meals."

I watched in fascination as the lump that was the chicken slid its way down his torso. If a snake could smile, I think Norian would have been smiling, right then.

Norian went to his office while I went to mine after we ate and I was signing papers and muttering to myself when Rigo found me. "Tiessa, this was supposed to be our day," he grumbled as he settled on the side of my desk.

"Funny how that got fucked up, isn't it?" I grumped and straightened a pile of signed papers. Grant and Heathe would have to sort through them in the morning and make sure they went to the proper places.

Rigo didn't say anything; he began removing clothing instead. His first, and then mine. He pulled me onto the floor after that and settled me on his lap, facing him. If I hadn't thought to shield and soundproof my study before things became noisy, just about anybody, with or without vampire hearing, would have known what was going on.

* * *

"Normally, I am happy to rise. That has changed." Rigo was talking before my eyes opened. I heard and understood, for the most part. He just wasn't used to someone taking this long to wake.

Blood Redemption

"Give her a minute—she wakes very slowly," Drew chuckled at the side of the bed. I caught his and Drake's scent, now—they were making up for last night. I was scowling when I opened my eyes.

"Honey, what do you want?" I gave Drake a baleful glance.

"Breakfast at the strawberry farm," Drew said. "Get your clothes on, itty-bitty pants."

Rigo managed to chase the twins out so we could get a shower; he didn't want to rush off to breakfast, either. When we arrived at the strawberry farm, I saw that Shadow had come to breakfast. At least his father and grandfather hadn't come.

"Baby, I want to talk to you after we eat," he said softly as Drake and Drew managed to herd me to a chair between Shadow and Rigo.

I felt like smacking my twins for doing this to me. This should have been Rigo's time. Yeah, I felt awkward over the whole thing. Cheedas and two assistants had been brought from the palace; they were happy to be cooking on the light side of the planet for a change.

"Raona, you are not eating." Cheedas tapped the island in front of me. That's where we were having breakfast—the overly large island in the kitchen.

"I'm not very hungry," I said. I didn't want him to feel bad—I had a monopoly on that emotion right then.

"Here," Shadow lifted our plates and folded us away. We ended up in my suite.

"This isn't awkward or anything," I pointed out, folding arms tightly across my chest.

"Lissa, this is a fucked up mess." Shadow set our plates down on my bedside table and reached out for me.

Chapter 6

I wasn't sure I wanted to be touched by anyone from Grey House right then. "Baby, please don't pull away from me." Shadow wasn't letting me get away. "I know Dad and Grampa have managed to do major damage. Tell me they haven't killed our love. Tell me that."

He pulled me against him and kissed the top of my head. I was crying by that time. Shadow was telling me how much he loved me. Telling me he should have come himself, instead of allowing his father and grandfather to deliver the news. Especially when I was so weak.

"I won't be going back to Grey House," I tried to wipe tears off my face. Shadow did it for me. "And when am I supposed to answer to the fuck up on Cloudsong? When, Shadow? Your grandfather and father dragged me into that mess, didn't they? I don't see them here, apologizing."

"They want to, but I didn't think you'd be willing. Not for a while." His gray eyes were troubled as he tried to lift my face to look at him. I was having difficulty with that.

"What are you going to do with Melida? What do your father and grandfather plan to do with her?"

"Ship her out of Grey House as quickly as possible, but we have to get this other thing resolved first."

"And what if we're forced to hand our profits over to Cloudsong for the next fifty years?" I asked angrily. My Casino owners wouldn't stand for that, and I didn't expect them to.

"Dad and Grampa hope to make some sort of deal— offering five years instead of fifty, and see where that gets us."

"Nobody here would settle for even one year, let alone start the bidding at five," I tried to extricate myself from Shadow's embrace. "The Casino owners make good money, but they'll leave this place behind if they find out this is in the works. Cloudsong may cut its own throat where Le-Ath Veronis is concerned."

"I'd like to go back in time, snatch Findal up and beat the hell out of him," Shadow grumbled, pulling me closer. "And I know I shouldn't be thinking this, but I'd honestly like to punch Dad and Grampa Glendes both."

"Yeah, I know about the betrayal from the father bit," I bumped my forehead against Shadow's chest.

"We can go stand outside the Green Fae village," Shadow suggested. He'd known what I was talking about. That's how we ended up standing under my favorite tree while a light rain fell around us.

Shadow has some wizard's trick where he can shield himself and anyone standing with him from the rain, so we were dry as we watched the village. Little was going on since it was raining—the Green Fae work in sunlight, mostly. It gives them their power.

Since we didn't see any sign of Toff and Redbird, I folded Shadow to my beach house, where Poradina and Evaline were. The apprentice surrogate Larentii was there with them, so I introduced myself.

"Thank you for sending Daragar," Poradina was extremely happy with the Larentii, I could tell.

"I didn't have anything to do with that," I gave her an honest answer. Shadow had a light in his eyes as he watched the two women. Well, it was a bit soon, I think, for him to start talking surrogate with me. He and I had other business to take care of before we considered that—if we ever did consider it.

"Yes, Connegar mentioned this to me, when I was learning with another surrogate. I asked to be assigned and

Chapter 6

Connegar, Reemagar and Ferrigar all thought it a good idea." Daragar smiled brightly.

He was more than eight and a half feet tall and had the bright blue eyes all Larentii had, although his blond hair was nearly white. He had it short and it was so thick it stood straight up on his head.

"Are you doing well—do you need anything?" I asked.

"We are doing very well." Poradina liked where she was, I think, as did Evaline. "I was worried we'd be stuck somewhere in the dark, with nobody paying attention to us. Everybody pays attention to us. Karzac and Daragar check on the babies constantly and make sure we're healthy. Karzac doesn't mind telling us if we're not eating right, too." Poradina was grinning.

"Yeah, there's no way to hide anything from him, all right," I agreed. "You don't get into an argument with him, either. I wouldn't know what it was like to be right all the time, like he is."

"What is it like—to have so many mates?" Evaline asked.

"Amazing, most of the time," I answered truthfully. "Until they all disagree with me at once, anyway."

"I haven't met this one." Evaline nodded toward Shadow.

"Yeah, well, this is Shadow Grey."

"One of the Grey House Wizards?" Evaline sounded impressed.

"Yeah. One of those." I didn't sound so impressed.

"I'm in the doghouse right now," Shadow admitted, a wry grin on his face. He hadn't spoken before this.

"You are residing with domesticated pets?" Daragar wasn't sure of the idiom.

Blood Redemption

"I'd probably be more comfortable," Shadow rubbed the back of his neck.

The comesuli cook was about to serve lunch for Poradina and Evaline, so Shadow and I left. "You never did have breakfast earlier," Shadow said, as I made my way toward my private study. I wasn't surprised to find Norian lurking outside my door.

"Were you lying in wait?" I asked as I opened the door.

"As much as I could," Norian smiled.

"She hasn't eaten anything," Shadow pointed out as I walked in, causing Heathe and Grant to stop what they were doing.

"I'll get a meal from the kitchen," Grant offered.

"I'll go with him," Heathe said and both my assistants walked right out again before I could ask them what was going on. Shadow kissed me, said he had work to do and folded away.

"We still have problems on Trell," Norian said later over a sandwich and a cup of soup—Grant and Heathe had brought back enough food and drinks for all of us. "There's evidence of an influx of money into the royal treasury, and a new temple is under construction in a city near the capital."

"Any murders or reported disappearances?"

"None reported, but we're getting rumors that the crown isn't releasing all information," Norian grumbled.

"Isn't that a violation of their agreement with the Alliance?" I asked, munching away on my toasted cheese sandwich.

"Of course it is. All member worlds are obligated to report crimes, so any population visiting will have that information before they set foot on the planet," Norian went on. "It would be common courtesy, even if it weren't in violation of their pact with the Alliance."

"Is Lendill there now?" I asked.

"I sent him there when we finished on Darthin."

"You didn't give him any time off?" I watched Norian as he chewed a bite of sandwich thoughtfully.

"Lendill is something of a workaholic and neither of us received time off. Just because I'm not somewhere else doesn't mean I'm not working."

"I didn't say that, Norian Keef," I pointed a wedge of sandwich in his direction.

"Don't point that at me unless you want me to eat it."

"If you're that hungry, you can have it."

"Will you feed it to me?"

"Norian."

"Lissa Beth."

I was thankful Shadow left before we started on Alliance business. I wasn't sure how he would react to Norian's desire for me to transport him to Trell that afternoon. "Does the Trellian crown know you have ASD agents there?"

"No. We got a tip on this days ago, but Darthin took precedence. We have people following up with Black Mist, but they're lying low right now, so we don't have much."

"Those difiks," I muttered.

"I was thinking much worse names. I asked Taff and Mora to pack a bag for you. I know you have that hearing on Cloudsong in a few days, but you can take off for that. Meanwhile, perhaps Trell will take your mind off those things."

"Uh-huh. And I'm sure the Alliance media everywhere isn't having a field day with that information," I grumbled.

"They are. You just haven't been watching the vids. Everybody is having a fit that Grey House is being dragged into this, but they're not defending you at all. They think all these Casinos are making you wealthy beyond reason, so there's very little sympathy. In fact, some journalists are saying that Cloudsong should just settle for what they can get from you."

"Norian, did you set out to turn my day into a pile of steaming crap? Did you?" I'd just lost my appetite and dropped the half sandwich onto my plate.

"Breah-mul, that wasn't my intention."

"What was your intention?" I snapped at him.

Cheah-mul, I was only trying to inform you. That is my job. I know you have not watched the vids in days."

I hugged myself and allowed my head to drop onto my desk. Grant and Heathe left the room at Norian's urging. He then came to the side of my desk and sat there, begging me to straighten up. I didn't cooperate.

"Lissa Beth, they cannot beat you in a fair fight, so they are digging at you the only way they can. If you allow them to hurt you like this, then they win. Do not let them win."

"Norian, you're not the one whose name gets dragged through the muck on every vid screen in every Alliance household," I said, shivering when I sat up straight.

"You forget about the vid screens outside the Alliance that also pick it up," Norian tilted my chin up so his eyes could look into mine. "We are both wounded, *deah-mul*. Inside. We have to stand tall and pretend it doesn't matter to those who do not know us."

Norian had now used the third portion of the declaration of love—he'd called me breah-mul, cheah-mul, and now deah-mul. It meant *my breath, my heart* and *my*

Chapter 6

soul in the language of Wyyld, one of the Twenty Charter worlds of the Alliance. I figured it was easy to rhyme songs in that language.

"Come with me, Lissa Beth. Trell is waiting for us."

Chapter 7

*T*rell

Lissa

"Does the Alliance have a problem with privacy?" I had hands on hips as I stared at another line of low-walled cubicles—six this time—inside the ASD office located in Xindis, Trell's capital city.

Lendill was there to meet us, after getting a communication from Norian that we were on our way. He chuckled at my dismay over the situation.

"There are four showers and all of them have doors," he said, grinning.

"Oh, so they think semi-privacy is all right, then?" I wrinkled my nose at Lendill.

"Better than nothing," he was still grinning. "It's nice to see you, Raona. None of the other Liaisons were so involved in our investigations. Frankly, none of the others had any talent, either. They only gave half an ear to Norian, their signatures on permission papers and that's about it."

"You didn't give me that option," I glared at Norian. He had the nerve to give me a cheeky grin.

"If you hadn't hauled me off to Twylec and then proceeded to destroy the Solar Red Temple all around me, then we wouldn't be here now. You showed me what you could do, so I chose to capitalize on that. You can't blame me—I have to use all assets available to do my job."

"I leave the running of Le-Ath Veronis to others, just so you can have your way, Norian Keef?" I was making a face at him, now.

"I like getting my way. It's so much better than not getting my way." Norian sighed blissfully.

"I ought to smack you," I grumped. Lifting my bag, I tossed it onto my borrowed bed from ten feet away.

"I've never seen any other woman do that." Lendill was impressed.

"I can do the same with you—or Norian. Personally, I'd rather toss Norian."

"Lissa Beth, stop complaining. We have several things to check on, tonight. We'll get dinner while we're out."

Norian lifted his bag and delivered it to his cubicle, next door to mine, in a more traditional manner. Lendill, just as before, had taken the last space, farthest from the door.

* * *

"What can you tell me, Lissa Beth?" Norian lifted an eyebrow as I scented my way through the large apartment.

"Six people were here regularly. All tainted in some way."

Chapter 7

"Tainted?" Norian was now very interested. We'd left Lendill behind—he hadn't gotten much rest lately, so Norian told him to get an early meal and go to bed.

Lendill seemed happy to comply. Norian had gotten addresses from Lendill before we left the ASD office, however, so he and I went to check on them.

"When I smell a taint around their normal scent, that means they're bad—done something they shouldn't—I can't explain it better than that," I said, looking out a wide window onto the street below.

Night had fallen and the streetlamps were glowing, illuminating the light snow swirling to the ground. Winter had come to that portion of Trell and it was bitterly cold.

Norian had asked Taff and Mora, my two assistants, to pack warm clothing for me. I hadn't even thought to *Look* to see what the weather was like. I would have walked out without a sweater, even. Norian opened my bag earlier, pulled out a coat and helped me into it before we left headquarters.

"Lissa Beth, if we walked up to someone on the street who had done murder, are you telling me you can scent that about them?"

"I can usually tell," I said. "It overlays the scent of their blood. I don't know how it works. It just does."

"Why didn't I know to hook up with a Queen Vampire before?" Norian murmured.

"Not all of them could do this," I said, watching the snow get heavier—I could see larger flakes in the lamplight. "Most of them have been called Queen if they weren't susceptible to compulsion. This is how it was explained to me shortly after I was turned. I was told that if the queen was good, then she was an asset to the race. If she was bad, she had to be killed. At the moment, I'm the only Queen Vampire that exists, so there isn't a plethora to choose from."

"I heard you were almost killed anyway."

"Norian, don't go there," I shivered at the memory.

"Not your fault, breah-mul." He was now behind me, rubbing the back of my neck carefully. "Come on; let's see if we can pick up the same scents elsewhere."

Three more apartments were on the list and I picked up the scent of two from the first place at all three of the others. There were seventeen scents in all—the last place turned out to be a condo, with all three apartments side by side. Nearly all the individual scents held some sort of taint, with the exception of two. I only smelled the blood of those two at the last place. Norian wasn't surprised when I told him.

"Do you think they died here?" he asked, as we stood in the bare living area. All furniture and clothing had been carefully removed from each place.

"I don't smell their deaths here," I answered, looking around.

The walls in this area were white, but all three bedrooms had been painted a red so dark, it was nearly black. To hide blood spatter, no doubt. I showed Norian where the blood spots were and he made a call to someone, asking them to come in the following day and take samples.

"We'll soon know whether we can ID anyone by the blood," he sighed. "I can usually scent blood, but I have to be in my other form."

"Do you do that a lot? Change to investigate a scene?"

"No. Too many chances of being seen," he replied. "Is there anything else here?"

"No."

Chapter 7

"Then let's get dinner and turn in. We've had a long day."

* * *

Black Mist Headquarters

"What do you mean you can't find her?" Viregruz stared at his two most powerful warlocks. "We know she's away from Le-Ath Veronis. Those comesuli of hers should learn not to gossip."

"We hear that even her mates can't find her," Zellar grumbled. "My informants tell me she has come up missing several times and none have been successful at tracking her. Except the Larentii, perhaps, and you know we're not going anywhere near them. There's no way I want my atoms separated."

Viregruz merely nodded at Zellar's assessment—even he knew not to approach the Larentii.

"Keep working on this—I'll pay a very generous bonus if you can get any useful information. I want this kill myself, if possible." Viregruz tapped the ends of his fingers together, letting his claws slide out a bit. "Bring me something young for my meal," he added. Zellar and his fellow warlock hurried to obey.

* * *

Trell

Lissa

Norian chose the restaurant and asked for a serving of prime rib—rare. I think he and Winkler would get along very well in the food department. *Do all shapeshifters have a high metabolism?* I sent to him as I dipped into my chicken dish.

"I think so," he answered aloud. It made me wish he had mindspeech—it might be more comfortable for him. I could

141

give it to him—I held that ability—but that was a step I wasn't ready to contemplate, yet. Norian watched me carefully as he consumed his meal. He ate what I couldn't finish, too.

The snow was thicker, wetter and colder when we left the restaurant, so Norian asked me to get us back to ASD headquarters the quick way. After we left everyone behind who might see us, I did.

The cold doesn't bother me much, but I didn't like slogging through wet snow and Norian liked it even less. I discovered that Norian doesn't like being cold, period. His snake crawled right into bed with me to warm up before he slithered back to his own cubicle to sleep later. I was glad I could hear Lendill snoring the entire time.

* * *

Grey Planet

"Dad, she didn't force me away from Le-Ath Veronis and she didn't yell at me." Shadow raked a hand through dark hair as he looked at his father. They were sitting in Glendes' private study and Glendes was watching his grandson and his son. "But if this goes badly on Cloudsong, I think I can forget ever being with Lissa again."

Shadow sighed and stood. Glendes had one of the few southern-facing windows cut into the mountain that held Grey House, and Shadow moved toward it to stare down at the valley beneath the mountain. He could see it as it truly was—past the shrouded cloaking spells that presented a blackened hulk of an asteroid to anyone without a very strong wizard's talent to see.

"We can present our case to the crown's legal counsel, but it isn't likely they'll listen to the facts that Lissa isn't legally bound to Grey House. They only see the monetary value in this." Glendes echoed his grandson's sigh. "All the worlds that we do business with are non-Alliance, and they are watching this closely to see if we honor the contractual obligations. If we don't, then this will definitely affect our business dealings in the future. The others will not care whether Le-Ath Veronis is impacted legally. Many of them see it as a gambling world only—they aren't willing to look past the surface to understand that the comesuli and most of the vampires who live there have nothing to do with the casinos." Glendes toyed with an ancient inkbottle on his desk.

"They'll negotiate for the number of years—fifty is unreasonable and they know it," Raffian added. "Five is much more likely, but even that will not sit well with anyone from Le-Ath Veronis. Adam and Merrill are already looking into this. They can weather this storm, but other owners may not. Some will lose all their investment if they have to pay out even a year's worth of profits."

"How can they even be connected to this?" Shadow tossed up a hand.

"Because the crown owns the land the casinos are built on," Glendes replied. "If Lissa had sold the land and all rights to it in the beginning, we wouldn't be worrying over casino owners. There is a clause in the agreements with the owners, stating that Lissa can commandeer all the proceeds from those casinos if she sees fit, as ruler of Le-Ath Veronis. It was meant as a stopgap in case any of the owners or investors turned out to be corrupt. She can seize the casino and distribute proceeds to injured parties, in addition to forcing the owners off Le-Ath Veronis. This has proven to be the legal loophole that Cloudsong has grasped in their greedy claws. Lissa can legally demand all the profits from the casinos for the amount of time Cloudsong requires."

Shadow cursed under his breath. "You know what Melida was doing this morning, Grampa? Do you?"

Glendes knew how angry Shadow was, and he didn't want to stir that anger any more than necessary. "What was she doing, child?"

"Swooning in front of Selkirk at the breakfast table, telling him she felt ill and needed to stay in bed. Selkirk didn't want anything to do with her and when Cleo tried to get close to see if she could find any problem, Melida took off toward her suite like a frightened grouse. She doesn't want Cleo near her for some reason, although Cleo is better than any healer anywhere."

"Perhaps Melida is aware that Cleo is Lissa's niece," Raffian suggested.

"She probably knows that Cleo and Kyler are both Lissa's nieces," Glendes agreed. "And she likely knows that both my daughters hold a great deal of power. She doesn't want anything to happen to this baby. The child will keep her alive, if her father learns what she truly did."

Glendes had spoken with Ferrigar. The Larentii Wise Ones had looked into the matter and then provided information to Ferrigar, Head of the Larentii Council, who'd then brought the news to Glendes. Ferrigar was connected by ancient blood to Grey House—Ferrigar's daughter had married a Grey and helped him form Grey House millennia before. Ferrigar still lived; his daughter had given up her life when her husband died.

"This still doesn't do anything for Lissa, except penalize her for even being with me," Shadow growled. "Our name

Chapter 7

isn't being dragged through the muck over this whole mess, but hers is."

"She's a high-profile Queen from the Reth Alliance," Raffian pointed out.

"You think she wanted that? Do you, Dad?"

"No, son, it's just the way things are. Tamaritha of Twylec didn't get that much attention, though she was swallowed by a Ra'Ak on a live vid feed. The picture didn't go fuzzy until afterward. Nobody saw what Lissa did to the others. Even we don't know what she did. All we know is that she left her body behind for a few weeks."

"Drake and Drew said that the Ra'Ak pooled their strength to destroy Nemizan's sun. Lissa managed to move Nemizan and its sister worlds to another sun."

Glendes' eyebrows rose at Shadow's explanation. He might have doubted Shadow's words, except he knew Drake and Drew couldn't lie. None of the Saa Thalarr, their Spawn Hunters or Healers could.

"Has she done anything to prepare for her defense on Cloudsong? The hearing is in two days," Raffian pointed out.

"Nobody knows anything and that ASD Director has hauled her off to Trell to take care of Alliance business there. When has she had time, Dad?" Shadow huffed at the question.

"Do you think she's just going to show up and take whatever is handed out?" Glendes had his own legal counsel—several fifth-level Grey House Wizards handled his legal affairs. They had all sorts of paperwork and arguments at the ready, not least of which was that Melida and Marid hadn't been completely honest or forthright when Melida had come to them, already pregnant. Glendes' contract specifically stipulated Grey House heirs and no others.

Blood Redemption

In Grey House's opinion, that violated the contract in the beginning and weighed heavily toward a writ of detachment. Either way, as soon as Cloudsong's judgment was passed, Melida would be shipped back to Marid and no further dealings would occur between Grey House and the Wizards of Belancour.

* * *

Karathia

"Has my granddaughter done anything to prepare for this hearing?" Wylend looked pointedly at Erland.

"No. She hasn't discussed it with any of us, either. I have no idea what she's going to do and frankly I am concerned."

"Not least from the fact that she can demand the profits from your casino," Wylend muttered.

"My monarch, if that was all that concerned me, I would shut my doors tomorrow and walk away," Erland snapped. "They cannot touch what I already have, and I have enough— not just to support myself, but to support Lissa and my child as well. I will not desert Lissa, just because the imbeciles on Cloudsong have ventured far into the realm of unreason."

"Do you think it will make a difference if her grandfather and her mate from Karathia come to show support?" Wylend asked.

"If I were Cloudsong, I would be concerned," Erland nodded.

"Then we will certainly go. My meetings for that day can be canceled. Let Cloudsong sweat when the King of Karathia shows up in their Hall of Hearings."

* * *

Trell

"Director Keef." Norian stared at the image on the vid screen. Norian was speaking with Ildevar Wyyld, High

Chapter 7

Chancellor of Wyyld and Founder of the Reth Alliance. Lissa and Lendill had gone out to find something to bring back for dinner, so Norian was alone at headquarters when the call from the Founder came.

"Deonus Wyyld," Norian dipped his head to Ildevar. "How may I be of service?" Norian raised his head to gaze at the ruler of the founding world for the Alliance. Ildevar was old—much older than the Alliance itself if the rumors were true, and still looked very young, except for his eyes. Ildevar Wyyld's eyes held the depth of a very long life.

"I wish for you to be present at Queen Lissa's hearing upon Cloudsong. If the judgment goes against her in this proceeding, I want you, as a representative of the Alliance, to let Cloudsong know that they will never be welcomed into the Alliance for perpetrating this injustice. We have no sway over the legal systems of any non-Alliance world, but we do have the authority to deny any membership—in perpetuity. If you are forced to supply this information, I give permission to leak it to the media as well. I suggest that you have a hidden camera on your person, so the proceedings may be recorded. I wish for a direct feed to be funneled to me as it happens."

"Of course, Deonus." Norian nodded his head respectfully.

"Carry a communicator in your ear, in case I wish to send information," Ildevar added.

"It will be done, Deonus."

"Very good. I know I can always count on you, Director Keef."

"Thank you, Deonus." The vid screen went blank and Norian breathed a sigh of relief.

Blood Redemption

Ildevar Wyyld and The twenty Charter Members who made up the Grand Alliance Council all knew what Norian was, but that secret remained with them and Norian was grateful.

* * *

Lissa

"Lissa, I have been instructed to attend the hearing with you, as an Alliance representative," Norian informed me when Lendill and I returned with mutton stew and thick pieces of bread to go with it.

Lendill had found a little restaurant in one of the older neighborhoods of Xindis, which served good, plain fare. We warmed our drinks in the small zap oven in the tiny kitchen afforded by the Alliance—the cups of tea had gotten cold on our brief walk back through the snow and freezing temperatures.

The snow had continued off and on throughout the night and part of the day and now was nearly six inches deep. My feet were nearly frozen when we returned to headquarters. Norian hadn't wanted to go in the first place, because of the low temperatures.

"So, you want to be there when all this happens on Cloudsong, huh?" I wasn't looking forward to any part of this. Not at all. If I were honest, I was frightened that I might lose my temper, and bared claws and fangs in a public place was never a good idea.

I sure didn't want to give away any of my casino owners' money, either—Cloudsong had no right to that. When this debacle was over, we were going to call a special meeting of the Council and have a discussion about the original contracts, rewriting the parts where I could commandeer the profits if I saw fit.

Chapter 7

We should have placed wording there to begin with, saying that I could only do that if I found the owners guilty of breaking the law or in violation of some rule or other. As it stood, I had complete control over that, for any reason.

Cloudsong had exploited that loophole so they could reap the benefits. It didn't surprise me that the Alliance was sending Norian—this could cut into the taxes paid to them by Le-Ath Veronis.

"Lissa Beth, you are staring at nothing and not eating," Norian pointed out after a while. "Your food is getting cold."

We sat at the small, round table in the tiny kitchen area. Lendill grabbed my mug of the Trellian version of tea and went to warm it again. I'd dumped plenty of sugar into it at the beginning, just to make it taste better. Trellian tea was bitter with a capital B.

* * *

"I can take us quicker," I muttered through chattering teeth as Norian and I stood beneath an awning, waiting for a train to take us to Rezael. The city lay two hours away by train, and Norian and Lendill suspected a Solar Red temple was under construction there.

"Shhh, let me handle this," Norian muttered. We were standing in the freezing weather, surrounded by other Trellians taking the trip with us. At least the crush of bodies kept the wind off us and Norian paid extra for a private compartment so we wouldn't be crowded inside the train. It pulled up just as I was considering grabbing Norian, folding him to Rezael and letting him pitch his fit when we got there.

Norian had to scan the chip in his wrist to get into our compartment, so nobody else could get in with us. Our compartment had comfortable seats that could fold into beds, a small table and a private bathroom. I didn't need it, but Norian might.

"Come on Lissa Beth," Norian patted the side of his wide, nicely padded seat when I was about to settle into the chair opposite his.

"Norian, what do you want?" I sighed.

"I want you to get me warm, I'm freezing," he muttered.

"Yeah? Whose idea was this, anyway?" I wasn't sure that I shouldn't just let him sit there and shiver.

"I want a nap, and this is the best way to get it. I love train rides," Norian said, slipping out of his heavy coat and setting it aside. "Come on; help the Alliance out a little." He patted the side of his seat again.

"I've been helping the Alliance out. A lot."

"You can do this—it won't hurt at all."

"Uh-huh." I went to sit on the edge of his seat.

"Let's get this off." He pulled my coat off and piled it atop his before pulling me against him and wrapping his arms around me. He did feel chilled. "Now," he said after he'd gotten comfortable, "tell me a story."

"What?" I pulled away to stare at him.

"Please. The sound of your voice will help me sleep. It doesn't matter what it is," he added, pulling me against him again.

"Fine," I grumped. "Have you ever heard *The Legend of the Three*?"

"Never heard of it," he mumbled, closing his eyes.

"Only a few of my kind know it," I said with a sigh. "It goes like this: In the beginning, the One created the Three. Those three were Wisdom, Strength and Love. The Three had many others beneath them eventually, at many levels of power and ability. The Powers That Be and the Nameless

Chapter 7

Ones are at the lowest levels beneath the Three." Norian snuggled closer.

"One day," I continued, "the One and the Three discovered a blight had infected their ranks. Some of those in many levels had banded together and turned against them, seeking to destroy what had been created. The Three were given the task of pursuing those destroyers and finding a way to turn them back to the Light, or devising a way to destroy them. Not an easy thing to do, since the ones they hunted were not only immortal and powerful, but were recruiting allies among the created races. The Three began to choose their armies carefully—part of their duty is to seek out and right many wrongs in their pursuit of the invasive evil. Among those who recognize them, the Three are called *The Mighty*. They are commonly known as The Mighty Mind, The Mighty Hand and The Mighty Heart."

"So what happened?" Norian blinked sleepily at me.

"The battle is still going on," I shrugged. Norian yawned and closed his eyes again. He was asleep in ten minutes and we made the entire, two-hour trip just like that—with Norian wrapped around me and breathing softly against the side of my neck.

I was awake the entire time and thinking. About the upcoming hearing and judgment on Cloudsong. About how wrong it all felt. Then I did some *Looking*, trying to decide what to do about it all. I patted Norian's cheek when we pulled into the station.

"No, love, don't move yet," he mumbled against my neck.

"Norian, everybody else is getting off."

Blood Redemption

Norian cursed softly and opened his eyes. I helped him stand; he grabbed our coats and herded me sleepily toward the doors so we could get off.

I smelled one of our rats the moment we exited the train, and that's what saved us. I had Norian turned to mist instantly while the laser pistol fired right through us.

* * *

"Now, tell us everything you know," Norian smiled unpleasantly at our would-be murderer inside a tiny ASD office in downtown Rezael.

I'd already placed compulsion on the creep to answer all of Norian's questions. Creep wasn't much to look at, with a narrow face and a long nose. Thinning hair and a sparse moustache rounded out the picture. His dark eyes followed me nervously while he answered Norian's questions.

"Seturna Odnard ordered me to kill you as you exited the train. We had information that you boarded in Xindis."

"Seturna Odnard, of Solar Red?" Norian bared his teeth. I could only imagine that he'd be hissing if he were the lion snake.

"We are to call ourselves Brothers of the New Dawn," our creep, whose name was Pebrus, whined.

"So, Pebrus, Brother of the New Dawn, where might Seturna Odnard be found? Who gave us away? Do you have a name?" Norian suspected a mole and he was doing his best to grind this guy down to get a name.

"Seturna Odnard is at the temple. We have been working with someone named Tork," Pebrus gave the answer.

"An assumed name," Norian looked up at me. "We have twenty-nine agents on Trell. We had thirty, but one has been missing for a while. Could be any one of them, though. With the proper resources, they might be able to trace my chip number." He'd used it to pay for our train ride.

"Did you suspect a mole before now?"

"Of course I did. I've known we were infiltrated for some time. The Charter Members are investigating their staff and Lendill and I have been trying to help with that. We've found two so far, but none of them knows about any of the others, so we have to track them one at a time."

"Honey, that sounds like a mess."

"Lissa Beth, it is a mess." Norian went back to questioning Pebrus, but he was just a flunky to Seturna Odnard—somebody who was expendable if he was killed while trying to kill us.

"I don't want to turn him over to the local authorities," Norian informed me after he'd gotten as much as he could from Pebrus. "We could kill him, but I don't want to do that yet."

"We can put him in my dungeon," I offered. Pebrus, who'd been listening, cringed at the mention of a dungeon.

"It won't be like the ones Solar Red operates," I told him. Solar Red tortured their prisoners and their dungeons were notoriously filthy and dark. My prisoners might get intense questioning under compulsion, but they had clean, decent quarters. If they were sentenced to die, their death was swift and as painless as we could make it.

Norian nodded his acceptance, so we folded to Le-Ath Veronis, which shocked Pebrus no end. I laid compulsion not to talk about how he'd gotten where he was, and Drake and Drew came running when I sent mindspeech.

Some of Rigo's Rith Naeri helped and we got Pebrus placed inside his new home beneath my palace. Drake and

Blood Redemption

Drew tried to convince us to spend the night, but we were hot on the trail of Solar Red in Rezael, so we left again.

* * *

Trell

"Seturna, the news is everywhere concerning the attack at the train station, but they haven't reported finding bodies and Pebrus hasn't reported in." The one who called himself Tork stood inside Seturna Odnard's private office to give the news.

"The news is accurate? There is proof of the attack?" Seturna Odnard frowned at his informant.

"Yes, Seturna. The spies we have embedded within the local authorities say the laser blasts are legitimate—the train car had to be repaired before it could continue on its journey."

"But no bodies were found."

"No, Seturna. Not even blood was found, which is puzzling."

"And what do the witnesses say?"

"They only saw the laser blasts—they didn't see who fired the pistol or the ones being fired upon, it happened so quickly, and they were all falling to the floor to avoid getting hit."

"So, there's either treachery afoot and someone knows and managed to keep it away from us, or something else is going on." Seturna Odnard watched his mole carefully. They'd gone to great lengths to get this one and set him up. Odnard had no desire to lose him now—he was much too valuable.

* * *

Lissa

Chapter 7

We'd found our way into Seturna Odnard's study while he was talking to the mole, and even though Norian couldn't send mindspeech, I could feel his anger. It was white hot and uncomfortable.

We listened to part of the conversation between the mole and the Seturna—they didn't get any information from the attempt on our lives—things had happened much too quickly. I had to get Norian out of there and fast, however; I had a feeling that the moment I dropped him, he would make the turn, he was so furious. I had to find a deserted spot so he could do that, and then I had to get him calmed down. There were things he needed to know.

I flew through the ceiling and then away from there as quickly as I could. Snow was falling again; thick white flakes dropped through my mist as I rushed along, searching anxiously for a safe place where Norian could turn. The tiny ASD office might now be watched, so I didn't go there. I found an empty hotel room instead, and hoping that the hotel staff wouldn't send any guests there, dropped Norian inside it. I remained mist, too, as he quickly turned to lion snake, then tried not to cringe as he hissed and shook his tail angrily before throwing his body against a wall.

"Norian, stop that—someone will hear!" I did some hissing of my own as I materialized. Norian flung himself once more at the wall with a loud thump before he turned in my direction, his hood spread and mouth open to display lengthy fangs. "Norian, listen to me and listen carefully. You only think you know who that was. I can still use my scenting abilities while I'm mist and you can trust me when I say that the spy wasn't Lendill."

Chapter 8

*T*rell

Lissa

Norian hadn't changed back to his humanoid form and was now snaking his way toward me. "Norian, I think we should go and find the real Lendill. Chances are he's still in Xindis right now, working away. At least that's where I hope he is. I hope they haven't gotten to him yet. I have a feeling they plan to replace him with the doppelganger we just saw a few minutes ago. I think the one we saw is your missing agent—he probably knew what Lendill looked like and had his features altered."

"You're kidding?" Norian stood in front of me, completely naked and still angry.

"Honey, I'm sure they made that guy exactly like Lendill in every way except one. Scent doesn't lie and that guy not only had a different scent, but he had taint all over him. You don't get that tainted in the space of a few hours. It would take years to get that bad. Come on; let's go looking for the real thing. I have a feeling he's in trouble."

Norian finally capitulated, dressed himself and I folded him back to Xindis. It's a good thing we went when we did— Lendill was in the fight of his life. The whole ASD headquarters had been ransacked and Lendill was involved in a shoot-out.

If Norian and I hadn't shown up, they might have killed Lendill—he was in the middle of two sets of enemies, huddling behind a brick column outside headquarters when I grabbed him up as mist. I dropped him and Norian on top of the building and then zipped down to street level to take out a few snipers.

* * *

"Lissa Beth, you could have left at least one of them alive so we could question them," Norian grumbled later, as six bodies were lined up—all headless—inside ASD headquarters.

"They were all shooting, what did you want me to do?" I did some grumbling myself. Yeah, Norian was right, but my adrenalin had been pumping and I took them all out before I even realized we might need one of them.

Lendill had been shocked when Norian told him what we'd seen. "Now what do I do? They'll be hunting for me for sure." He was pacing and fretting over the whole incident.

"Do you recognize any of these?" I pointed to the six bodies. Norian shook his head. They were all Solar Red, according to him.

"Then I'll try a little trick I learned from the Larentii," I said, and walked over to one of the heads. Normally, I'd have matched up body parts by scent, but these had something blocking their smell—as if someone worried the scent might incriminate them.

I was forced to match clothing, instead, and I kept the scenting problem to myself—no sense in worrying Lendill or Norian more than they were already. I set about using power to change the appearance of the head and body I'd chosen, until we had a third replica of Lendill. "There," I said. "Now, let's scatter two or three of these fuckers around, make it look like a takedown and then dump the others on Tykl."

Norian had been watching me with shocked fascination as I'd disguised the attacker to look like Lendill. He also called somebody and told them where the three bodies would be on Tykl, in addition to asking them to investigate the entire mess there at headquarters. We'd have to find another place to stay.

None of us was happy when we had to leave most of our clothing and supplies behind—it would look suspicious if we didn't. I took one complete change of clothes with me, as did Norian and Lendill.

I folded them back to the hotel in Rezael, after borrowing a credit chip from Flavio. He'd been wakened from a sound sleep but it couldn't be helped and I *Pulled* the credit chip in and let Lendill use it, after altering his appearance. He now looked like the third most beautiful man I'd ever met.

"Lissa Beth, life just keeps getting stranger and stranger around you," Norian had fists on hips when we got inside the hotel room.

"Honey, you have no idea how strange things can get if you stick around, and we haven't even made a dent in that thirty years yet," I informed him.

Blood Redemption

"I'll need new equipment," Lendill ventured to say. Honestly, the poor man was probably still in shock. I know I would be if I found out somebody had manufactured a twin who was meant to take my place, and then gotten attacked by those who wanted my twin to take over. Plus, the fact that his face no longer looked like his own had to be the biggest surprise of all. At least he was extremely handsome now and likely would have to fend off women wherever he went.

"Can we get what you need on Le-Ath Veronis?" I asked.

"Probably."

"Good. We'll go there. I desperately need to soak in the hot tub and we have that fucking hearing on Cloudsong tomorrow."

"As long as you get me back here the minute it's over," Norian huffed. "We have work to do here. I need to contact one of the twenty."

Well, maybe he was on a first name basis with all of them. How was I to know? I truly didn't care, either. I folded us to Le-Ath Veronis.

"No, I made him look like Flavio. That's Lendill Schaff." I'd explained it for maybe the fifteenth time since we showed up in the kitchen of my palace to see if we could find something to eat.

Rolfe was there and watching us. He even sat with us to have a snack, once he discovered it was Lendill and not Flavio. The Head of Earth's Vampire Council still carried a lot of clout.

Norian and Lendill went off to grab equipment, Rolfe promised to find Lendill a bedroom and I yawned the whole way to my bed. Drake and Drew discovered I'd come back— I'm sure Rolfe sent mindspeech but I didn't call him out on

Chapter 8

it. I had two Falchani in my bed when I reached my suite, and they let me sleep. Eventually.

* * *

"Raona, wear this for the hearing." Taff and Mora were making suggestions on what to wear to Cloudsong. I had a headache—big surprise. Norian had come and was trying to herd me around. Not only that, but nearly all my mates had shown up, including Karzac.

Roff rustled his wings as he watched me fret; Drake and Drew were dressed in full battle leathers, with both blades strapped across their backs. Erland and Wylend had come; Gavin wore his old shuttered look. Garde was blowing smoke and the Larentii were watching everybody.

The casino owners began to filter in. At least they were forced to stand in the hallway outside my suite; my guards wouldn't let them near me. I had no idea what they thought about all this and I'd been afraid to *Look*.

Nobody had come to report to me either, regarding any of this. I think I was thankful for that.

Mora ended up handing me a light-blue silk tunic with dark-blue loose trousers. A belt that matched the trousers was wrapped around my waist, then shoes that matched the belt were slipped on my feet. At least I would be color-coordinated when things went to hell in a handbasket.

One of my Larentii folded everybody who wanted to go, which turned out to be quite a crowd. Grey House had brought around fifteen—Glendes, Raffian, Shadow and the other Master Wizards were there, plus their legal counsel, I presumed.

Melida and Marid—I had to *Look* to determine who they were since I'd never met them, were already there, waiting.

161

Blood Redemption

There weren't many seats inside the Hall of Hearings for an audience, either—only the major players were allowed to sit.

And then we had to rise for the entrance of the King of Cloudsong, his remaining son and the judge appointed by the King to preside over this circus.

We got to sit again once the King sat. If he ever came to Le-Ath Veronis, I intended to make the fucker stand.

"We have levied charges against Glendes of Grey House and his grandson, Shadow Grey, who signed a contract accepting all financial obligations pertaining to Melida, daughter of Marid of Belancour and her deceased husband, Findal. We also levy charges against Lissa, Queen of Le-Ath Veronis, Shadow Grey's first mate. Cloudsong recognizes that a mate's obligations are the same as your own, therefore, she is also named in these charges."

The judge rattled off the information in a monotone. It made me wonder if he ever got excited about anything—he was in his seventies, had a long, wrinkled face that would have made any bloodhound proud and eyes that looked as if they needed cataracts removed.

"We wish to point out that prior to the marriage between Shadow Grey and Melida of Belancour, Lissa of Le-Ath Veronis broke affiliation with Shadow Grey," one of the Grey House lawyers stood and announced. "Therefore, she should not be named in these proceedings."

"Cloudsong does not recognize verbal divorcement," the judge spouted and that was that. Didn't look as if they recognized much of anything, if it was beneficial to them in the long term.

"But there was never a contractual marriage between the Queen of Le-Ath Veronis and Shadow of Grey House. It was an informal arrangement only." Merrill had stepped up to speak on my behalf, looked like.

"There was an exchange of rings, was there not? Cloudsong recognizes that as binding, whether there was a written agreement or not," Judge Bloodhound said.

Geez, this guy had an answer for everything. Whether he actually had laws on the books to back it up was another question. "The Queen of Le-Ath Veronis will remain an active participant in these proceedings."

"Then we wish to point out that we were not notified of any undisclosed obligations on the part of Melida of Belancour before the contracts were signed," the Grey House lawyer said. "We received a listing of obligations from her father, Marid of Belancour, and nothing of this magnitude was mentioned."

"But he informed us when we notified him of his daughter's mate's perfidy that he was unaware of it until we gave him the proof we had. Therefore, he could not have given you that information. You then signed the contract, taking on all of her debts. This is one of her debts and we intend to see that justice is done. We could be asking for the life of the Eldest of Grey House. We are being generous, since we realize that Grey House had no involvement in Prince Brandelin's death and choose to ask for monetary damages only from all pertinent parties."

Well, there you go. I was a pertinent party.

"Then it is our duty to point out that fifty years of profits is excessive in the extreme," the Grey House lawyer said. "You say yourself that we had no involvement in the Prince's death. We are innocent of any crime, by your own admission. Yet your option is to bleed us dry and destroy our family?

Blood Redemption

You seek to obtain your justice by committing an injustice yourself."

"What price will you place upon the Prince's life? He would have ruled a good fifty years—that is the average rule of any monarch upon Cloudsong. That is what we base our demands upon," the judge wasn't budging an inch on this. "You say this will destroy your family. I have heard that Le-Ath Veronis is quite profitable. We will accept fifty years of profits from there as complete judgment in this case, leaving Grey House free of debt."

That had me standing in a hurry. They wanted to put all of this on me? I couldn't believe it. Angry didn't begin to describe what I felt right then. I think they were all lucky the fangs and claws didn't come out.

This was what they were aiming for all along, by dragging me and Le-Ath Veronis into all this. I think the King of Cloudsong realized I was furious. I did my best to reel in my temper, and phrased my words carefully.

"King Kenderlin," my voice carried across the room to where he sat on a richly carved throne, "would you drop this case if your son were still alive?"

"I would not only drop this case, I would pay to have my son again," he huffed. "Do not trouble that wound, or the judge will levy a heavier fine against you."

"Uh-huh," I grumped. "Excuse me." I folded away.

* * *

"You planned this, didn't you? Find some obscure law to drag my granddaughter into this, because the riches would come rolling in. Or so you think." Wylend came to stand next to Lissa's empty chair. Someone, likely one of the Larentii, had covered her disappearance and now a replica of Lissa stood beside Wylend, who wasn't fooled for a moment.

Chapter 8

"You are?" The judge rumbled.

"King Wylend Arden, of Karathia," Wylend announced.

"The King of Karathia is here?" Kenderlin almost came out of his chair. "I did not know that the Queen of Le-Ath Veronis had a living grandfather."

"As you can see, she does. That is why I am here, to ensure my granddaughter is treated fairly."

"You do not frighten me, warlock," the judge scoffed. That made Wylend cross arms over his chest.

Norian, who had tiny cameras affixed to his clothing, was transmitting the entire proceeding live to Ildevar Wyyld. As yet, Ildevar had made no comment and the earpiece Norian wore remained silent.

"Then you have never dealt with my kind," Wylend remarked casually.

* * *

Lissa

"Em-pah, you can back up, now, I've got this," I dragged Brandelin of Cloudsong behind me, bewildered as he was at having been pulled out of an exploding building at the last possible moment, more than three months before.

I'd gone *Looking* during my train ride, determined that Brandelin's living would have absolutely no effect on the timeline, and held that as my trump card. "Here's your heir, King Kenderlin. Now what was that you said about dropping this whole thing?"

"This cannot be my son," Kenderlin stood and snarled.

"Father, what are you saying? I was just inside a burning building, when this woman came and pulled me out of it. Are you rejecting me? Do you wish for Jenderlin to succeed you? I think the others died back there," he pointed in a confused manner behind him.

165

Blood Redemption

"Brandelin?" Kenderlin was now looking closer at his son—at the smudge marks on his skin, the partially burned clothing and the smell of smoke that clung to the Prince. I was standing there, wondering what to do next.

"She can always return him to the fire," Wylend intervened smoothly. I reached out to take Brandelin's arm, wondering if Wylend's bluff would work.

It did.

"No—wait!" Kenderlin was heading toward his son. "Tell me what happened on your tenth birthday. Tell me!" He commanded.

"I climbed up the pear tree, fell and broke my arm," Brandelin muttered. "I was afraid to tell you and walked around with a broken arm for three days."

"This is my son," Kenderlin said in wonder.

"That still does not compensate us for pain and suffering," the judge was getting back in on this.

"But your King said that the return of his son would mitigate the charges," the Grey House lawyer pointed out.

"He is not presiding over this hearing, I am," the judge informed all of us. Well, he just made it to the top twenty on my shit list. "For pain and suffering, thinking the Prince dead, we levy the equivalent of five billion Alliance credits, in gold or other viable tender, against Le-Ath Veronis."

Yeah, I stood there and gaped. Five billion Alliance credits, in gold? That was a lot of pain and suffering.

"Here is your gold." Kifirin arrived suddenly, smoke pouring from his nostrils. A huge stack of gold ingots appeared before him just as suddenly. The pile of gold was as tall as I was, and nearly six feet square. That was a lot of gold. I wondered if he'd emptied Le-Ath Veronis to get it. "Never trouble my mate again, or you may not live over it."

166

Chapter 8

"And you are?" I swear; this judge should learn when to shut up.

"I am Kifirin, Lord of the Dark Realm." And with that, Kifirin disappeared just as swiftly as he'd appeared in the first place.

Kenderlin came to examine the gold. Brandelin was still in shock, I think, and had no idea what was going on. Jenderlin, Brandelin's younger brother, looked ill. I figured he was wishing he were anywhere except where he was.

I thought I'd gotten my shock for the day when the asshole judge still demanded payment, after I'd brought the Prince back from the dead. I should have known better. Melida was suddenly in my face.

"You could have brought Findal back with you, and you didn't," she was shouting and crying at the same time and then she slapped me. Maybe I should have kept my mouth shut. Maybe. I didn't.

"Yeah?" I shouted right back at her. "Did you think for even one minute that Black Mist intended to let him live? Did you? They don't pay out unless there's no other way. Did you know that when you and Findal made your deal with them? Did your daddy know what you intended to do with the money? Did he? Stupid bitch," I snapped and walked around her to get out of that sanity-challenged hellhole.

"I have an announcement," Norian shouted over the ensuing din inside the Hall of Hearings. That stopped me in my tracks—I was just about to get the hell out of there and go sulk somewhere.

They'd intended all along to make me pay, although I hadn't had anything to do with any of this. Now Norian wanted to talk? What the hell was he doing?

167

Blood Redemption

"I am here as a representative of the Alliance," Norian went to stand in front of the judge. "I was sent by the Founder and Twenty Charter Members to observe these proceedings and record your judgments in this case. They have been witness to this travesty and they now ask me to inform you that Cloudsong will never join the Alliance. A copy of the writ will be forwarded to you." Norian turned on his heel and headed in my direction.

"Wait," Kenderlin was trying to shout over the noise that resumed after Norian had his say. Norian didn't stop; he just kept walking in my direction.

"Well, honey, that was some speech," I said, taking his hand. I folded both of us the hell away from there.

* * *

Le-Ath Veronis

"You like sitting on rooftops?" Norian looked green, perched as he was on top of the highest dome of my palace.

"Honey, I'll take you down, but I'll be coming right back up," I told him. He seemed relieved when I dropped him off on the steps leading to my palace before misting back to do more roof sitting. Kifirin came to sit beside me. At least heights didn't make him uncomfortable.

"Honey, I appreciate you showing up on Cloudsong. Did you empty all the gold from Le-Ath Veronis?" At least he wasn't blowing smoke at the moment. He was Kifirin, too, and not the god right then.

"You did not listen to my words," he actually smiled at me. "I said, 'here is *your* gold.' I didn't lie—it was theirs—I pulled it from Cloudsong. They paid themselves. Unfortunately, many of their lodes are now empty and unless I miss my guess, Cloudsong will become an isolated world. I cannot imagine that many will wish to work for the crown,

Chapter 8

when their treatment of you is made known. No wizards will come to protect them, out of fear for their lives. The opposing faction that wished the Prince dead will again wage war against the crown. We will see how they fare without outside help."

"What will happen to miss bitch pants?" I grumped. I could still feel the slap she gave me and it pissed me off every time I thought about it.

"The only reason she isn't floating on the breeze as separated atoms is because she is pregnant," Kifirin replied. "She struck a Larentii's mate. Connegar and Reemagar are still angry about that. Meanwhile, I think Glendes of Grey House is hammering out a writ of detachment and handing Melida back to Marid of Belancour as quickly as he can. I wish them luck with one another."

"I'm not going back to Grey House." I repeated my words to Shadow.

"Avilepha, you do not have to go anywhere you do not wish to go," Kifirin murmured and pulled me onto his lap.

"They never intended to ask Grey House for anything. They were coming after me," I sighed. "As if I would drain all the profits from the casinos for them." I shivered in Kifirin's embrace. My head hurt so bad from stress and anger I thought it might explode.

"Reason cannot be named as one of their assets," Kifirin placed fingers against my forehead. Yeah, he can place a healing sleep just as well as any Larentii. Better, maybe.

* * *

"I need to take her back to Trell—we have business there," Norian walked next to Kifirin, who carried an unconscious Lissa in his arms. Kifirin stopped in the hallway, leveling a gaze at Norian and breathing smoke.

"Or not," Norian backed away.

"Never do that again," Erland grabbed Norian's elbow and pulled him backward as Kifirin continued down the hall. "Do you have any idea what Kifirin is?"

"Perhaps you should explain it," Norian grumbled. Erland folded Norian to the library, where Lissa's other mates were holding a meeting.

* * *

"I can't find anything that this impacts," a tall, brown-haired man raked fingers through his hair as he stood before a good-sized crowd. Norian recognized Lissa's mates and a few others from the hearing. Many he didn't recognize, however. He sat down to listen.

"We're not hearing from Belen on this and she pulled Brandelin out just before he died." A platinum blonde woman spoke up next. "I know that is how we've gotten some of our members—Winkler, Aurelius and Thomas Williams, to name the most recent."

"What are we discussing?" Norian whispered to Erland, who sat next to him.

"There are some who have the power to bend time. They just can't use that ability to impact any part of the timeline," Erland whispered back. "Remind me to see if we can't find somebody to give you mindspeech."

"Connegar placed the image of Lissa when she folded away, I just don't know how they're going to explain Prince Brandelin's sudden appearance," the blonde woman spoke again. Norian hadn't been watching Lissa at that moment—he'd had his eyes on the judge and the King of Cloudsong.

"Were there any cameras inside the Hall?" Someone else spoke up and Norian thought that Drake and Drew looked very much like this man.

Chapter 8

"That's Dragon, Drake and Drew's father," Erland explained. "Time to confess—you had cameras, didn't you, Norian Keef?"

"I had cameras—the Charter Members wanted the information so they could deny membership in perpetuity if justice was denied in the case," Norian stood. "The feed went directly to one member, who requested it." Norian sat again, hoping he wasn't in trouble. He was certainly outnumbered at the moment.

"Griffin, do we need to negate that information?" The blonde woman asked the tall, brown-haired man. Norian watched as the man's eyes became unfocused for a few seconds. He came back with a sigh.

"No, Kiarra, we don't need to do a thing about this." In fact, Griffin was almost smiling.

"Griffin is Lissa's father, and fine outside that role. As her father, he's the biggest asshole ever," Erland settled in to gossip. Norian was now staring at Erland in alarm.

"You're joking?" Norian said before he could hold back the words.

"I *am* Lissa's father, and calling me an asshole is being kind," Griffin was now standing over Norian, who was ready to turn if things went badly. "There's no need to allow the snake to manifest. You are in no danger here."

"Tell me what all these people are, and Kifirin, too," Norian said. Griffin walked away, leaving Erland to explain things to the ASD's Director.

"When I tell you, you won't be able to tell anyone else—knowledge of the race protects itself," Erland grinned. "I know you've already heard the words *Saa Thalarr*. It means Hope and Vengeance in Neaborian."

"Neaborian is a dead language," Norian said.

"Did you know there are people living on the planet again?" Erland grinned. "But that doesn't have anything to do with the Saa Thalarr. They were created to combat the Copper Ra'Ak, you know."

* * *

Lissa

"Lissa, you should wake and eat something." Karzac settled on the side of my bed and brought me back to consciousness with fingers to my forehead. Too bad doctors everywhere didn't have that talent. No drugs needed, thank you.

"Honey, what are you doing here?" I mumbled, doing my best to force my eyes open.

"Lissa my love, your mouth always works before your eyes or the rest of your body."

"Honey, you are so funny," I huffed, cracking open a single eye to stare up at him.

"I have never been accused of being anything close to humorous," Karzac stifled a smile.

"I'm buying you lessons in stand-up," I forced my other eye open.

"I will skip my classes," Karzac rolled his eyes at my suggestion.

"Karzac, why aren't you naked?" I reached up and tugged on the collar of his shirt. I had a feeling that Grace and Devin shopped for him—I couldn't see him taking much time for that sort of thing.

"Is that what you want, my love? You want me in your bed?"

"Yeah."

Karzac leaned down to kiss me, and then kissed me again. He removed my clothing before he removed his, and

Chapter 8

what happened afterward was worth every second of the undressing. We were extremely late getting to dinner.

＊＊＊

Trell

"Lissa Beth, I want to be jealous." Norian hauled me away from the dinner table the minute I set my napkin down. We were now inside the hotel room in Rezael after rousting Lendill from his office on Le-Ath Veronis, where he'd been doing even more research.

I'm not sure that guy ever took a break. He'd still looked like Flavio, too, so Reemagar came and adjusted the disguise. Lendill now looked like Flavio's cousin instead of Flavio.

"Why are you jealous?" Lendill had already gone to bed inside his bedroom—we had a three-bed suite inside one of the nicer hotels in Rezael. Reemagar had accomplished that for me, too, fabricating a new credit chip for each of us, and all of it tied to an account that Adam set up for us at one of the banks on Le-Ath Veronis.

The funds would eventually be paid out of my account; Norian said the Alliance would reimburse the expenses. I didn't really care because we ended up in a nicer place.

"I want to be jealous of every one of your mates, breah-mul. They are welcome in your bed." Well, Norian might be wrong on one account—I hadn't heard a word from Shadow. I wondered if he and his family were wiping their brows in relief and working to get me out of their system.

"Norian, what do you want? I don't know whether I'm prepared to add to the mate department."

"You do not care for me."

"Honey, I didn't say that. If I didn't care for you, you'd be shredded instead of getting petted when you make your way into my bed, invited or not."

Blood Redemption

"Will you pet me now?"

"Honey, come on," I grabbed his arm and dragged him toward my bedroom. "Just keep in mind that petting is all you'll get."

Norian settled into my bed and curled right up as the lion snake. What do you do when a two-hundred-pound lion snake curls up in the center of your bed? "Honey, if I roll over on you, it'll be your own fault," I said, trying to scoot him over.

He didn't budge an inch. Instead, he settled his head on my stomach and closed his eyes in bliss when I stroked his face. When I woke the next morning, his head was right under my chin—I'd rolled over on my side and he hadn't turned a scale in response.

"No, cheah-mul, not yet," Norian changed in a blink and wrapped his arms around me when I tried to slide off the bed. His arms were warm around me in the chill air of our hotel room—Lendill had set the temperature, so he obviously liked it cooler. He had no way of knowing about Norian's penchant for warmer air.

"Norian, you're naked." I was pointing out the obvious.

"Yes. Isn't it wonderful?" He nuzzled my chin and neck, then wandered toward my mouth.

"I thought we were only petting."

"You are not petting anything at the moment." He lifted himself over my body. "Don't turn me out. I'm begging you."

"You have that begging thing down pretty good," I pointed out and misted away. His head was stuck inside my shower minutes later—yeah, he was still naked.

"Norian, you get a kiss. That's it," I said, moving toward him. He settled for that and walked off grinning. His ass is really nice, and I watched it walk out of my bathroom.

Chapter 8

Grey Planet

"Grampa, she won't take money or any other kind of compensation." Shadow just wanted to get out of his grandfather's office.

"We can pay for a portion of the gold." Raffian made the suggestion.

"Drake and Drew say that Kifirin pulled that gold from Cloudsong's own veins of ore. They paid for that themselves. Besides, Lissa would just throw it right back at us," Shadow retorted.

"At least Melida is off our planet," Glendes sighed.

"A suggestion was made to me, and it made sense when it was presented," Raffian went on. Shadow watched his father—Raffian was excited about this idea and wanted Glendes to agree.

"What suggestion is that and who made it?" Glendes turned to Raffian.

"Kyler made it, but I think it may have come from her Larentii." Raffian had a wry smile on his face.

"What is the suggestion, then?" Glendes' daughters, Cleo and Kyler, hadn't been speaking to him lately.

"She suggested that we apply to join the Alliance. We don't do business with any Alliance worlds, because they don't allow outside trade. We'll still be able to work with the worlds that aren't members, because there aren't any laws against grandfathering in current clients, we just have to abide by the rules of trade as set by the Alliance, but we already do that, Dad." Raffian was pitching his case to his father. Glendes lifted an eyebrow at the suggestion.

Blood Redemption

"What do you think the economic impact will be? I know Le-Ath Veronis pays a percentage of their income," Glendes was intrigued by the idea.

"A small percentage to pay for benefits, and we'd have an entirely new market for our work. We wouldn't have to worry so much over vetting our clients first," Raffian said.

Shadow watched the exchange between his father and grandfather, without commenting. They'd gotten completely away from the subject, and that had been what to do to lure Lissa back to him.

He felt like folding away and working this out on his own—or perhaps with Drake and Drew, but he didn't want to strain the relationship with his father and grandfather more than it already was. Now was the time to make amends with everyone involved and for Shadow, Lissa was first on that list. He breathed a relieved sigh when Glendes turned back to him.

"I know we've wandered away a little," he smiled at his grandson. "We'll do our best to bring Lissa back to you. We just have to figure out how to do it."

* * *

Black Mist Headquarters

"Here is the information you wanted." Zellar handed a note to Viregruz. Viregruz lifted an eyebrow at his pet warlock as he carefully unfolded the small slip of paper. Only a short, handwritten message was depicted. Viregruz smiled.

"Get the Liffelithi for me—and quickly. I'll be more than happy to hand over most of the money we received from Solar Red and San Gerxon to take her out, just to get this done as swiftly as possible. They'll need a shield, too, to get a ship inside the Alliance. I expect you to provide that shield

176

Chapter 8

until our target is hit. You can withdraw it immediately after."

Zellar felt a momentary pang of conscience. The Liffelithi held a weapon that had been outlawed from one end of the universes to the other. If the Alliance suspected they had it, they'd have mobilized their army already and gone after it.

Liffel was a nondescript world and home to several races of dwarves, all of whom fought constantly. The inhabitants' willingness to war with each other was the reason the planet's application to join the Alliance had been rejected on many occasions. One particular faction had gained possession of this weapon when all the others like it had been dismantled and destroyed by the Alliance.

Viregruz had discovered its existence—the ones who held it had contacted him discreetly, letting him know that for a price, it could be *borrowed*. Viregruz was about to see how effective this weapon might be and that concerned Zellar. He shook off the worry, however, and went to do as Viregruz bid.

Viregruz watched Zellar leave, rereading the note one last time before tearing it into tiny bits, which he swept into a waste bin. This was the Queen's fault, if she didn't watch over her population better than this. She should have known that someone close to her would likely pass the information along, not even thinking that it might end in the Queen's death. Viregruz knew where the Queen was, now. All he had to do was pay the Liffelithi and her death would be swift. Viregruz smiled widely and sat back in his seat.

Chapter 9

"*L*issa Beth, are you good with names?" Norian was now the Director of the ASD and not a lion snake who'd spent the night in my bed. Lendill was standing next to him and they'd cooked something up, I could see it in their eyes.

"I have almost total recall," I said, frowning at Norian.

"Good," he smiled. Norian can certainly turn on the charm when he wants. "We've called a meeting of all our operatives this afternoon," he said. "And I'm depending on you to tell me which ones have taint about them—who might be in on replacing Lendill or anything else that ties my tail in a knot. I'll introduce Lendill as my new assistant, Rych," Norian added.

He'd pronounced the name Rych like "rich." "Is that short for anything?" I asked, crossing arms over my chest.

"Rycharde," Norian was still smiling. "We're thinking about making it permanent."

"Honey, what are you doing? Does Lendill really want this?" I was skeptical, all right.

"It works, at least for the moment," Lendill sighed. "New face, new name, I suppose."

"Then let me do this," I said, and went to Norian, placing my hands on his face and gathering power around me. When I dropped my hands, Norian had mindspeech. "Now you," I did the same thing for Lendill/Rych.

"What did you do?" Norian didn't know, yet. Neither did the newly named Rych.

"Gave you mindspeech, but you can only communicate with me and a few others—you won't be able to do anything with somebody who doesn't have the gift." Norian's eyes went wide in shock. That's how Rych sent first.

Does this really work? he sent to me.

It really works, I sent back. Rych laughed—a full laugh that I hadn't heard before. This truly was a gift for him.

Lissa Beth, do you hear me? Norian finally had his head wrapped around this, I could tell.

Honey, I hear you and you can even communicate like this while you're in snake mode, I replied.

"This will make things so much easier," Norian breathed. "Come on, let's do a little snooping."

We did some snooping, three blocks away from the Temple of the New Dawn that was still under construction. A market district surrounded the new structure and just about anything could be had up and down that street. We got breakfast sausages rolled up in baked dough and we ate first, before Norian began asking questions.

Chapter 9

"Have there been any disappearances?" Norian asked a vendor who sold silk scarves.

"Rumors are everywhere, and we all look to the news vids for better information, but there's nothing coming from the news services." The scarf merchant sniffed as if he suspected the news vids weren't accurate. He was right.

"Is there anyone you know who has come up missing?" Norian pressed on.

"A vendor down the way disappeared two eight-days ago," he said. "I didn't know his family, so I haven't made any inquiries about his disappearance. He could be ill or called away on some errand. I don't wish to jump to conclusions."

Our vendor wasn't sure what to tell us, exactly, since he didn't know who we were. Therefore, I placed compulsion. Things went smoothly after that.

"Everyone is frightened," the vendor stated, after I ordered him to speak the truth. "We don't know whom to turn to, any longer. The people who are missing—nobody has seen any of them again. Children are missing, too. We don't like it, but the ones who have contacted the journalists also end up missing."

When we got as much from him as we could, I placed compulsion to forget that we'd been there before moving on. *I say we take out the fuckers now*, I sent to both my companions. My language caused Rych's eyebrows to rise momentarily.

I promised the Twenty that we wouldn't have a repeat of Twylec, Norian practiced his newly acquired skills of mindspeech. *It's to protect you, Lissa Beth.*

Blood Redemption

You tell them everything? That had me stopped dead in the middle of the busy walk, forcing people to move aside all around us since foot traffic flowed continuously.

Only the one, Norian grumped as he took my arm and we started moving again. *How will it look if you are seen near that sort of thing regularly? Rumors fly about you anyway, breah-mul. We do not wish for more troubles to land on your doorstep.*

"Nobody ever worried about that before," I grumped aloud. Norian pulled me closer to him.

"We worry about it, now," he hissed in my ear. *Refizan certainly remembers a little Vampire Queen. Even though the cameras went dark or fuzzy during the Conclave on Nemizan, do you think they aren't talking about that anyway and speculating wildly? Cheah-mul, you are in enough danger. Let us protect you when we can.*

Norian's words almost made me stop again but he prevented it, keeping a tight grip on my arm and pulling me along with him. Rych had moved to my other side and I walked in step, flanked by both of them.

We talked to three more shop owners before taking a break for lunch. I'd had to place compulsion with each of the three in order to learn what Norian wanted to know. It wasn't good—any of it.

"Where are we meeting with your people?" I asked, as we ate at a small table inside a café. Norian was cold, I could tell, and he wanted to eat inside rather than staying outside and ordering from a vendor's cart.

"About six blocks from here, at another hotel," Rych answered. Norian's mouth was full, so he let his assistant take up the slack.

"Do any of them know where we're staying?" I asked.

Chapter 9

"They think they do—I've got a suite set up not far from here, under Norian's name." Rych was proud of himself, I could tell. He grinned as he bit into his sandwich.

I nibbled at my food. I was far away, though, in thoughts anyway. All the vendors we'd spoken with had mentioned children disappearing. I didn't like that one bit and wanted to go right to the temple and pull any out that might be there. Norian was doing his best to hold me back.

"We'll take care of business later, when it's dark and we know which of our agents are moles," Norian tapped the edge of my plate, bringing me back to my uneaten food. "Eat your lunch—I don't need a collapsing Liaison." I sniffed at his words and lifted my sandwich.

* * *

Norian gave an improvised speech, telling twenty-nine operatives that we were making some progress in this case, but it was going slowly and we weren't likely to find anything truly incriminating for a while.

I'd gone *Looking*, just to make sure there weren't any cameras or listening devices on any of them, but they probably knew better than that. Nobody had anything.

Norian was misleading them, too, putting any moles' fears to rest that we didn't have any solid proof yet. When his speech was over, I mingled with the crowd and told Norian and Rych through mindspeech just who the bad guys were. Six of them were tainted and Norian had their names by the time they walked out the door.

That evening, he placed a call to each of the six operatives, asking them to meet him at our bogus hotel room. Rych answered the door and each of the six were led to a bedroom for a private conference with Norian.

Blood Redemption

I was inside the bedroom with Norian and watched as each one was bitten by a twelve-foot lion snake that leapt at them the moment they walked through the door. All six died of poisoning and all six were transported, courtesy of yours truly, to Tykl. Someone would pick up the bodies later.

Rych/Lendill never saw the snake and never asked questions, either. We all knew what was going to happen to those operatives when they were invited to the suite. Perhaps Rych thought I did it—he'd seen me work when Norian and I had come to help him while he was under attack.

"Now, on to other business," Norian shrugged into his coat later. "Lissa Beth, you named every one of the six we suspected," he added. "Rych here," he clapped his assistant on the back, "had already gotten hits on all of them; we just wanted confirmation. Now, feel free to take us to the dungeons of the Brotherhood of the New Dawn." He grinned at me.

I turned all of us to mist and got the hell out of there.

Norian probably didn't want me to kill the guy, but I did it anyway. No way was he going to live after raping a nine-year-old. That brother of the New Dawn got sent to Tykl in two pieces, just as dawn was breaking there. He got to keep company with the poisoned mole operatives.

* * *

"Lissa Beth, if you're done now, we need to have a few words." Norian was back to hissing after I dropped eight children off at an emergency room and sent them inside, some of them nearly unable to walk, they were so brutalized.

Rych took himself out of our hotel suite so Norian could have his few words. I figured the words were going to come from his side and all the listening was going to come from

Chapter 9

my side. Well, I had experience with this. I thought about sending him to work with Gavin for a while.

"Lissa Beth," Norian paced in front of me. I'd chosen to sit on a nice sofa inside the living area of our suite. If he intended to yell, I wanted to be as comfortable as I could be while he did it.

"Norian Keef," I muttered.

"Lissa Beth, I want to hug you and yell at you at the same time," Norian stopped his pacing for a moment and stood in front of me. "They'll know something is up when one of theirs disappears. You should have left the prisoners there," Norian began his chastisement. "You need to learn control. We have to take them unawares, if we can. This will allow them time to pull together and form a battle plan."

"Then why didn't you stop me before we went? You know I'm not going to sit still and watch them mistreat babies."

"I know why this upsets you so much. Please try to see it from my perspective. It is my duty to take them down. Half of them could be on their way off-planet by now and we'll lose contact with them. I have a handful of my men at the space station, but we don't have all the names involved in this yet. Do I need to point out the problems with a blown cover?"

"No, you don't have to point that out," I turned my head away from him and hugged myself as tightly as I could. "But you killed six moles yourself, earlier. Do you think your cover wasn't already blown?"

"We haven't moved against them yet. Until now. They thought the moles were protecting them. Now they'll try to make contact and none of the moles will respond. New Dawn will know for sure. If they don't attack that bogus hotel suite we set up by tomorrow night, then they're incompetent."

"We can be there, waiting on them as mist," I offered.

"Lissa Beth," Norian ran a hand through his hair in a frustrated gesture. "Neither I nor Rych like to be mist for more than a few minutes at a time. We've talked about this—we're used to being more solid and substantial."

"You just don't want to give up control," I grumped.

"That, too," Norian nodded at my assessment. "We've been doing this for a while and turning to mist is an unsettling experience."

"Then why drag me into this? You don't like the way I do things—leave me at home. I have enough crap happening there to keep me busy for a while." I still wasn't looking at him.

"I know your life is complicated and I know you're not spending enough time running things on Le-Ath Veronis. Nevertheless, you're our best bet for taking these Solar Red spin-offs down quickly and quietly. I have to use what I have at my disposal."

"And the Queen of Le-Ath Veronis is at your disposal, because the Founder and Twenty Charter members thought she should be." I turned to look at Norian, now. "Don't think for a minute that I don't see their hand in this. I don't jump when they say, they can dump Le-Ath Veronis and we'll be out of the Alliance. Why don't you just go ahead and say it, Norian?" I laid all my fears before him. It had worried me from the beginning; I just hadn't said anything about it until now.

"You make it sound as if they're blackmailing you."

"Aren't they?"

Chapter 9

Norian gave a frustrated sigh and turned away. "Lissa Beth, they use whatever they have to protect the Alliance. Surely you can see the reason in that."

"Uh-huh. I just used what I had to protect some children who were being tortured. You let me know by mindspeech when you need me the next time, Norian Keef." I went straight to mist and then to energy and got the hell out of there.

* * *

"I don't know where she is." Norian sat across the tiny café table from Rych and sipped his tea.

"Boss, I don't like to tell you your business, but you probably should have told her what you wanted in the beginning." Rych was venturing onto uncharted seas by pointing out what he considered Norian's flaw in the plan.

"Hmmph," Norian grumbled.

"You think she'll really come if you call?" Rych went on.

"I hope so," Norian stared into the dark liquid inside his mug. "If she doesn't, I'm not sure what to do—what we can do. She told me she feels coerced and that's not what I wanted. She thinks Le-Ath Veronis will be thrown out of the Alliance if she doesn't jump and run when we tell her to."

"Boss, none of the others did anything close to what she's done for us. If not for her, I'd probably be dead and some look-alike would be sitting across from you right now. Where do you think you'd be, then?"

"Most likely headed toward oblivion," Norian muttered. "I figure I'd be dead too, if you want the truth."

"What are you going to do?"

"I'll contact the one and see what he says."

"I don't envy you."

Blood Redemption

"I know." Norian shrugged into his heavy coat and Rych was right behind him as they left the café.

* * *

Temple of the New Dawn

"You've become a liability, since the ASD knows the real thing is dead." Seturna Odnard examined Tork's face as he stood on the other side of the Seturna's desk. The study had been lavishly decorated—Odnard intended to have a long and comfortable stay on Trell.

"Then send me elsewhere. I can still benefit the brotherhood."

"Perhaps. But there's something I'd like you to do, first," Seturna Odnard steepled his fingers and smiled at Tork.

"Name it and it will be yours," Tork nodded. He knew how precarious his position had become with Odnard and the others. He was lucky he wasn't already inside one of the temple's dungeons, awaiting torture of some kind. They all took pleasure in it—it was what drew them to the religion in the beginning.

"Good. We lost one of our brothers earlier tonight and several of our prisoners. We want you to kill the Director of the ASD—we feel he is behind this. Unusual for him to tip his hand so early, but perhaps he is playing a deeper game. We'd like him killed before the plan goes into full effect. Money is currently keeping the crown quiet. Eventually we'll control that, in addition to everything else here. Kill Norian Keef for me and you'll not have to worry about who your face resembles."

"How would you like him to die?"

"As painfully as possible."

"I think I can manage that." Tork gave a quick nod and left Odnard's study.

Chapter 9

Odnard waited for a few moments before tapping a code into his private communicator. When it was answered, Odnard gave a short message. "I have a tail on the director—I expect him to be dead by tomorrow evening."

"Good," came the one-word answer.

* * *

Tork cursed quietly when he discovered the hotel information he'd been given led him on a false trail. The room was empty. The hotel staff informed him that a meeting was held there earlier, but no clothing remained, or any other indicator that the room had been occupied. He'd have to locate his contacts and do some tracking to find the target. He'd paid the hotel staff well for this information, too, which made him even angrier.

* * *

"Bring her here—I'll explain things," Ildevar Wyyld sounded frustrated.

"When, Deonus?" Norian wasn't sure what to think about this turn of events.

"As quickly as you can get her back. Arrange for a ship if you have to—it wouldn't hurt to leave things as they are on Trell for the moment. Let them worry that you'll strike again and when they can't find you, so much the better. Let them spend their energy trying to track you and the others down."

"Of course, Deonus." Norian nodded to the image on the vid screen. The screen went dark—Ildevar Wyyld terminated the communication from his end. Norian blew out a breath. He was about to find out if mindspeech would summon his Liaison.

Norian was worried, too, that he might have fractured any chance at a relationship with her. He'd always heard it wasn't a good idea to work with a mate or even a potential

189

mate. That fact was staring him in the face and he didn't like the looks of it, if the truth were known. *Lissa Beth?* He sent out mindspeech. He was about to learn the truth, one way or another.

* * *

Black Mist Headquarters

"We can afford to lose a few," Tetsurna Prylvis agreed with Viregruz. "None of mine suspect anything. You're sure this will be over quickly? Our target will not have time to escape?"

"Absolutely," Viregruz steepled his fingers. "How many do you have, there?"

"Less than three hundred. All easily replaced."

"I only have a handful, now—my main operatives died in the battle outside ASD Headquarters. At least the Vice-Director was killed. That was our objective, after all."

"Our people performed very well together," Prylvis agreed. "Their sacrifice will serve our purpose completely."

* * *

Lissa

It had only been a few hours since I'd left in a snit. Honestly, I didn't expect him to come calling so quickly, yet the mindspeech reached me in some far-off corner of the universes. I knew he wasn't in trouble with the senses I had while I was energy. I'd told him I'd answer his call, so I kept that promise.

"What do you need, Norian Keef?" I appeared in front of him only a few seconds after he'd sent out the call. He looked somewhat frazzled to me, but then he'd pissed me off, so I wasn't about to go to him and try to make him feel better.

"Lissa Beth, we've been called to Wyyld—Deonus Wyyld wishes to speak with you," Norian informed me.

Chapter 9

"Oh, so they want to give me my walking papers already?" I wasn't in a charitable mood to begin with and this just made it worse.

"Breah-mul, I don't think they have any intentions of doing that. Deonus Wyyld wants to talk to you. Maybe set your fears at rest over this. Honestly, I had no idea you thought we were blackmailing you."

"What was I supposed to think, Norian? You walked into my palace like you owned the place and started throwing orders around. Tell me how else to respond to that? I have a lot of people on Le-Ath Veronis who came, simply because we were members of the Alliance. I have no desire to let them down after we persuaded them to come."

"Look, there's a ship waiting to take us as soon as we can get to the space station. No, I don't want you to take us in that way you have," he raised a hand to hold off the comment I was about to make. "Rych and I will come with you, if you're worried about Ildevar Wyyld."

"I'm not worried for me," I grumped. "Am I supposed to pack up?" I turned toward my bedroom inside the suite.

"Rych already did that for you. He and our bags are waiting at the station."

"Not wasting any time, then," I muttered, turning back to him.

"Cheah-mul, I would like nothing better than to erase this night from both our minds. All I want is to come and hold you against me and that's the last thing I think you want right now."

"Norian, do not try to make me feel guilt over this. Do not," I said and folded both of us to the space station.

The trip to Wyyld took twelve hours and I didn't speak to Norian or Rych the entire time. We arrived at the

Blood Redemption

Founder's Palace in the middle of the night, so we were taken to a guesthouse outside the palace and allowed to go to bed.

I guess we'd gotten three hours' sleep—if we slept—I kept waking up, thinking it was because I was so angry with Norian. I should have *Looked.*

Should have.

Would it have changed anything? Probably not, because any interference on my part would have definitely changed the timeline and that was forbidden. It didn't keep me from screaming and cursing, not only at Norian and anybody else I could think of, but at myself as well, for not being there to do what little I might have been able to do when Black Mist blew Trell to tiny bits with a Ranos Cannon.

* * *

"How can you stand there calmly, when six-hundred-million people just died?" I was shouting at Belen and Kifirin now, who'd both shown up. Norian was afraid to approach me when I started having my fit, and I was worried that I might be forced to reimburse Ildevar Wyyld for rebuilding the inside of his guesthouse. I'd shredded the place.

"Avilepha, you had no control over this. Those people would have died, whether through this attack or due to another cause. Be assured that the decisions the Trellian aristocracy made had them well on their way to destruction. Whether it was now or in ten years' time, it would not have mattered." Kifirin was holding a hand out to me.

"But this is my fault." I sat on what was left of my bed and tried to stop shaking and crying.

"Little sister, you did not order those deaths. One whose soul is filled with hate did that," Belen said. "What you need to see to now is the one who revealed your location to your

Chapter 9

enemies. This came from Le-Ath Veronis, beloved. You must find the source before you consider going back there."

"Someone gave out that information?" Norian was about to become outraged. "But only those at the palace knew. Her mates and such."

"Then start the questioning with them," Belen said. "Do not weep, dear one. No one holds you accountable for this." Belen's face, normally serene, looked weary to my eyes, but then I was busy wiping tears away, so what did I know?

Six-hundred-million—including the children I'd pulled away from Solar Red—all gone now, in a matter of moments. Belen folded away, but Kifirin stayed behind. He put the guesthouse back together—I wasn't going to do it. Ildevar Wyyld had called me away from Trell and I wasn't smart enough to watch over the place after I left it. This was my fuck up.

"Avilepha, listen to me—you will know when the time is right for you to act on such things—it is the way you were made," Kifirin was kneeling in front of me after fixing what I'd destroyed in the guesthouse. "You were restless, yes, but it was not calling out to you as it should have been, if you needed to help. Stop blaming yourself, my love." He raised a hand to touch my face and I didn't jerk away from him.

Norian didn't want to leave, I could tell, but Rych, who could now use his old name again if he wanted, pulled him away and left Kifirin and me alone.

"Kifirin, how many times are we going to make love when I'm still crying?" I sniffled as he got me settled on the bed.

"As many times as it takes," he murmured and brushed his mouth over mine.

* * *

Blood Redemption

Kifirin was gone the second time I woke; it was late afternoon when I jerked upright in bed with a gasp. Kifirin must have put me in a healing sleep to keep me down that long. I heard Norian and Lendill talking in the tiny kitchen down the hall. Hoping that the people of Trell hadn't suffered when they died, I slid off the bed and forced myself to clean up and dress.

"Look who's awake," Lendill said.

"Can I call you Lendill, now, or are you sticking with the other name?" I sounded grumpy, even to my own ears. How was I supposed to be? Sunshine and light?

"You can call me anything you want, little Queen." Lendill nodded to me. "Would you like something to eat?"

"I really don't feel like eating," I said. I got tea and toast anyway, and Norian watched me closely until I nibbled on the toast. Ungratefully, I admitted to myself that our argument was now moot—it didn't matter anymore that our cover was blown. "How many of yours did you lose, Norian?" I asked instead.

"Lissa, do not add their deaths to that pile of guilt you're racking up against yourself," Norian chastised me and then winced. "Breah-mul, I did not mean it to sound like that." Lendill was now staring at Norian after he'd let the endearment slip in front of him.

"Get used to it, Lendill Schaff," a new voice sounded outside our kitchen. The owner of the voice walked in and I immediately placed myself between Norian, Lendill and the newcomer, fangs and claws out, eyes red and hissing for all I was worth. I was staring at a Copper Ra'Ak in humanoid form.

194

Chapter 10

Wyyld
Lissa

Several things happened at once; Lendill stood and bowed low, Norian was trying to get to me (which was mighty brave—nobody should try to approach a vampire when they're hissing, with claws and fangs bared) and the Ra'Ak was trying to explain.

"Lissa Beth!" Norian was doing a little hissing of his own (he comes by it honestly). "This is Ildevar Wyyld!"

I turned my reddened eyes on Norian for the barest second before turning them right back to Ildevar Wyyld. "What did you have for breakfast this morning, Deonus Wyyld?" I hissed around my fangs.

"I didn't have breakfast this morning, but I have a sheep every third day, or a cow or something similar, upon occasion," he smiled at me. "I knew I couldn't fool you, little Queen." He smiled—actually smiled—at me.

"Uh-huh," I mumbled sarcastically. "I've only met one of your kind who wasn't murderous in the extreme."

"You know of one other?" Ildevar Wyyld looked at me, a speculative light in his eyes. He wasn't bad looking as a humanoid—with dark-blond hair, brown eyes and dimples when he smiled. Tall, too—around six feet or better.

"Yeah. But that information won't be coming from me." Gilfraith's secret was safe. I began to wonder, though, why Kifirin had left me there, if he knew there was a Ra'Ak—surely, he'd known what Ildevar Wyyld really was.

"Lissa, I would very much like to speak with you in private on this matter," Ildevar Wyyld informed me, beckoning with a hand. I didn't want to go anywhere with him.

"Little Queen, you are safe, I promise. I realize that a promise might not mean much to you, but if you knew me better, you'd know that I keep my word. I have known Norian for a very long time and you see he is still whole."

"He might not be for long," I gave Norian a dark look. How could he not know what Ildevar Wyyld was? How could he not?

"Now, I cannot have you harming my Director," Ildevar was smiling again. "Please. I have held this position since the beginning of the Alliance and have been what I am much longer than that. Hear me out at least, before you make up your mind about me."

"Fine," I sighed. Norian frowned at me, but he and Lendill left the guesthouse. Ildevar waited several minutes before he said anything.

Chapter 10

"They are out of hearing now. I know you know what I am, little Queen. Norian and Lendill only suspect that I belong to an ancient race. They have no idea what I really am. Please, sit and make yourself comfortable," he gestured with a hand. "I know your vampirism makes you strong, but to me you seem small and frail. Please sit. Would you like more tea?"

"No," I said and sat on a stool at the small kitchen table. I got tea anyway and watched Ildevar Wyyld closely while he made it. That seemed to amuse him. He laced it generously with honey before placing the fresh mug in front of me and sitting at the table on the opposite side.

"I am Ra'Ak." That was his first statement. I snorted in response. It made him smile. "I know you have met my younger cousins," he went on. "I and a handful like me are from an earlier time. When the Copper Ra'Ak were the protectors, so to speak, of the Black Ra'Ak. Coming from Earth, you might call us muscle."

That statement amused him no end, I could tell. "Not that we didn't possess intelligence. Many of us did and employed it, even, from time to time. Is your tea to your liking?" He nodded to my mug—I still hadn't tasted it. I did so now.

"It's lovely," I mumbled ungratefully, setting the cup down again.

"Good. I haven't lost my touch." He rested his elbows on the table. "The Twenty Charter Members of the Alliance are exactly what I am, Queen Lissa. A Copper Ra'Ak, before the fall of the Copper Ra'Ak. The youngest among us is two hundred thousand years old. I am three times his age. When our cousins started breaking away from Kifirin's teachings—yes, I know who he is and that he was here earlier—Norian told me. Well, to make a lengthy tale shorter, we did not like the direction our race was headed, so we broke away before one of ours set himself up as Prince and began watching all his underlings. He never touched us. It meant breaking away from Youon, the Black Ra'Ak King as well, but at the time, he was ignoring what his Copper subjects were doing. He continued to ignore them until they became unmanageable and eventually destroyed their Black brothers. By that time, the twenty others and I were already set up here—all our worlds are close together in case we need to help one another. We settled on what was then sparsely populated worlds. That has changed as you can see. We have thriving populations, now, and sustainable industry. We protect our humanoids."

"You don't eat any of them? I've spoken with Youon. Even he says they feed six times a year from the worlds not worth saving." I was still a little huffy, I'm afraid.

"We also feed six times a year. From the criminal population. We choose our target carefully and go after them. Crime is low on our worlds as a result. Tell me you did not take blood from humans and I will accept your self-righteousness."

"I did take blood from humans. I never killed to do it," I snapped. "And becoming vampire to begin with was never in my plans, your high and mightiness." We were just about done, here. I rose from my seat.

"Wait. Please, sit," he held a hand out toward me. "Calm yourself. I did not mean to upset you or open wounds. You seem to have more than your share of those."

"Well, did you plan to become Ra'Ak? In the beginning?" I was poking at him, now.

Chapter 10

"No. That was definitely not in my plans. I was selected, of course, as it is supposed to be. An old cleric—that's what I was, of a now dead religion. Not unlike how the vampires turn theirs, I believe. They are supposed to take someone of good character and death must be imminent? Isn't that right?"

"That's what the rules say. They didn't apply in my case."

"They were ignored, in your case," Ildevar nodded, his brown eyes gazing at me sympathetically. I didn't know whether to buy that or not.

"I have the abilities any Ra'Ak has and yes, please try to accept that I mean you no harm and in fact intend to be kind. Our Copper relatives, once they decided to break away from our traditions, went after the strong and corrupt instead of the honorable and steady-minded for their turns. They intentionally evolved the race into the killers they are now. I hear you are responsible for nearly destroying the race."

I watched his face as he made that statement—there was no evidence he disliked that fact.

"Yes. I was responsible. That is why I consider any Ra'Ak an enemy. Except for one. If what you say is true, then he must be a throwback to a better time."

"I might wish to meet him sometime," Ildevar said idly, toying with Lendill's abandoned mug of tea.

"You'll have to prove yourself to me before I ever approach him with that idea, and he's no longer Ra'Ak, actually."

That statement made Ildevar Wyyld's eyebrows lift in curiosity.

"Then perhaps if you trust me enough one day to introduce me to your friend, I'd like to discuss how he's no longer Ra'Ak with you. We'll table that for now. You know what Norian is, I presume."

"I know what he is."

"I think of him as a distant cousin to my kind, then. I would like to name him as my heir, but there is the problem of his mortality. While he'll live for centuries, he'll die eventually, unless something is done. I wanted to ask you to make him vampire, so he would become immortal and rule Wyyld should I choose to retire."

That brought a loud snort from me. "You do not care for him? You do not wish to do this?" Ildevar actually looked hurt.

"Ildevar Wyyld, you haven't caught up with the last few pages of this novel," I informed him. "If I give Norian blood, he'll become immortal, all right. You see how I can walk around in daylight?"

"I assumed your Larentii accomplished that for you."

"That's what people are supposed to think," I said, dropping my eyes.

"The Larentii are not involved?"

"No. Neither is Kifirin."

"He was my second guess."

"Well, he didn't have a hand in it, either."

"Will you tell me how this was accomplished, then?"

"Initially, my father gave me blood. That allowed me to walk in daylight. I've evolved, since then." That was putting it mildly, but I didn't want to go into twenty questions with a Ra'Ak, no matter how benign he seemed.

"And your father—how did he do this?"

"Have you heard of the Saa Thalarr?" That was my trump card, and I played it now. Ildevar's eyes widened in shock. He'd heard of the Saa Thalarr, all right.

Chapter 10

"That is what your father is?"

"He's retired, now."

"Ah." Ildevar was settling down, now, getting used to this bit of news. "Did that make you one of them?"

"No. They have no claim on me."

"Interesting."

"Yeah. Don't think to get to them through me, either. It won't happen."

"I would not ask such a thing." Ildevar now sounded hurt. "I know of their long struggle with the evil that the Copper Ra'Ak became. I know they were created to keep them from destroying all the races. I have no argument with them or their purposes. What I am asking is for you to trust me, if you can. I care for Norian, if I care for anyone. He is a kindred soul, in his shapeshifting. I hope we come to have that in common, little Queen. He cares for you—I know this much—and if you would consent to make him immortal, to take my place one day, then I would be most grateful."

"I was already considering it," I grumped. I may have been pouting a little, too, but it seemed to amuse Ildevar Wyyld.

"Then I hope I have not interfered and changed your mind. Although I did detect a bit of a quarrel between you, did I not?"

"People disagree all the time."

"Yes they do. But if they care for one another, then the quarrel should have no impact on their relationship."

"It depends on what the quarrel is over."

"You wish to spar with me?" That made him laugh.

"Not particularly. And it isn't because I'm afraid of you." I raised a hand to hold him off.

"I've watched the vid from Refizan too many times to count, little one. I know what you can do and I do not wish to challenge you."

"Well, I saw what the Ra'Ak did to Le-Ath Veronis, when they killed the last Queen." I didn't tell him that I was that queen, reincarnated. I figured that would muddy the picture. I still had a hard time dealing with it myself.

"Yes—the dark races have no reason to love my kind." He nodded in agreement. "Of course, most of the dark races are dead. Only the vampires, werewolves and a handful of others managed to survive. Norian is one of those races that somehow made it through, but then his kind are not tasty enough for my cousins."

"Wow. That didn't stop them from destroying Le-Ath Veronis or Harifa Edus."

"I know. The vampires and werewolves opposed them. The others hid. It is that simple, little Queen."

"And the High Demons stood by and watched." I was nodding too, now.

"Yes. A shame, actually. They might have intervened and brought things back to the way they should have been. They did not and here we are. There are no females among the twenty, did you know that? If we couple with a humanoid, it can damage them. We have to be extremely careful if we take anyone to our bed."

"No, I haven't thought about that," I shivered at the idea of it.

"Do not concern yourself—I am very careful and my partners leave intact and happy. I have learned to do this, over the years."

"Oh, good." How else was I supposed to respond? This was letting secrets out of the bag right and left and I wasn't

Chapter 10

sure I wanted to know those secrets—ever. "So—do you not kiss your partners?" Okay, I had to know.

"We claim it is a phobia, so we do not. You know of the Ra'Ak kiss, obviously."

"I've seen it done. It wasn't pretty."

"On Refizan?"

"Yes." Ildevar tapped his fingers absently on the table at my admission.

"But the vampire turn isn't pretty, either," I offered.

"It is the way we were made," Ildevar acknowledged.

"Yeah. Some days I want to kick Kifirin," I grumped.

"If I suggested that, I suspect I might be dead within minutes," Ildevar was back to smiling. I didn't say that I slapped Kifirin—twice, I believe. I didn't want to give anyone ideas, especially when Ildevar was right—Kifirin wouldn't take that from anyone else. "And so we are back to Norian. He wishes to learn who upon Le-Ath Veronis gave out the information that you were on Trell. That in itself resulted in those deaths. Had the information been withheld, they would still live."

"I'm afraid to find out who it was," I admitted reluctantly. I hadn't gone *Looking*, either. In fact, I wanted to put all of it off as long as possible. That was pain waiting to happen, and I'd had more than my share lately.

"Yes, it can bring harm, when you learn that someone you care for brought this to your door." Ildevar was right—I wasn't in the mood for fresh betrayal right then. "I suggest you allow Norian and Lendill to handle this for you. They will find this out. Meanwhile, there are many who now believe you dead. You may wish to be selective when you pass along the information that you are not. Now, I will leave, I will have better quarters prepared at the palace and a meal served. Norian is lurking outside, so I will inform him of the new arrangements."

Ildevar stood and stretched. "Do not fear me, little Queen. I would like to say you are my friend, one day. And the mate to my heir. As to your fears that we would blackmail you, those are unfounded, although it is my wish for you to continue to work with Norian. With both of you working to destroy the enemies of the Alliance, I will sleep better."

"You could do it yourself," I pointed out.

"But that increases the chances of discovery. We have hidden ourselves for thousands of years. We do not wish to frighten the Alliance and we certainly have no desire for any of our ruthless cousins to come calling. I gave you this information for a reason, Lissa. You have the power to destroy me, should you choose to do so. I hope we can come to trust one another." Ildevar Wyyld walked out of the small guesthouse, closing the door softly behind him. Norian and Lendill were back inside within minutes.

"Breah-mul, we're moving to the palace. Leave your things—someone will bring them," Norian spoke softly as he tried to herd me out the door without being obvious about it. We walked outside, and it was a beautiful day. A garden bloomed around us and the scent of roses came to me.

Flowers. That's what did it. Six-hundred-million lives had been snuffed out in seconds. I crumpled to the ground and started weeping. Norian was kneeling on the grass beside me, taking my face in his hands and kissing me.

He lifted me up after that and I had no idea what he was saying as he carried me the entire quarter mile to the palace. I'm sure Ildevar Wyyld's home was beautiful, but my first impression of it will always be through tears, with Norian kissing my forehead while he carried me.

Chapter 10

* * *

Le-Ath Veronis

"She isn't dead." Those were Connegar's words to the inner circle. Drake and Drew breathed a sigh of relief at the announcement. Shadow was there and looking pale. He was afraid Lissa had died when Trell did and he hadn't had a chance to make things up to her. Garde was pacing and blowing smoke while Erland did his best to calm the High Demon down.

"Then where is she?" Gavin demanded.

"Somewhere safe. Someone on Le-Ath Veronis gave the information on her whereabouts to a Black Mist agent. I can tell you where the agent is, but you must deal with the one who handed the information over. This will not be easy." Connegar raked long, blue fingers through thick, blond hair. Reemagar was standing nearby and nodding slightly at Connegar's words.

"Did one of us let it slip?" Tony was standing now.

"No. But someone close did, inadvertently. Although it was not an intentional breach, it must still be dealt with. We cannot have this happening again. Six-hundred-million died, in the hopes that Lissa's enemy could get to our mate. We cannot let anyone outside this room know she is still alive."

"But the entire palace is holding its breath," Roff pointed out. Cheedas was in mourning, he knew that much. The old cook was inconsolable.

"Then place compulsion not to reveal the truth," Connegar replied. Roff nodded his thanks. Lissa would not want Cheedas to suffer needlessly.

"Where is the agent?" Rigo stood. He was prepared to take care of this, immediately.

Blood Redemption

"In a dress shop in Casino City," Connegar replied. No less than thirteen of Lissa's fourteen mates were folded to the dress shop in question.

* * *

Pearlina Rin was hanging a new shipment of blouses onto racks when the newcomers arrived. Some of them she recognized right away and did her best to release the poison in the vial inserted beneath her skin.

She hadn't counted on the efficiency or the ability of the Larentii, however, who had the tiny container out and handed to Rigo swiftly. Gardevik came forward then and grasped her by the throat.

"You will tell us everything you know," Reemagar placed compulsion, careful not to destroy Pearlina's mind with the power exerted. He was angry and Larentii were extremely dangerous in that state.

Connegar worked to keep his fellow Larentii under control. Reemagar was very close to releasing Pearlina's particles and they had to question her first.

* * *

Roff watched Cheedas, Grant and Heathe. They all thought Lissa dead. This would be his first time placing multiple compulsions. "You will not reveal the truth to anyone outside the inner circle," Roff laid the command. He knew his compulsion wouldn't work with Grant and Heathe—they were both older than he as vampires. He also knew they were good at keeping secrets. He suspected someone else of releasing the information about Lissa and it made his heart hurt.

"What is it?" Grant sounded hopeful.

"Lissa is alive. The Larentii confirmed it," Roff replied.

Chapter 10

"Thank goodness." Heathe sank onto the sofa inside Lissa's private study. Roff had brought them inside to deliver the news. Cheedas was weeping, but they were tears of relief, now.

"Where is she?" Grant asked.

"They wouldn't even tell the rest of her mates." Roff was certainly upset over that. He wanted Lissa on Le-Ath Veronis. He wanted to protect her, just as the others did. He knew Rigo was about to explode from a lack of information. He was Lissa's newest and he'd gotten precious little time with her. Shadow, too, was extremely upset and angry.

All of Lissa's mates wanted her back so they could put their hands on her, yet she was elsewhere and that information was withheld. Roff hadn't failed to notice Kifirin's absence, either.

Regardless, the rest of them were determined to find the one responsible for handing information to Pearlina. Gavin and the others were currently getting that information from the Black Mist operative, who was being questioned in the dungeons.

* * *

"He has wizards and warlocks under his command? You are sure of this?" Erland didn't like what he was hearing. "Do you have any names?"

"I only heard one name," Pearlina admitted reluctantly. The stupid Black Mist bastard had assured her that none could get past his compulsion. He hadn't counted on the Larentii. They were fools—all of them, and now Pearlina was about to pay the price for spying.

"And the name was?" Erland pushed.

"Zellar."

Blood Redemption

Erland sent mindspeech to Wylend as quickly as he could without being obvious about it.

"How many other wizards or warlocks?" Erland continued his questioning while receiving mindspeech from Wylend, who was issuing a bounty on Zellar immediately.

"I only know of three." Pearlina pouted.

"Who gave you the information about the Queen?" Gardevik snarled. He was about to snatch up the bitch and squeeze her until she died.

"That comesula that comes into my shop to buy. Thinks of himself as female and buys dresses. That one. I don't know his name." To Pearlina, all comesuli were male.

Gavin had been listening patiently while the others questioned the Black Mist spy. He slammed his fist into the stone walls of the dungeon, breaking rock with the blow. He knew now who the culprit was, as did the others.

* * *

"Rolfe, what do you tell Giff, regarding the Queen?" Wlodek had been brought in for this. He liked it as little as the others, but this was where it started. Rolfe, as Spawn Hunter for the Saa Thalarr, could not lie. He wouldn't have been able to ignore Wlodek's compulsion, either, had the former Head of the Council chosen to employ it.

"Anything she asks," Rolfe admitted. He was beginning to worry. The Saa Thalarr all knew, as did the Spawn Hunters, that Lissa was still alive. The Larentii had confirmed it.

"And she wanted to know where the Queen was, didn't she?" Wlodek sat on the edge of Lissa's desk, toying with a handheld comp-vid lying upon it.

"I had no reason at the time to keep that information from her."

Chapter 10

"She likes to gossip with the dress shop employee where she buys her clothing." Wlodek wasn't accusing Rolfe. He might have done the same in Rolfe's place.

"I suspected as much—she spends much time there, when she shops."

"And much money." The inner circle had already researched the financial records.

"Yes."

"The shop employee was a Black Mist spy. Giff supplied information on the Queen's whereabouts. Trell was blown to bits when Black Mist tried to kill Lissa."

"Kill me. I beg you not to harm Giff." Rolfe slid to his knees in front of the former head of the Vampire Council.

"Rolfe, I think that will be for the Queen to decide. In the meantime, you can either place compulsion on Giff or we can lock her in the dungeon. Which would you prefer?" Wlodek looked down at Rolfe's bowed head. Rolfe would be the one to suffer over this. Along with six-hundred-million people, whose lives were snuffed out in a blink.

"I will place compulsion." Rolfe sounded defeated.

* * *

Wyyld
Lissa

"Lissa Beth, can we have dinner in your suite?" Norian stood beside me as I gazed over the gardens outside Ildevar Wyyld's palace. Ildevar had servants, but they were few and discreet. Guards were stationed along the outer walls, but there weren't many inside the walls. Ildevar protected himself, I was pretty sure.

Norian was dressed better than I'd ever seen him dress. Fine fabrics replaced the sturdy uniform he normally wore, which consisted of black pants, boots and gray shirt. He looked good in a white silk tunic with a long, finely woven green vest. Linen pants in a darker green rounded out the outfit—it was the Wyyldan style of dress. The servants wore a plainer, pared-down version of it. Ildevar was dressed similarly to Norian, I'd noticed.

"You stay here, when you're not on assignment," I said, only now realizing it. It made sense—if Ildevar wanted Norian as his heir.

"I do. Deonus Wyyld was one of the few who was kind to me when I was young. He offered a place to stay and told me to keep it."

"You look nice," I fingered the fabric of his vest.

"You look beautiful. But you always look beautiful."

"Honey, I don't think I looked very good with fangs and claws out," I sighed.

"That is what you are. Just as I am what I am, when I turn."

"Are you ever in a place where you feel comfortable turning?" I wanted to touch his face, but held back.

"I've gone to the jungles on a few worlds when I have time off. I can turn there without worrying about it. When I turned inside your palace and crawled alongside you, that was a first for me. It was the first time I was able—and welcome—to do that with people all around me. I didn't know that Le-Ath Veronis would be the place to welcome a shape-shifting lion snake."

"Ask Drake and Drew to turn for you, sometime," I said.

"The Falchani? I didn't know they were shapeshifters." Norian put his arm around me as we both surveyed the gardens below. My suite was three stories up, with a lovely view. Ildevar, Ra'Ak that he was, seemed to appreciate flowers and ornamental shrubs just as much as anyone.

Chapter 10

"They're not—not normally," I answered Norian's question regarding the twins. "Those dragon tattoos aren't just for show, you know."

"They turn to dragons? How?" Norian turned me to look at him, and I was folded into his arms, my hands against his chest. Green eyes studied my face while a whisper of a smile tugged at his mouth.

"It's what they are. I'll tell you about it soon, I promise."

"Lissa Beth, why do I get the idea there's more here than even I suspect?" He pulled my head against his shoulder.

"Because you're a smart man," My voice was muffled against his vest.

"Have dinner with me in your suite."

"All right. You just want me to feed you, don't you?" I pulled away to watch his face.

"You know it." A cheeky grin followed that remark.

"What are we having?"

"Lamb, I think."

"I hope it's cooked."

"It is."

"Good."

* * *

"Honey, I don't know that you can swallow this. Let me take it off the bone, first."

Norian, in his lion snake persona, was impatiently waiting for me to feed him. I tore off pieces of tender lamb and fed him by hand. He kept his fangs back and ate what I offered. He was also dipping his forked tongue in a wineglass.

"What am I supposed to do with an inebriated snake?" I asked. He was getting into the wine pretty good. When he was finished eating and drinking, he draped himself over my shoulder while I ate.

"You're not finished already?" I'd pushed my plate away and now had a naked Norian Keef draped over my shoulder. His arms came around me as he kissed the side of my neck.

"I'm not very hungry," I said, attempting to shrug away from his embrace.

"Yes you are," he coaxed. He moved around until he was sitting on the small table I had inside my suite. I had to avert my eyes from certain parts of him. "I can feed you," he offered.

"Norian."

"Lissa Beth. Breah-mul. Cheah-mul. Deah-mul. If I don't take you back to Le-Ath Veronis in excellent health, all the people waiting for your return will have my head."

"I wouldn't want to be the one trying to take it," I answered honestly.

"Come on, eat a little more. Then I want to sleep with you."

"Uh-huh."

"You know I do. And sleeping isn't all I want to do." He was back to kissing my neck and trying to unbutton my blouse.

"What if I'm not ready?"

"I'll get you there."

"That wasn't what I meant."

"I know." His breath fanned my temple as he deftly unbraided my hair. "I think I'll have to feed you later." He had a hand on a breast, pushing my bra aside and stroking a nipple.

"Norian?"

"What, love?"

Chapter 10

"If you're already undressed, what am I supposed to do?"

"Play with this." He placed my hand himself and kept on kissing.

* * *

What do you say when your Ra'Ak host is there, smiling as if he'd won the lottery the following morning at breakfast? *Hi, how are you? Yes, we fooled around?* Norian was piling a plate with food and shoving it in front of me.

"Honey, I can't eat all that," I protested.

"You didn't finish your dinner last night."

"I was hoping you'd forget."

"Lissa Beth."

"Norian."

Ildevar Wyyld faded from the room like a shadow at twilight. Norian was kissing me between feeding me rolls and bits of ham. He turned, allowing his clothes to drop away, and I was feeding him. He loved being hand-fed in his lion snake form.

I wondered if that went back to his childhood, somehow. Did his mother feed him like that? Maybe I'd check on it, if I could get Norian to answer questions. I ran fingers over his head and down his body. He really liked that.

We were interrupted moments later by mindspeech from Lendill. *We know how Trell was destroyed—it was a Ranos Cannon, held by the Liffelithi,* he sent. *The Agency located their ship as it was leaving the Alliance, and we have coordinates.* Norian turned in a blink, and I was standing, ready to go. Norian dressed quickly, and Lendill joined us in seconds.

Blood Redemption

"Are we going?" Lendill asked. He was ready to go; I saw that right away. He had a weapons belt strapped around him and looked to be all business.

"Let's go," Norian nodded to me. We went.

* * *

The Ranos Cannon was carried inside a monster-sized ship, which was making its way toward Liffel as quickly as it could. The ASD had located the ship as it was speeding toward home, and I'd folded us to it after Lendill showed me where it was on his handheld. The three of us stood inside the ship's cargo hold, which had been renovated to contain the nastiest weapon ever.

While we stared up at the huge cannon that could obliterate an entire planet in seconds, Norian explained conversationally that there was an old saying about Liffel—that two Liffelithi couldn't get along for more than two ticks. After that, they were enemies, until other enemies came along.

Lendill then did his best to describe ranos technology to me—how it worked, who'd invented it—all sorts of things. I was only interested in one thing, though. I was about to take it apart.

Then we'd deal with the ones who'd blown Trell to bits. As it was, the ship's sensors had finally discovered us and sirens were going off everywhere—that meant the security team was on its way. I had the three of us shielded quickly and was prepared to turn to mist if necessary.

Shots were fired initially as a horde of Liffelithi dwarves descended on us, but the laser blasts were ricocheting off my shield and bouncing into the hull, which didn't do it any good, actually.

Chapter 10

I was proud of Norian and Lendill—they hadn't drawn a weapon and stood calmly beside me, cool as the proverbial pre-pickled vegetable while chaos occurred outside my shield.

Somebody was shouting for weapon-toting dwarves to stop shooting in less than a minute. I watched the one who'd shouted the command—a rather short Liffelithi dwarf, wearing a very large hat.

Napoleon came to mind as he swaggered toward the perimeter of my shield and poked it with a finger. Norian glared at him as I moved to the inside of my shield, standing opposite the captain.

"Can you hear me?" Napoleon poked my shield again.

"I hear you, all right," I said, crossing arms over my chest.

"Good. Come out of there, give yourselves up and we'll consider allowing you to live."

"I could say the same to you, except I don't want to lie," I told him. "I don't intend to let you live."

"I don't know what's holding this shield up, but it has to run out of power eventually," Napoleon said while running his hands across the invisible barrier. "We'll have you then, and since we're being truthful, you won't live either." His teeth were good—I saw that when he offered a nasty grin.

"Well, gee, that's too bad, huh?" I snapped. "Before I kill you, I want to know who's behind the Trell massacre. Go ahead; tell me it was Black Mist."

I somehow had the idea that Black Mist had provided protection or shields on the way in, and then canceled their efforts on the way out. It was a signature move for them.

"I won't divulge any information to you," Napoleon huffed.

Blood Redemption

"You will tell me everything you know," I commanded, compulsion thick in my voice. The schmuck should have known not to stand so close—he got hit with my compulsion from close range.

"Black Mist offered us a great deal of money. The head of my clan made the deal and didn't tell me how much. I merely carried out his orders."

"So, somebody else to go after," I mused, watching Napoleon. Norian and Lendill came to stand beside me; Norian wanted to turn to his lion snake so badly I could feel him vibrating. "What's his name?" I asked. "This dwarf who took Black Mist's money?"

"Giryoth," Napoleon muttered. That information hadn't been given willingly at all. Of course, he didn't have a choice.

"We'll pay a visit to him presently. In the meantime, I'm destroying your toy."

I went to energy and gathered light around me. The Ranos Canon melted. Liffelithi were running and screaming immediately; the heat I gathered was melting the walls and the floors of the ship.

Napoleon ran away with his crew—I hadn't told him not to. I then disabled every escape pod on the ship with a thought. Norian, Lendill and my body remained inside my shield, which was as cool as a spring day as we watched the ship fall apart around us.

Napoleon's men screamed and died—either from the heat or by exploding as they were sucked through holes forming in the hull of the ship. Once outside the pressurized ship, their bodies flew apart—they no longer had anything to hold them together.

I think Lendill went to his knees at one point, his mouth hanging open in shock as he watched. The whole thing took

Chapter 10

ten minutes, after which I slipped back into my body and folded the three of us to Giryoth's palace.

Chapter 11

L *iffel*
Lissa
Giryoth's assistant cursed us and the seemingly useless guards outside Giryoth's private quarters when we appeared inside his office without warning. "How in the name of revenge did you get in here?" he shouted.

He could have been Napoleon's brother—he was short, too, maybe weighed a little more, with hair dyed a dark green. It matched his uniform—a dark-green jumpsuit with gold doo-dads on the left breast.

"We folded space," I answered truthfully. "We're here to see Giryoth."

"You will not get in to see him," he pulled a laser pistol from a side pocket and aimed it at us. Well, too bad for him. He was headless in less time than it took to draw a breath.

Blood Redemption

He'd forgotten the first rule of attempted homicide—never bring a gun to a vampire fight. I stepped over his body, heading for the doorway that lay beyond his desk. I took a brief look around me—judging by the opulence surrounding us, Giryoth was extremely wealthy. I figured Black Mist had made him a lot wealthier, after they'd blown Trell away. Well, he wasn't going to spend that money if I had anything to say about it.

"Norian, what does the Alliance do with the money and assets seized from criminals?" I asked calmly as we stepped inside Giryoth's private study. He wasn't there but I heard noise just beyond—somebody was having sex, I could tell.

"They take the funds into their coffers and pay restitution to those affected by crime," Norian replied as we walked toward another door. It was locked, so I kicked it in, hard enough that it broke from its hinges and crashed into the opposite wall.

"What in the name of the blood feud is going on?" Giryoth thundered, leaping out of bed. Well, somebody had a bedroom installed behind his office. Made it easy to sexually harass the secretary, I guess.

It's difficult, too, to appear serious and menacing if you're not very tall, completely naked and purple with rage. Giryoth's companion was cowering in the bed, the sheets gripped tightly in her hands. She was pretty and Giryoth was wealthy. Go figure.

"How much did Black Mist pay you to kill six-hundred-million people?" I asked as politely as I could. I was doing my best to reel in my temper. Norian and Lendill stood at my shoulder and Lendill had one of his laser pistols out. He wasn't going to need it.

Chapter 11

"How the hell did you get in here?" Giryoth shouted. "Windon! Get in here, now!"

"Windon will have to pull himself together, first," I purred, allowing my claws to slide out.

"Who are you?" Giryoth was only now beginning to worry. His companion was far ahead of him—she was already making breathy, shrieking noises.

"I am the Queen of Le-Ath Veronis. Six-hundred-million people died on Trell because Black Mist was aiming at me. Too bad you missed, huh?" I took a step toward him. Giryoth shuddered and took a step back.

"And I am the Director of the ASD," Norian was right beside me. "I can only imagine that I was supposed to die as well. As you see, you failed to kill me, too. Shall we leave you here and let Black Mist know?"

"No," Giryoth whispered, backing up a little more, his eyes widening in terror. Yep—death was right in front of him and he was still more frightened of Black Mist.

"What are you going to do, Lissa?" Lendill muttered. I turned to look at him.

"I have an idea," I said, and folded Norian, Lendill and Giryoth to Wyyld.

* * *

Wyyld

"Are you sure this won't upset you?" Ildevar Wyyld asked as he eyed Giryoth, who had no idea what was coming. Ildevar had sent Norian and Lendill off to research the whereabouts of Black Mist. That was a ruse—he'd told them he and I would take care of Giryoth. Ildevar was going to do the honors, and I was going to watch.

"I've seen it before, remember?" I replied with a shrug.

Blood Redemption

Giryoth was looking from Ildevar to me and back again, fear plain on his face. Well, he should have thought about consequences before killing Trell.

"I must thank you for providing for me," Ildevar bowed slightly in my direction. Giryoth didn't have time to squeak before Ildevar was his lengthy, coppery self and had Giryoth swallowed in less time than that. It's a little disturbing, knowing that it's a humanoid sliding down a Ra'Ak's throat instead of an animal or cooked meat of some kind, but Giryoth had it coming.

"Did you remove his clothing for me?" Ildevar was back to humanoid.

"No, we found him like that," I sighed.

"They digest easier if they are naked," Ildevar remarked. "Now, what do you intend to do with the rest of Liffel?"

"Well, the population has been diminishing on Evensun," I said.

"Ah."

"I thought I'd send them there. We'll see how one batch of murderers does against another batch. And then I intend to blow Liffel to little, tiny bits. As a message to Black Mist."

"When did you intend to do this?" Ildevar looked at me, a speculative gleam in his eyes.

"In the next few minutes. I think Norian may be reevaluating his relationship with me. As you may, too."

"Do you care for Norian?" Ildevar raised an eyebrow.

"Of course I do. We wouldn't have—well, we wouldn't have," I turned my head, feeling embarrassed.

"There is nothing to be ashamed of. You have multiple mates. It is reasonable, when there are so few females among your kind."

Chapter 11

"Yeah, well, if somebody had told me that when I was younger, I would have thought they were crazy." I folded away to do my errands.

The criminals went to Evensun. The others, and there weren't many—mostly children, I sent to an underpopulated world just outside the Alliance. They were begging for immigrants—a devastating disease had destroyed many of their inhabitants. Then I went to energy and blew Liffel to atoms. The news was all over the newsfeeds by the time I returned to Wyyld.

* * *

Black Mist Headquarters

"I'm assuming the ASD turned the ranos cannon on Liffel," Viregruz nodded toward Zellar, who'd brought the news of Liffel's destruction to Black Mist's founder. "Doesn't matter," Viregruz continued. "Cancel the transfer of funds— I'll double your bonus," he nodded to Zellar. "You did very well, and this has turned out better than anticipated."

Viregruz moved to stare out a window—night had fallen and very few people wandered along the darkened sidewalk below.

"I, uh, have other news," Zellar muttered, hanging his head. "From one of our spies."

"What news is that?" Viregruz jerked his head toward Zellar.

"Our target—well, targets—are still alive."

Viregruz shouted his displeasure, and the echoes could be heard from blocks away.

* * *

Wyyld
Lissa

Blood Redemption

"Lissa, if I didn't know you better, you'd frighten me." Those were Norian's words as he nuzzled my neck.

"Norian, this probably isn't a good time," I sighed.

"Are you saying you didn't do the right thing?" He and I had already talked about what I'd done, except for the part where I gave Giryoth to Ildevar for dinner. Norian thought we'd executed Giryoth. That was true; it was just in a manner he hadn't expected.

"I did my best," I muttered. "That doesn't mean it still doesn't upset me."

"I know. Breah-mul, I know you are not used to this, and that is fine. I want my mate to have a soft heart. Where I'm concerned, anyway."

"Honey, I wish I could have been with you when you were growing up." I tucked a lock of hair away from his eyes. It had fallen down and was tickling his eyebrow.

"I wish you could have been there—especially when I was in my teens and my hormones were raging."

"Uh-huh." I looked into his green eyes—they had flecks of gold in them. They were the same eyes he had as a lion snake, only those eyes were slitted. Norian smiled at me and settled his mouth over mine.

"Lendill asked if we were going to marry, while we were here. I told him I wanted to and that Ildevar wants it, too. He told me earlier, breah-mul. He wants me to be his heir, but only if you give me the gift he mentioned. What gift is that?" he was nuzzling my neck again.

"My blood." I pushed him away. "I have to give permission for you to take it. Is that what you want? How much do you love me, Norian?"

"Lissa," Norian blew out a breath. "You have no idea what was going through my mind when I saw you the first

Chapter 11

time. And I yelled at you anyway. You just grabbed my arm, hauled me off to Twylec and proceeded to show me what you could do, taking care of my worst problem immediately, when you should have just slapped me through a wall. The second time I saw you, I knew I was gone. You were pouting at me, cheah-mul. If you hadn't been surrounded by your mates in that hot tub, I would have been all over you, although I was half-afraid you'd shred me. You're the only one who has ever touched me with affection while I am my other self. I cannot describe what an ecstasy it is to be stroked while I am that. If you doubt my love, deah-mul, tell me how I can prove it to you."

"Does drinking blood frighten you, Norian?" I had to know—we could put it in juice or something, if it bothered him.

"I will do this and walk through fire for you, if that will keep you with me."

I ended up taking a wineglass and nicking my wrist. Norian got my blood mixed with red wine and I gave him his ring and the words of permission. He drank and fell asleep.

That is the way of it—the body goes through a transformation during sleep. Norian would sleep for a while and when he woke, he would be immortal. I carried him to bed.

* * *

Earth

Gryphon Hall

"Rolfe, you are not the one responsible." Kiarra looked at the vampire-turned-Spawn Hunter. "I have no idea if Giff intended to harm the Queen, but that is between the Queen and your mate. I don't believe the Queen will be overly harsh,

225

especially if Giff was unaware that she was divulging sensitive information. Have you told her what happened?"

"I have been unable to," Rolfe hung his head. "I did place compulsion for her not to reveal anything else concerning the Queen or anyone at the palace."

"How is Yoff?" Kiarra changed the subject, asking about Giff's child.

"Yoff is well and growing." Rolfe gave a half-smile, but Kiarra knew it was forced. "When do you think we will be called out to kill spawn again?" Rolfe asked.

"I don't have an answer for that. Nothing has come to our attention lately," Kiarra replied. "Be assured we will let you know." Rolfe nodded and folded away.

* * *

Le-Ath Veronis

"I asked. That's how I know," Markoff said with a shrug. Roff stared at his brother. He'd sought Markoff at the winery his brother helped run. Roff hadn't been able to stand it any longer and had gone to ask Markoff if he thought Giff intended to harm the Queen. He couldn't bring himself to ask Giff; he dreaded hearing what the answer might be.

"Giff said she thought of Pearlina as a friend, and didn't hold any information back. There was no specific intention to harm the Queen, although I think she knew in the back of her mind it could turn out that way. I did not tell her what that information cost Trell."

"I am afraid to say as well and I have no idea what Lissa will do when she finds out."

"You cannot let this devour you," Markoff placed an arm around his brother, though Roff was much taller than Markoff now. "Dariff just shakes his head in confusion over the whole thing."

Chapter 11

Dariff was Markoff's child and close to Giff's age. He and Giff had grown up together.

"The difficulty is that we were all warned by Gavin, Tony and the Falchani not to reveal any information regarding the Queen. Giff knew better. I do not know what she was thinking."

"Things have been unsettled since Toff was taken."

"Yet I hold hope that my child will come home one day. As does the Queen."

"Yes, betrayal by a member of your family is the hardest to accept, is it not?" Markoff patted Roff's shoulder and moved away. "Lissa's own father placed Toff in harm's way and now she barely speaks of him. I hear he is not welcome on Le-Ath Veronis."

"That is true, although she has not formally banished him. I worry for my child, Markoff. I don't think the Queen will be unjust in her judgment; it is the Council I worry about. This may be treason in their eyes, and they may not be kind."

"I had not thought of that," Markoff blew out a sigh.

"There are a handful of crimes that the Council is compelled to vote on and those are treason, murder and drinking from a child. The death penalty is involved in each of those crimes. Markoff, I am frightened."

"How would you feel, brother, if this were not Giff, but another who almost caused the death of our Queen?" Markoff was attempting to be objective, though it was also causing him pain.

"I would be angry, and out for blood." Roff rustled his wings. "But this is my child and my heart bleeds."

"I know it does. Dariff and I are holding our breath until the Queen returns. Do you have any idea when that might be?"

"None. And Rolfe goes about the palace like a ghost. This has brought great harm to him. How did this happen? Tell me what brought this to our door?"

* * *

Wyyld
Lissa

Ildevar Wyyld wasn't taking any chances. He was performing the ceremony himself, just as quickly as he could. Norian and I stood in front of him as he gave the words of binding. Norian got his ring—I placed the gold claw crown signet myself. Norian had a ring for me—don't ask me where he got it. It slid onto the finger where Gabron's had once been.

Yes, I knew that Aryn had once been Gabron. Kifirin had accomplished that, somehow. But he had done too much harm to our relationship, and I didn't know if things would ever be right between us. In the meantime, I pretended not to know.

Ildevar smiled at Norian and when the ceremony was over, the Twenty Charter members folded in and witnessed Ildevar's naming of Norian as his heir. Norian received a second ring for that—it bore the crest of Wyyld. Ildevar wore one identical to it.

"Congratulations, honey," I gave Norian a peck on the cheek.

"Is that all I get?" He pretended to be hurt.

"Norian, the Twenty Charter members are watching, I hissed. Norian grinned.

Chapter 11

"Perhaps you should take some time for yourselves," Ildevar suggested, placing a hand on both our shoulders. He was smiling benignly at us. It boggled my mind, seeing a Copper Ra'Ak act in a civilized manner. The other twenty were the same—they were sipping wine and talking. Lendill was there, of course, and he was beaming.

"I never thought to see Norian mated," Lendill said.

"And I have my doubts about you," Norian teased his second-in-command.

"I thought I was going to have to call you Rych for the rest of your life," I did a little teasing, too.

"Thank the stars that didn't come to pass." He still kept the face that we'd given him, though. He said he liked it better. Well, it certainly drew more women.

"Norian, let's go looking for your family." I don't know why it came out of my mouth, it just did. I suppose it was my way of ignoring the fact that I was expected on Le-Ath Veronis—a betrayer had to be named and an accounting taken, and I didn't want to face that pain right away.

"I don't even know what planet I came from," Norian muttered.

"Honey, I can find that. We'll just have to locate your family after that. All right?

Do you want to do this?" I couldn't believe the hope in Norian's eyes.

"Come on, pack your bag and we'll go." I dragged Norian away. Lendill was smiling and talking with Ildevar Wyyld when we left.

* * *

Phinerris

"Are you sure this is the right place?" Norian glanced around the hotel suite we'd booked. Phinerris boasted good

229

food, great wine and provided grain crops to many Alliance worlds. They were blessed with rich soil, a mild climate over most of its surface, three large oceans, plenty of seafood and the usual humanoid population. With a few exceptions.

A thriving community of shapeshifters lived there. They resided on the outskirts of the city where we'd rented our hotel room. They had farms there, and raised wheat. Yeah, lion snake shapeshifters grew wheat.

I thought back briefly to the wheat field I'd dug Winkler out of, shortly after being turned vampire. The sun had come along after I'd gotten him out and almost fried me. I couldn't recall being in a wheat field since then.

I'd *Looked* to find Norian's birth planet, but intended to go through regular channels after that to find his family—I really wasn't in any hurry to go back to Le-Ath Veronis.

"I almost died in a wheat field once," I said as Norian hung his shirts inside our small closet. We'd brought enough clothing for four days; I hoped it was going to be enough.

My thoughts had turned back to lion snake shapeshifters and the wheat they grew on Phinerris as I watched Norian perform mundane duties. I was still trying to wrap my head around the fact that I'd just added to the mate department, too. I had enough mates to field a football team, with a few reserves.

"Breah-mul?" Norian turned to me. I had to explain about the wheat field. He was staring at me when I was finished.

"It's nothing to worry over," I said, patting his face. He didn't look as if he believed me. "Do they have records that go back to when you were taken?" I asked, changing the subject.

Chapter 11

Norian was one hundred sixteen, according to his calculations. I wanted to know if we might be able to trace his parents through the records—surely they'd reported his disappearance.

"We may have to do some digging. Phinerris has had good record-keeping technology for centuries, now. Everything depends on whether they keep those records in an accessible form for the public."

"Well, let's hope they do. Are you hungry?" I looked up at him. He smiled nervously at me. I think Norian, now that it was a possibility, was both excited and terrified to find his family.

"Honey if your family is here, we'll find them. Surely they'll be happy to see you."

"We'll find out first, before we approach them." Norian herded me from our hotel room. We found a restaurant nearby and Norian ordered half a chicken, I think, but only ate part of it.

As it turns out, we should have shared an order—neither of us did justice to our meal that night. Norian crawled into bed as lion snake and huddled against me, his head resting between my breasts the whole night. I did my best to reassure him, but I don't think either of us slept much.

* * *

"Those records are archived." That was the normal, bureaucratic answer we received the following morning when we asked about records from one hundred plus years before.

"How can we access them?" Norian asked. He didn't want to pull out his ASD badge, as this was unofficial business.

"Fill out an application, pay a fee and wait three days," came the bored response. The Phinerran didn't care and it showed. He was tall, thin and stiff, as if he'd been working the same job far too long.

"Is there a way to rush this through?" I asked.

"You have to get permission from the Director," tall and thin was getting snippy with us.

"Then take us to your director, and do it now," I laid compulsion quietly. Norian was sweating over this and I hoped I wouldn't have to pick him up and carry him out. That wouldn't raise any eyebrows. Uh-uh.

Tall and thin drew in a breath before leading us to an inner office. We found the Director speaking to someone on a communicator. "Ipsford, what is the meaning of this?" The Director grumbled as he terminated his call.

"You're going to help us out," I laid more compulsion. "We need to get into archived records and we need to see them now. We will be happy to pay the fees." Well, we didn't want Phinerris going broke because we circumvented their decidedly inconvenient, bureaucratic system.

"What are you waiting for, Ipsford, take them to the archival depository," the Director almost shouted at Ipsford. "And scan their credit chip while you're at it."

"Thank you," I nodded to the Director. "And you never saw us," I added. He offered a curt nod and went on with his work as if he hadn't seen us. Sometimes—not always but sometimes—compulsion did come in handy.

"Go back a hundred and twelve years," Norian was almost vibrating, whether from nerves, fear or both, I couldn't tell. I didn't want to point it out by asking him to calm down—I didn't need a freaked out lion snake in the city archives. That might be difficult to explain.

Chapter 11

We went through all the records of child abductions and disappearances for that year—twice. Then we went through the following year—twice. Nothing. I was worried and Norian was about to have a meltdown.

"Honey, calm down, we'll find them. If not here, then we'll go knocking on doors. I still have my nose, after all." I looked up at him—I was sitting in front of the computer; he was too anxious to sit. "Let's go backward instead of forward," I said, and went to one hundred thirteen years before.

"Honey, look—three abductions very close together." I pointed out each of the records. Three children, all taken from farms in the space of three days. Somebody wanted kids and wanted them fast. One child was seven, another five, and the last one was three.

"But none of the ages listed were my age," Norian muttered. He really was vibrating with nervous energy, now. I was worried that I might have to fold him out of there.

"Nori, they might have been wrong. Or something else might have happened. You know for sure that four was your age? You remember that part well?"

"I was four," Norian insisted.

"Honey, what about your name? None of these kids is listed as Norian."

"Norian wasn't my name, but I don't remember what my name was," he sighed and bumped a fist against his forehead. "All I remember is people calling me Keef. That's where my last name came from. They kept asking me my name and I kept saying Keef. The Norian part I got from the ASD—it belonged to the ship I was transported on. It was called *The Norian Sind*, after an old king. It was a smuggling freighter and I never did learn where it was from."

233

Blood Redemption

"So, Keef could have been a nickname," I wanted to beat my own forehead but held off—Norian was upset enough as it was. I looked at the three names again. "I think we should check these out, Norian."

"Fine, but if they don't pan out, we'll be right back here, looking again." Norian sounded as if that might be the last thing he wanted to do. Honestly, I think he was ready to call it quits and have me get him out of there.

"Come on, honey, let's go check and see if any of these families are still around." I took the information with me and we went back to Ipsford.

After paying even more money to search current records while more compulsion was laid, of course, Norian and I had three addresses. I thought that boded well; the names were still the same as before, so these people were long-lived. Normal Phinerrans lived to be around a hundred and ten. These had to be older than that. I just didn't know how old.

"What are we going to tell them?" Norian was becoming more of a basket case as we went along.

"Honey, where's my Director of the ASD?" I asked gently.

"What?" Norian's fingers were tugging his hair. Tightly.

"Never mind. Let's go check this out," I said, and folded us to the first address.

We walked up a wide lane to a large farmhouse. Built of stone, it looked as if it had stood for hundreds of years, weathered just about everything and seemed prepared to weather even more.

Wheat fields lay in the distance, surrounding several barns and outbuildings. I didn't see any domesticated animals, however. No dogs or an equivalent—no cattle, sheep or other animals. I figured I knew the reason; I couldn't

Chapter 11

imagine that any shapeshifter who turned into a snake got along well with other animals—none of which might understand they weren't in any danger.

An old-fashioned knocker was on the door, so I tapped it lightly and Norian and I stood outside, waiting. A woman answered the door. I'd convinced Norian to split the difference on the ages, and go for the five-year-old who'd disappeared.

"Hello," I said to the woman who answered the door. "My name is Lissa, and this is Norian," I nodded toward Norian, who was shaking slightly. "We're doing an investigation on the child disappearances more than a hundred years ago. We were wondering if there's anyone here who might remember anything about them."

I knew right away that Norian wasn't related to this woman, but then we didn't know who she was.

"Oh, that was a sad thing, and still affects the family," the woman replied. "I'm just the housekeeper—the family is all out getting a harvest in. Do you have a card or any information?"

"We don't," I replied. Norian was sending desperate mindspeech—he didn't want to be connected to the ASD right then and he didn't want to frighten these people. "Do you think we might come back later? We can work around their schedule with no trouble."

"Do you think they might reopen the case?" The woman looked hopeful.

"Possibly," I nodded. Well, she was talking to the Director of the ASD, after all—and the Liaison—me. We could do some snooping, if it might reconcile some families.

"Then come back tonight after dinner—around eight bells, if that's all right."

Blood Redemption

"We'll be here," I agreed, and Norian and I left.

* * *

"Honey, you can't have a meltdown, I need you," I got Norian into a warm shower after folding us to the hotel. Norian just put his arms around me and squeezed. If I hadn't been vampire, he might have crushed a rib or two.

I got him into bed for a short sleep and went out looking for something I could bring back for dinner. He was still asleep when I got back, so I left him like that for a while.

It was while we were eating cold sandwiches later that Norian told me something I should have thought out myself. "Breah-mul," he said, "the full moon here on Phinerris is tomorrow night. I'll have to make the turn, so you ought to get me somewhere so I won't give myself away."

"Honey, I forgot all about that," I admitted, chastising myself mentally. "Do you do what the werewolves do, and go out to hunt?"

"Sometimes, if I'm hungry. Usually I just wander around, or climb a tree or something. If anything threatens me, well, it could get bitten. That's why I stay away from people around that time."

"Good to know—stay away from Norian on the full moon—check," I said.

"Deah-mul, I know not to harm you," he muttered. "I don't lose all my sense."

"Also good to know," I nodded.

We got ready and went back out to the wheat farm we'd visited earlier. A man answered the door, and he was around three hundred years old, if my nose was correct. He didn't smell like Norian.

Not kin, I sent to Norian, who did his best not to jerk at the sudden mindspeech. We spent a pleasant evening with

Chapter 11

the family of lion snake shapeshifters—none of whom were related to Norian. We talked about looking into the old files and trying to determine what happened to the children, just so there might be closure for the families.

They sounded hopeful. They also offered drinks and snacks, but Norian and I declined, leaving after two hours. We got all sorts of information on when the child from their family disappeared, only they made it sound as if it were their ancestors instead of immediate family.

The mother seemed most hopeful. I think the father was resigned to the fact that he would never see his child again. I felt really bad for him—at least I knew where Toff was.

* * *

"That was useless," Norian was extremely disappointed, I could tell, as we got ready for bed.

"But did you see the hope in that mother's eyes—that she might see her son again someday? That gives *me* hope, Norian. Hope that if we do find your parents, that they'll be so glad and relieved to see you. That's what I hope for." I gave him a kiss.

"Lissa Beth, if you weren't here with me, I wouldn't have the courage to stay."

"Honey, we'll go out and check the younger child's parents tomorrow. Then you can find a place to snake around tomorrow night and if we don't find your relatives, we'll go see the last ones the following day."

"I know," Norian sat heavily on the bed.

* * *

"This is nice." I looked up at the tall, three-story, stone house. The first one we'd visited was spacious enough, but this was a manor. Like the other, it too was centuries old and built to last. The wood frames and shutters around the windows were freshly painted in a pale green, picking up a similar color in the stones.

The manor was covered in a dark slate roof, with three chimneys jutting from the top. Flowers lined the perimeter of the house in wide flowerbeds, with hedged walkways to and from barns and outbuildings in the near distance. It was picturesque, no doubt about that. We knocked on the door and a woman who appeared to be another housekeeper opened it up to us.

"We were expecting you—the Silbars called us last night. Please come in," she said and motioned us inside. We were led into what looked like a library on the first floor at the back of the house, and there was a man there, waiting on us. I drew in a breath, recognizing his scent, just as my skin itched furiously and he drew a laser pistol from behind his back and fired.

Chapter 12

I had Norian turned to mist in a blink and the laser blast went right through us. I was so angry I might have taken our assailant's head off when I materialized, but I held myself back, knocking the pistol from his hand first and then tossing him into a wall and holding him there.

"You stupid ass, you almost killed your brother," I hissed in his ear—the one that wasn't making a dent in the library wall, that is.

"My brother is dead," he managed to mumble. Yeah, I had him crunched up against the wall pretty good. The painted surface was going to have an imprint of his body in it when I let him go, I think.

"You sound so fucking sure of yourself," I countered. "Where are your parents?"

Blood Redemption

"Out in the field, supervising the harvest. I took the communication last night. Do you know how many false reports we've gotten over the years? People saying they had information, only they wanted money. At first we paid. I've made sure the last few that came didn't get out of here alive."

Well, that was fine and good, provided he wasn't killing the innocent. I jerked him away from the wall, practically threw him into a chair and stood in front of him with my arms crossed angrily over my chest.

"Do you have any idea what kind of trouble you might be in, if you'd harmed either of us?" I snapped at him. Good heavens, he even looked like Norian. It made me wonder what his parents looked like.

"None, if I buried the bodies in the right place." Yeah, he was about to make the turn, looked like.

"Norian, I think you're going to have to convince your brother, here, that he doesn't need to bite either of us," I said, looking from homicidal sibling to Norian and back again.

Norian was staring, unable to move. I think his mouth was open, too. I reached over and tapped the underside of his chin. He closed his mouth. "This is my brother? Reedy?" He was looking closely at his brother, as if he were looking for something familiar.

"Don't give me that," Reedy, if that was his name, hissed. Yeah, it was too close to the full moon and the snake wanted to take over.

"This is Norian Keef, Director of the ASD," I hurried to make an introduction, before things got farther into the danger zone. "And I am Lissa, Queen of Le-Ath Veronis. We don't need your money. We came to find Norian's family.

240

Chapter 12

Therefore, if you'll shut up and listen, maybe we can all learn a few things."

Reedy was still glaring at us suspiciously. Yeah, I might, too, if two people showed up without warning and claimed to be a monarch and the head of the Alliance Security Detail.

"My ID," Norian produced his badge from a pocket. Reedy frowned as he looked at it.

"Could be fake," he muttered.

"These aren't." I let my claws slide out, and I pointed one of them at Reedy. "I can smell your blood, Reedy, or whatever your name is. Now, I truly don't want to be responsible for killing Norian's brother, but it sounds like you have a little blood on your hands already. I suggest you get your parents in here. We need to have a pow-wow before the moon comes up and you all get scaly and hissy."

"How do you know anything about that?" Reedy still didn't sound convinced.

"Let's take a little trip," I suggested, and folded all of us to Le-Ath Veronis, where the full moon, thankfully, was six days away.

"Little girl, tell me where you have been." Cheedas had hands on hips as we showed up in his kitchen.

Reedy looked around him, shock showing in his face. "Where am I?" he whispered.

"You are in my kitchen, in the Queen's palace on Le-Ath Veronis," Cheedas snapped, lifting a ladle and waving it at Reedy. "And you should have more respect for my Raona, or you will not receive the best of food."

"He can make good on that threat," I said mildly, smiling at Cheedas. He smiled back at me.

"Are you staying for dinner, Raona?" Cheedas asked.

Blood Redemption

"No, honey, we have to get Norian's brother back home before they call out the dogs," I said. "He was just having a hard time believing we are who we say we are."

"Avilepha, you should come home soon," Kifirin appeared beside me, shocking Reedy further. Kifirin blew smoke as he looked around me at Reedy. "Lay a hand or a scale on my mate and I will kill you slowly," he said.

"You're threatening me?" Reedy huffed.

"I do not threaten. That is a promise." Kifirin's smoke grew heavier.

"You probably don't want to talk to Kifirin that way. You're one of the dark races, after all, and he won't waste a minute doing away with you," I informed Reedy. Truly, it was for his own good.

"Kifirin? I heard he was a myth." Reedy kept digging the hole deeper. If I didn't stop him, he'd bury himself in a self-made grave.

"Yeah? Well, lion snakes might be myths to some people, too, yet the reality is right here, is it not? Let's go find your parents, you stupid shit." I folded us away again.

* * *

"Mother, I couldn't stop them. This one claims to be Queen of Le-Ath Veronis, and this one says he's my brother." Reedy rushed to give out information when we landed in front of Norian's mother. The family scent was all over her. She'd given Norian his eye color—I saw that right away.

We stood on the edge of a large wheat field under a tent of some sort. A small table occupied part of the space, and it was covered with a water jug and cups. Machinery was working out in the field, harvesting the wheat crop and raising dust.

Chapter 12

"Nori, I think you're going to have to change." I looked at Norian, who shrugged before his clothing puddled around him and he rose up, hissing, his hood spread out. It resembled the mane of a lion, which most likely gave them their name.

"See, not so far-fetched anymore, is it?" I had a claw at Reedy's throat again. He was staring at Norian, who snaked to my side and lifted himself to drape over my shoulders.

"Honey, now might not be a good time," I kissed his head and he dropped down again.

"Is that my son?" Norian's mother was looking at him closely, now. "The pattern belongs to the family, but that can't be my Lirokalif."

"Is that why you called him Keef?" I asked. "The name was too long for him to say it properly?" Norian was gathering his clothing, after he put the claw crown ring on first. He got points for that, in my book.

"And we called Yaredolak, Reedy, for the same reason," Norian's mother agreed. "Is this my son? Is it? Will someone explain where he's been all this time?" She was about to have a meltdown, too, and Reedy just looked bewildered, now.

* * *

"The Alliance boarded the ship—it was a freighter smuggling other things besides me," Norian sat at a table inside a large kitchen at the family manor. Norian's mother, father and his doubting brother sat with us while Norian told his story.

"I couldn't tell them my real name, I could only say Keef, umma and pap," he went on. "They almost killed me when the full moon came along. Ildevar Wyyld showed up, made arrangements for me to be brought up and schooled and then convinced me to work for the ASD."

243

"And now you're the Director." Norian's father was still in shock.

"Yes. And only recently made Ildevar Wyyld's heir. After I married Lissa Beth." Norian put his hand over mine. The claw crown ring was prominent on his finger.

"But you've been gone so long, I'm not sure how to fit you into the family," his mother sighed.

"You don't have to fit me into the family. I just wanted to find you. Make sure I hadn't dreamed you, or something. With the way Reedy greeted me, it's probably just as well." Poor Norian. If he'd expected a tearful reunion, he wasn't getting it.

"It's the full moon, and we'll be going out in a while," Reedy was still acting grumpy.

"What is wrong with you?" I asked. "Norian isn't taking anything away from you. And now, your parents can rest easier, I hope, knowing that their child wasn't tortured, killed or held in somebody's zoo. Norian has a job to do, so he isn't going to be hanging around, depending on you to support him. And I'm still a little pissed over the fact that you tried to kill us without knowing whether we were good or bad. I get a slight itch, looking at you. Why is that, Reedy? I know you're fifteen years older than Norian. That would have made you nineteen or twenty, when Norian was abducted. Who did you make a deal with, Reedy?" I'd done a little *Looking*. Reedy had given away sensitive information.

Norian's father was now staring at his oldest son. "Nori, I think it's time we left," I said, rising. "You can turn here, or I can take you back to Wyyld or Le-Ath Veronis. Whatever you want, honey."

I looked At Norian's mother. "I *am* Queen of Le-Ath Veronis," I said. "If you'd like to visit with your son again, get

Chapter 12

a message to me. My assistants will know to pass it along immediately." I folded Norian back to Wyyld.

* * *

"My own brother gave us away?" Norian couldn't believe it.

"Honey, you were taken on a full moon. Reedy told the kidnappers where the three smallest ones were going to be. Who knows what he gained from all that?"

"Maybe I'll have him investigated." Norian was angry, now.

"Up to you," I shrugged. "Do you think Ildevar will mind if I dig through his kitchen for something to eat?" Norian's family hadn't offered us a thing.

Norian helped me look for food; we ended up with a rice dish with meat and vegetables. It was good. We ate at the island and Norian settled me on top of it before working his way between my legs. "Norian, we are not going to fool around in the kitchen," I grumbled.

"But I want to," he was kissing my neck and trying to unbutton my blouse. I fooled him—I folded us to my suite. He didn't seem to mind.

* * *

"Lissa, we have to go. Quickly." Those were Norian's words to me when I woke.

"Honey, that's the worst pickup line I ever heard." I cracked an eye open and stared at him. He was already dressed in his ASD uniform—black, gray and all business.

"Lissa, we'll have to work on separating business and pleasure later. Deonus Wyyld tells me we have to go to Tykl."

"The trash planet?" I was fully awake now. "Whatever for?"

245

Blood Redemption

"Somebody wanted to get to those bodies we dumped there before our agents could collect them all. We are attempting to find out why that is. Come, get dressed."

"Fine," I grumped and slid off the bed. Norian watched me the whole time I undressed to shower and then watched me dress again, before doing my hair.

"I didn't get to watch you," I pointed out. He gave me half a grin and tried to hurry me along. I guess lion snakes have some kind of herding ability—he was doing a good job.

Lendill was waiting on us, and they wanted me to get them to an Alliance ship orbiting Tykl. The bodies they'd found were on board. I had to concentrate to hit a moving target, but we did it. The Captain of the ship hardly lifted an eyebrow when the three of us appeared out of nowhere inside his office.

"We destroyed the small ship sent to pick up the bodies, but we don't know why they wanted them. We can't find anything on the bodies, either—no chips or anything else that might be used as a homing beacon, and there's no other reason anyone might know they were here. That information has been kept tightly guarded." Captain Galeda informed us as we walked swiftly toward the ship's infirmary. The three bodies they had were in cold storage there—they'd already been examined.

These bodies were three of the attackers I'd decapitated during the shoot-out with Lendill. "None of these were ours," Lendill said as we examined them. The heads were set near the necks from which they'd been severed.

"Were the decapitations done with a laser sword?" Captain Galeda asked.

"No." Norian wanted to smile; I just knew it.

Chapter 12

"We've gone over prints, eye scans, body scans—the works. There's nothing, except these tattoos." He pulled down lower lips to show three identical sun wheel tattoos. "No chips or implants, though. No strange DNA patterns, even. We've had the complete workup as far as blood and tissue go," the Captain added. "They all suffered from the same, rare disease."

The bodies still held whatever it was that blocked their scents, so I *Looked* for information instead. Captain Galeda's words had raised my suspicions, and now I knew why the scents had been blocked—likely by a warlock. I had my arms crossed over my chest, trying not to hyperventilate afterward.

Black Mist has allied with Solar Red, and they're both behind this, I sent to Norian and Lendill. Solar Red had a habit of placing sun wheel tattoos somewhere on their priest's bodies. And these three, well, they'd been enhanced—with vampire blood. That spelled Black Mist to me.

They didn't care that these priests would die eventually from the infusion of vampire blood—they wanted them strong to take Lendill down. It didn't matter what happened afterward. There was something else, too, that made my skin itch about these three.

Breah-mul are you sure? Norian sent back. He was still getting used to mindspeech—he always hesitated a little before doing it. *And what does that have to do with these three and the fact that someone came to find them?*

Black Mist has either wizards or warlocks, I'm sure of it now, I returned. *I think these bodies are sending out signals, only it isn't any kind of beacon you can use science to find. You'd need another warlock, I think.*

Blood Redemption

I suspected that Black Mist wanted them so we wouldn't figure out they'd been enhanced with vampire blood. I didn't want to tell Norian that if I didn't have to, though. If word of that got out, we could have panic across the Alliance.

We don't have any wizards or warlocks in the ASD—not on the payroll, anyway, Norian sounded grumpy, now.

Let me see if I can get Erland to come, I replied, and then sent out mindspeech to my Karathian mate.

Erland was there faster than I thought possible. "My love, what do you need?" he asked breathlessly. I had no idea if I'd interrupted anything important. He was dressed as he usually was—neatly and in the latest fashion.

"Honey, I think we have something here that a wizard might have had a hand in." Briefly, I explained what was going on with help from Norian, Lendill and Captain Galeda.

"You'll have to stand back from the bodies, this can be a little bright," Erland warned. Honestly, I'd never really seen him work before.

We got a good demonstration now. He held out his hands, whispered a few words that I didn't catch and the heads began to glow. Not the bodies, just the heads. Their eyes popped open and purple light shone from their lifeless depths.

"This is an extremely difficult and expensive spell," Erland dropped his hands after a while, allowing the light to disappear abruptly. "It is keyed to the warlock who created it. A finding spell. Unless I know which warlock created the spell, I can't determine the point of origin. Even Wylend can't do anything about this. We need the warlock's name."

"But this is how they found the others?" Norian stared at Erland.

Chapter 12

"Yes, and they know exactly where these are, too. This ship is in danger—when I checked these three for the type of spell cast, it triggered another spell. The caster knows that a wizard or warlock has checked the bodies. They didn't want that to happen."

I barely had time to throw a shield around the ship before we were hit. The ship still got knocked around—I'm sure the object had been to throw the ship into Tykl's orbit, which would cause it to crash.

"He won't be able to throw another hit like that—that was enough to empty any warlock's reserves," Erland straightened his clothing. The blast had nearly knocked all of us over and caused a few alarms to go off aboard the ship.

"Is there any way to nullify the spell on these three, here?" Norian asked after we were back to normal.

"Sure. This one is free. The next one will cost you." Erland flashed his famous, heart-melting smile and went to work.

"Honey, I ought to ask to watch you work more often." I sat next to Erland as he had a cup of tea in the ship's galley afterward.

"Love, that sounds boring." He bumped his forehead against mine before giving me a warm kiss. "Now, I need to have a conference with your grandfather." Erland set down his cup, rose and was gone in a blink.

* * *

Karathia

"Zellar doesn't have that kind of power and his is the only name we know," Wylend huffed at Erland's information.

"If I ever catch up with any of them," Erland didn't finish. Just the thought of warlocks allied with Black Mist made him want to cast a breaking spell against them. He'd

249

have to be close to do it but heads would explode, in a manner similar to what Lissa could do.

"You have my permission to use any force against them." Wylend knew exactly what Erland was thinking.

* * *

Black Mist Headquarters

Zellar didn't have to tell Viregruz that his effort had failed—he'd informed Viregruz before the spell was cast that it was too far and distance would weaken the casting.

Viregruz had guessed at the failure by Zellar's expression and the exhaustion that came with it. Zeller hadn't had this level of power before, but he'd tapped into the core of the planet. Removing that energy required the darkest of spells and once tapped, the energy would continue to drain away at an accelerated rate until the planet died.

Zellar no longer cared how the power was gained—it had become an addiction to wield so much of it. Besides, Viregruz was looking to relocate anyway. What care did they have that Mazareal would die within a decade? Zellar was paid very well for his services, and at the moment, Viregruz was still treating him as a favored employee.

Zellar knew it was due to his newly acquired talent and power—he just wasn't telling anyone where it came from. He was thankful, too, that Viregruz hadn't blamed him for Giryoth's failure to kill the Queen of Le-Ath Veronis and the ASD's Director. Zellar worried, though, that if he were involved in many more failures, Viregruz's attitude might change.

It helped, too, that none seemed to know that Zellar worked for Black Mist. Zellar's spies monitored the ones hunted by the ASD and so far, his name hadn't appeared on any bulletins. The King of Karathia had his name on a list for

Chapter 12

lesser crimes, but even he had no suspicions of Zellar's new talents.

"They will not find anything, Lord Viregruz," Zellar assured the vampire who'd created Black Mist. "Their science will not tell them anything. They cannot use tests to track a spell and they have no warlocks in their employ. My spies in the Alliance keep me informed."

"Yes, I know this," Viregruz agreed. "I'd prefer that it stay that way—the ASD shouldn't hire power wielders. That leaves us with an edge, my warlock friend."

"We should look again for another world—we must relocate soon," Zellar went on. He didn't tell Viregruz that in two months or less he would completely drain the world they stood upon. Its death would come slowly after that, but it would come.

"My friend, I am turning my thoughts to that. Had I known about the world that is called Le-Ath Veronis, I would have taken it before the bitch queen came along. That would have been perfect for us."

Zellar didn't comment. He had some information on that world and he knew Viregruz might not have been able to take it. Le-Ath Veronis had been uninhabited before the queen arrived. Now it grew and thrived.

Even Viregruz would have admitted that with no life, he and his other vampires could not survive. They would be forced to search for a world that had plenty of warm-blooded humanoids upon it.

"Shall I call one of the others to bring a meal for you?" Zellar asked politely.

"Of course. I am hungry. We will discuss relocation later."

Blood Redemption

Zellar dipped his head respectfully and went to find a servant.

* * *

Tykl

"Lissa, Erland told us where you were," the communication looked fuzzy on board the ship, but the audio was good. Grant and Heathe were both there in the not-so-clear image, with information to share with me.

"What do you have, honey?" I asked.

"Someone who identified herself as Narimalan Cordrifith has asked to visit Le-Ath Veronis," Grant reported. "She said you told her she could come if she wanted to visit with her son."

"That's Norian's mother," I drew a tired breath. Norian, Lendill and I hadn't had any rest since we'd boarded the ship, and it didn't look as if we were going to get any soon. "Arrange for her to come, and for her husband to come with her. I will not allow her first son—his name is Yaredolak by the way—to set foot on Le-Ath Veronis. Arrange for discreet guards, too—Norian doesn't know his family very well and I sure don't want them to hurt him or anyone else on my planet."

I'd taken the call inside a private cubicle—Norian and Lendill were doing business on other matters elsewhere.

Heathe went to his communicator while I waited; he scheduled a visit with Norian's parents in two days. He also asked my palace staff to prepare a guest suite for them. They would be given the best treatment while they were visiting.

"Why doesn't Norian know his parents?" Grant asked as he tapped away on his comp-vid.

"Honey, it's a long story," I said. "I'll tell you the whole thing someday. It isn't their fault. Or his fault. We may have

Chapter 12

to get to the bottom of this sometime soon." I terminated the communication and went looking for Norian to give him the news.

"Honey, your parents are coming to Le-Ath Veronis in two days. I hope you can spare some time," I told him, sitting on the chair next to his as he scrolled through information on his handheld.

Norian gave me a shocked look—his fingers stilling on the microcomputer in his hand. "Did they say why they were coming?" I think he had difficulty swallowing for a moment.

"Honey, I didn't ask my assistants to grill them—I assume they want to see you. We didn't talk much when we were with them the other day."

"I'm not up to more of the same. And I can tell you now; I don't have any desire to see my homicidal, child-selling brother again."

"I told Grant that he wasn't welcome on Le-Ath Veronis," I rubbed Norian's back. Deep down, this hurt him. More than he would ever show anyone, except for me, perhaps. He and I—we both had terrible things in our childhood.

"Honey, I have a question," I said as we sat there, shoulder to shoulder while I rubbed his back. Norian seemed lost in thought.

"What is it, breah-mul?" Norian leaned over and breathed on my neck before placing a kiss.

"In your duties as Director of the ASD, have you run across any poisonings of important people? Or people who were bitten by, say, a lion snake?"

If Norian had been thinking amorous thoughts, that stopped him in his tracks and he stilled completely.

Blood Redemption

"Cheah-mul, lion snakes are common to nearly half the Alliance worlds. They have been used many times over the centuries to bring about changes in leadership or to create chaos. The venom acts too quickly—there is no time to administer an antidote before the victim dies."

"But in the last one hundred years or so?" I was pressing for information. He still didn't see where this was going.

"Let me pull up the records." He was humoring me at the moment. He had several assassinations pulled up for me quickly—all occurring within the past ninety years.

One was on Tulgalan. Another on Otheliah. Those were the most important—charismatic leaders on both worlds had been poised to bring about sweeping changes. Both were killed before their plans could be brought to fruition. Others had died in the same way, all important but not as far-reaching.

"This doesn't include all the minor deaths—people in industrial circles or things of that nature, who died from lion snake poison. It seems to be a favorite among killers." Norian took his minicomputer back.

"Honey, how many perpetrators did you catch on those deaths?" He'd only been director for seventy-six years, so he might not be able to say for sure on any assassinations before that.

"None. All anyone had to do was release a lion snake inside a bedroom or an office. Those snakes are aggressive, especially if they are in a strange place. They'll attack anything that shows up."

"Think about this for a moment," I said. "You assume that someone wanted to add a lion snake shapeshifter to their menagerie. You thought you'd be put in a cage for the rest of your life. What if that isn't true? What if someone

Chapter 12

came looking for you and the others to get a killing machine? Did you ever find the snakes in these cases, Norian? Did you look?"

Norian's face turned gray as he stared at me. This had never occurred to him. He assumed the other two children had been shut away inside a cage. Perhaps they had, but then someone might have raised them—given them bits of warmth or affection here or there, just to get them to kill. They would be indoctrinated, now, and I had a good guess who'd done this, if things had happened that way.

"You think Black Mist not only has vampires but shapeshifters, too." Norian's voice was flat. "We never found those snakes. Just turned the hunt for those over to the local authorities, who were never able to find them, either."

"They wouldn't be looking for humanoids. They were looking for the snakes and the ones who'd set the snakes loose. Not an easy thing to do, huh? Nobody would have any records of anything like that being shipped in—even as illegal contraband. They'd have come in like tourists, I imagine, and left the same way."

"And the snakes, being sentient, could have placed themselves in the proper location. They wouldn't have been taken there by someone and then turned loose. They could have changed long before they arrived." Norian didn't like it, but he was now going in the same direction I was.

"I'll know a lion snake if I smell one now," I said.

"You know my scent, deah-mul?" Norian wrapped his arms around me and laid his forehead against my shoulder.

"Honey, I'd know you from a long way off," I said, running my hand through his hair.

"Breah-mul, you frighten me terribly at times."

Blood Redemption

"Oh, and you're not terror-inspiring?" I was teasing him now. Norian looked at me for a few moments before turning to lion snake. His tongue tickled when he flicked it beneath my chin. I folded us to Le-Ath Veronis.

"Honey, I can carry you, but you have to help me out, here," I said, trying to gather him up. That's not easy with a twelve-foot snake that weighs two hundred pounds—it wasn't the weight, it was the length. Part of him was coiled around my waist and the rest hung around my neck as we made our way to my suite.

Nori's head in snake form is more than twice the size of my fist, and he can beg with his eyes, too. "Honey, if this is what you want, then that's okay."

He was going to curl up beside me as a snake, instead of turning back to human and taking advantage of the situation. "But if I roll over on you in the night, don't say I didn't warn you," I said. He gave me a look of pure skepticism and closed his eyes.

* * *

Why do men always want to make love in the morning, when your breath is certainly not at its best? I'll never figure this out, and if mother nature actually exists, she and I may have a conversation, someday.

Norian didn't seem to care that I was rumpled and not feeling minty-fresh. Somewhere along the road he'd learned a little about pleasing a woman, because he did a mighty fine job.

"Why were you worried about rolling over on me? You don't weigh anything," Norian was back to nuzzling my neck before wandering down to more important features.

"Are you insulting me?" I asked. Norian's eyes turned back to my face. I found it amusing—he held my nipple

Chapter 12

between his teeth. He gave it a gentle bite before letting go to answer.

"Lissa Beth, you aren't one of those women who finds fault with every compliment, are you?"

"Was that what that was? A compliment? Drake and Drew think that calling me itty-bitty pants is a compliment."

"All right, give me a compliment, then." He scooted up beside me, and then pulled me against him.

"I like your eyes, in both forms," I said. "Your scale pattern is very nice. Is it the same in all your kind, or is it a little different in each one?"

"The scale pattern varies in individuals," he replied.

"And I like this part. Very much." I stroked the part in question.

"I was hoping you'd say that," he murmured against my mouth.

* * *

"I couldn't get vid images on anything other than the last two assassinations," Norian placed his comp-vid on my desk while I was trying to take care of a few things that in Grant's words "wouldn't wait."

I didn't tell him that he'd just covered up papers on important Council business. To Norian, everything else took a back seat to what the ASD was doing.

"What are these?" I was flicking through images on the comp-vid screen.

"Look at the eyes, breah-mul. I had to go back and ask for any anomalies in the visitors to those particular planets just before and immediately after the killings took place. See?" Norian jabbed his finger on the screen, causing one image to expand. I saw a clear headshot of a male, whose eyes—well—those eyes had me standing up in a blink.

Blood Redemption

"Oh, my gosh, Norian, what did they do?" The man we looked at seemed perfectly normal as a humanoid, except for his eyes. They were slitted—a reptile's eyes.

"Lendill and I think these may have been manufactured—that they took sperm or DNA from one of the kidnapped shapeshifters and created these to build an army. Cheah-mul—we may be facing who knows how many of these." Norian's eyes were troubled as I blinked at him in horror.

"Honey, this is awful. We're tracking rogue wizards, Solar Red, Black Mist and now lion snake shapeshifters that somebody created to go out and assassinate people cleanly? I think I have a headache." I slumped in my chair.

"Deah-mul, I didn't mean to make you ill." Norian settled on the edge of my desk and rubbed my forehead gently.

"Nori, your brother has an awful lot to answer for."

Norian didn't say anything to me.

* * *

I dressed the best I could without going too far, and wore the band of Tiralian crystal on my forehead. Norian, too, wore his ASD dress uniform. I had no idea he had so many medals and doo-dads. He gave me an embarrassed grin when I examined some of them on his chest.

A hover-limo had been sent to the shuttle station to pick up Norian's parents; we waited in one of four reception suites I had inside the palace. Aryn and Aurelius had gone as palace representatives to pick up our guests and they were ushered in while Norian's mother stared about her in shock.

"I thought you might have been lying to us," Rivelodar Cordrifith said as he was brought before Norian and me.

258

Chapter 12

"No. Some days I try to forget about all this—it doesn't mean a thing when there are more serious matters to attend to," I said. "I hope you and your wife are well."

"We are," Norian's father nodded.

"We have refreshments ready, if you'll come with us," I said. Norian was still tongue-tied, I think. I grabbed his elbow and he followed along, settling his parents on a comfortable sofa in more intimate surroundings. Aryn and Aurelius followed us as security.

"We, ah, wanted to come and talk to you about your brother," Norian's mother, Narimalan, said after drinks and tiny sandwiches were served in my library. I didn't say anything, waiting to see what she and Norian's father had to say.

"What's that?" Norian hadn't said much until now—he'd listened while his parents went on about relatives—living and dead. I figured Norian had already done his research, once he knew who his family was, but I didn't point that out. After all, if the Director of the ASD didn't have access to that information, then nobody did.

"We, ah, want you to leave Reedy alone. We know he may have made some mistakes," Rivelodar Cordrifith said, holding up a hand, "but he is our son."

"And Norian isn't?" I know I should have stayed out of it, but I couldn't.

"No—we know he is, but for years we thought he was dead. We didn't raise him; someone else did that. We can't change any of that now, and he's a stranger to us. We've talked to Reedy—he knows that he just can't kill indiscriminately, even if it's someone who might deserve it. He has to take care of things after we're gone; he has a fiancée now and we hope to have grandchildren before long.

Please understand our situation." Norian's father was begging us to go along with this.

"So, you want Norian to look the other way for his brother, the murderer, who not only arranged to have his brother kidnapped but two other children as well?" I know; I was completely incredulous. "Have you told those other families what he did? Have you?"

I knew all too well what having a child stolen away felt like. At least I knew where Toff was—those other parents had no idea what had happened to their children. And the fact that their children had probably been raised to commit crimes and perhaps to provide sperm or DNA to create others like them didn't sit well either.

"No, and we're begging you not to tell them—they'll kill Reedy." Norian's mother's voice was tremulous. "Reedy's engaged to one of the Travinseloh's daughters."

"You mean the fiancée might not be so in love with dear old Reedy if she finds out he sold her brother into slavery?"

"It was someone who wanted to keep them as a novelty," Rivelodar snapped.

"Yeah? Guess again," I snapped back. "Somebody has been using them to assassinate heads of state and important officials for the past hundred years or so. I know he's your son, but really, what else do you think he might do?"

"He was only nineteen when he made that bad decision," Norian's mother was in tears, now.

"Yeah. But he wasn't nineteen when he killed those people who came asking about the missing kids. Whether they were trying to bilk you out of money is irrelevant. All it would have taken is a call to the local constabulary and they'd have investigated. Instead, he did murder. Now, we're

Chapter 12

just supposed to conveniently forget about that, because you asked us nicely?" I still couldn't believe what I was hearing.

"We hoped that you'd see it as parents wanting to protect their child," Rivelodar muttered.

"Nobody protected Norian," I said. "Did Reedy say why he sold his brother? Did he say what he got out of it? And mind you, unless I miss my guess, the one he sold those children to is still alive and he knows where you are. What if he wants more lion snakes? What then?"

I was standing and shaking. Norian still hadn't said a word. I think he was lost in all this—he might have been taken back to a time when he was four or five, not understanding what was going on around him. Lost completely to a childhood that had brought him loneliness and pain.

"You're joking. Surely they wouldn't be so bold or foolish to come back—we've taken steps to guard against that," Rivelodar spat, standing up.

"Can you stand against Black Mist?" I asked. "Can you stand against them and their Solar Red Allies? Most likely, they have your two missing lion snake shapeshifters, and perhaps a few others manufactured from their DNA. We have pictures. What if they show up for the next batch of children your little community produces? Yes, I did my research, too. Except for Reedy, they wiped out an entire generation, didn't they?" My chest was heaving, I was breathing so hard.

"Lissa, don't upset yourself," Norian found his voice. "It is just as well that Ildevar adopted me, isn't it? I have no real parents. They'd rather have a murdering child trafficker for a son than one who has done well for himself. I won't press charges against Reedy. Not for past crimes. But I will be

261

watching," he warned his parents. "If he steps a toe out of line again, I'll haul him in and I'll see to it he's prosecuted completely for all his crimes. Let him know that Evensun is waiting for him if he ever crosses my path again." Norian stalked out of the room.

"If he or any of you harm Norian, I may not wait for the courts." I was just about to leave, too.

"I will handle it," Kifirin showed up, blowing smoke. "You will not have to trouble yourself, avilepha. You, both of you," Kifirin took a long, hard look at Norian's parents, "I suggest you resign yourself to what is to come—your oldest child will not be able to hold himself back—he has developed a taste for killing. Your choice will prove to be a poor one." Kifirin disappeared.

"Who was that?" Norian's mothers quavered.

"Kifirin, Lord of the Dark Realm," I said as calmly as I could. "I think he just passed judgment on Yaredolak. Aryn, Aurelius, can you see our guests back to the shuttle station? They won't be staying." I turned and stalked out, following the path Norian had taken.

* * *

"Nori?" I walked carefully into his office—I had no idea what I might find.

"Breah-mul?" Norian was holding his head in his hands.

"Honey, those are just people you don't know. And they don't know you." I pulled his hands down and leaned in to kiss his forehead.

"Are they going to stay?"

"I sent them to the shuttle station. Aryn and Aurelius know to send them to the space station. They can wait there for the next transport. They won't be welcome back here, honey."

Chapter 12

"Good. Lissa, what are we going to do about Solar Red and Black Mist? What are we going to do about their rogue wizards and those reptanoids?"

"Is that what you're calling them—reptanoids?" I sat on the edge of Norian's desk and lifted his head up, bumping my forehead against his.

"Lendill came up with that term when I talked to him about it and showed him the vids."

"Uh-huh. Lendill's just pretty darn handy, isn't he?"

"Until you came along, he and Ildevar were the only family I had."

"Well, you have a bigger family now. You might even get an invitation to go fishing with the Falchani twins if you stop monopolizing all my time."

"They fish?" Norian looked quite surprised.

"Among other things. If you've never been skiing, they'll take you for that, too." Just the thought of it made me smile.

"But I like monopolizing your time."

"Of course you do. Let's find something to drink."

Chapter 13

*L*e-Ath Veronis

"I know this doesn't mean anything in the midst of everything else, but Mazareal has reported problems with the atmosphere, dying crops and fluctuations in their climate reports—none of which have any logical reason behind them. They've been green for a very long time—and until recently, the sun has been stable, the planet stable and all that," Lendill waved his comp-vid at Norian when he sailed into Norian's office.

Lendill had returned to Le-Ath Veronis the day before and had gotten the update on Norian's former parents from Lissa. Norian still couldn't bring himself to talk about it.

"Can you get somebody else on that?" Norian asked absently. He was still backtracking on the reptanoids he'd uncovered—looking to find names and where they'd traveled from, hoping it would lead him to Black Mist's headquarters.

"I'll find somebody," Lendill punched up a list of available agents.

"Let me know what you find," Norian mumbled and turned back to his work.

* * *

Lissa

"We've been waiting for you to come back for longer than a few hours at a time," Drake, Drew, Gavin and Tony were all inside my office. Heathe and Grant had taken off the minute all four of them arrived.

I was studying the monthly tax reports and the disbursements that Kyler had made. I hadn't seen either of my nieces for a while—not since the whole Cloudsong debacle. That seemed like a hundred years gone, now, with everything that had happened in between.

"Why have you been waiting?" I pretty much knew the answer, but wasn't sure I wanted the information that came with that answer.

"To tell you who leaked your whereabouts to a Black Mist spy," Tony said. Well, he'd once held a position close to that of Norian's, so he was taking point on this.

"You found a Black Mist spy. Here, on Le-Ath Veronis." My voice was flat as I stared at four of my mates. They'd pulled in additional chairs so they could all sit.

"She's in the dungeon—the Council has already passed the death sentence, they're only waiting for you to talk to her if you want before sentence is carried out." Gavin provided that particular piece of information.

"And you're holding back the worst piece, aren't you? The one who gave her the information to begin with."

"Baby, it's hard, telling you this part," Drake said. "The Council wants to prosecute, but Aurelius and Aryn have

Chapter 13

convinced them to table this discussion until you knew everything."

"What charges are they planning to levy?" I asked. I wanted to shiver—the news was coming, and until now, I'd successfully held it away from me.

"Treason," Drew said. "That's all it is at this stage. A defense can be mounted."

"Of course it can," I said. I knew the Council. Knew that many of the oldest vampires on the Council had once been Heads of Vampire Councils on their respective former planets.

They hadn't kept their race alive and thriving by being anything less than ruthless. If a vampire made a misstep, they were eliminated. I'd seen it myself, first with Wlodek and then with Flavio. If I thought they might be anything other than merciless in this matter, my heart would be beating at a more normal rhythm.

"Tell me," I muttered, standing and turning away from all of them. A painting hung behind my desk that I seldom looked at, once I took my seat. Winkler had hired a vampire artist to paint it for me. He'd taken vid images of the Green Fae settlement, when the trees were flowering.

Little Toff was sitting on the ground, playing with a basket of blooms there among the trees. I figured Corent or Redbird had originally been in the image, but the artist had been instructed not to paint them. Only Toff remained. The whole thing made me want to weep.

"Giff revealed your location," Tony said. "She thought Pearlina was a friend. She knew it was wrong to tell anyone, but she did it anyway. She didn't think the woman was a spy."

Blood Redemption

If I'd been stabbed in the heart, it might have hurt less. "We've questioned Giff extensively, some of it under compulsion," Gavin went on quickly. I heard him as if I were listening underwater. "She knew it could harm you. She knew Pearlina might pass the information to others, because Pearlina likes to gossip. It's true she didn't know that Pearlina was a spy, but Giff was angry with you, cara. Didn't care if you might be hurt in all this."

"Did she realize that this might come of it? That six-hundred-million might die in my stead?" I asked. Silently, I cursed my father as I whirled and blinked helplessly at Gavin. Had Griffin seen this, when he'd so callously allowed Toff to be taken? Did he realize so many might die, because Giff would be angry with me—and with him?

If I dwelt too long on those thoughts, I might curl up and weep for a month. As it was, numbness had taken over. Giff hadn't thought past getting back at me, somehow, and so many were now dead from a few careless words.

"She didn't hear about Trell until recently," Drew said. "I think her cousin Dariff told her. Rolfe was asked to place compulsion not to reveal any other information she might have to anyone, and she has been confined to Rolfe's home and the surrounding area near his estate. We have removed Rolfe from his duties at the palace until this matter has been resolved."

"You're saying that Rolfe has been punished too." I turned and reached out to place a finger against the image of Toff's tiny face in the painting. "Even though he has no guilt in this matter."

"Lissa, it is better this way," Gavin said. "Rolfe is torn between two he cares for. This allows him to spend time with Giff until the matter can be brought before the Council."

Chapter 13

"Where is Roff? This has to be destroying him." I was emotionless, my voice detached. I was in my study and a million light-years away at one and the same time. How had things come to this? How? Did Giff now blame me so much for Toff's taking that she wanted me to die? Is that how things stood? Instead, and without thinking, she'd condemned an entire planet to death in my place.

"Roff is worried for his child," Gavin sighed.

"Lissa, what would you do, if this were placed solely in your hands?" Kifirin appeared suddenly at the side of my desk. I turned slightly to look at him.

"I would send Giff, Yoff and Rolfe to Kifirin," I said, meaning the High Demon world that Kifirin had named after himself. "They could live and work there, without fear of betraying any of my secrets. Glinda might welcome them into her home and Giff could go back to the work she likes—stuffing a queen's closet with clothing." I brushed away unwelcome tears.

"Then your heart is generous," Kifirin nodded to me. "I will not circumvent the rules as laid down for Le-Ath Veronis. I will not forget your judgment, however." He disappeared as suddenly as he'd come. Well, if a god wouldn't intervene, what hope did I have?

"Shall we set an appointment to interview the prisoner tomorrow morning? I don't think Norian is going to drag me away between now and then," I mumbled. For now, I wanted to be alone. Wanted to go to energy and leave everything and everyone behind me.

My mates might have wanted to give comfort, but there wasn't any comfort to be had for me. I could have hunted Griffin down and shouted at him—I could have blamed him for all this. None of that seemed to matter anymore. Nothing did. I faded to mist in front of all four mates before going to energy and flying away from Le-Ath Veronis.

* * *

Birimera

Gavin and Tony got the call to fight a pod of spawn, just as the other spawn hunters did. They all folded away when the call came in the middle of the night. Gavin dropped to the ground beside Tony—they were practiced at fighting in tandem.

Winkler appeared nearby, Thomas Williams right behind him. Turning to their werewolf state, they were prepared to do battle. Aurelius came, as did Rolfe, Jeral, Drake and Drew.

More than a thousand spawn had been unleashed upon unsuspecting Birimera, deep in the agricultural area surrounding the equator. Drake and Drew had blades out, ready to fight; they would only turn to Dragon if they were forced to do so. All spawn hunters made ready to do battle as the spawn advanced toward them.

* * *

Le-Ath Veronis

Lissa

I didn't return to Le-Ath Veronis until shortly before I was scheduled to interview the Black Mist spy in my dungeon. Walking into the kitchens to find something small to eat perhaps—I didn't want to go to a formal breakfast—I found Cheedas and his assistants too upset to cook. Cheedas was wiping tears away as I appeared beside his wide granite island.

"Cheedas?" I reached out a hand.

"Raona," Cheedas threw himself at me.

Chapter 13

"What's wrong, honey?" I stroked the dark hair that now held much gray in it. Cheedas was getting old—I had to face that.

"Raona, have you not heard?" Cheedas pulled back from me. "The entire city is in mourning."

"Honey, tell me," I said, my breath too short to get the words out properly. I was suddenly terrified.

"Rolfe and the others went to fight those awful things," Cheedas wept on my shoulder. "Gavin tells me that Rolfe did not even attempt to fight them when they came—he just stood there and let them take him. He died, Raona. There was barely anything left of him when the others killed the spawn attacking him."

My legs gave way beneath me and Cheedas and I both fell. It couldn't be. Couldn't. Rolfe—our Rolfe—the Northern Star, guard for Heads of Councils and a Queen—he could not be dead. He was death on any attacker—nothing withstood that tall vampire. It was why he'd been chosen to protect Wlodek and Flavio. And then me. Rolfe could not be gone. I was weeping with Cheedas as we huddled on the kitchen floor.

* * *

"Lara'Kayan?" Only two people called me that—Karzac and Thurlow. This wasn't Karzac. Lara'Kayan meant *forever love* in Neaborian. I had no idea where I was, lying on a bed supported by a floor and nothing else. Clouds floated past me as I blinked up into Thurlow's face.

"What am I doing here?" I asked, pulling myself up and leaning on an elbow. The blue of the sky was like a Larentii's skin, it was such a perfect color.

"Lara'Kayan, you were about to separate permanently from your body," Thurlow said. "You were in such pain. I am

271

holding your pain away from you at this moment, so that you will not leave us. We have much to do, my love. You cannot leave your children before they are born. How can they love a mother they will never know, if you leave us?"

I blinked at Thurlow. I'd forgotten about Garde's and Erland's surrogates. Forgotten about my own babies. How had I done that? How? "I know you loved Rolfe and the others," Thurlow went on. "How do you know they will not come back to you? Have you spoken to your Larentii mates lately?" If he'd wanted to push his point home, he couldn't have chosen a better way to do it.

"But the pain is so awful," I whispered, lowering my eyes.

"I know. I feel that pain every day, when I look at you and you turn away from me," Thurlow said. "It was of my own doing, long ago and in my first life," he added. "It was my lot to love you this time. To feel something of the pain I dealt before. I beg you to release me from that pain, love. Come to me. We will find a way through all of this, I promise. I and the others will stand with you in this. I will help you get through this and help your mates who also suffer. Belen has given permission, love."

"Permission for what?" Thurlow was releasing the pain back to me—I could feel the beginnings of it now.

"To allow you to feel the love and power of the light side beings. Belen and I are only two among many. We will give you hope, Lara'Kayan. You must trust us. That is what we ask."

"You ask me to trust you?" I didn't understand.

"That there is love, though love is lost. That there is hope, though hope is lost. That there is faith, though faith is lost. That nothing is ever truly gone from us—everything we

Chapter 13

lose we will find again. Somewhere. Time is meaningless, *rhizha' sarroulis*. And it is the only thing standing between you and what you think you have lost. Therefore, if time is meaningless, then it is not truly lost, is it?" Thurlow smiled at me, revealing a small dimple in his left cheek. I reached up to touch it. He caught my hand, kissing the palm before he let me go, his eyes closed in pleasure.

He'd called me *rhizha' sarroulis*. I knew what it meant, although I'd never heard the words. It meant *soul's completion*. That I was part of him and he a part of me. Only the light gods used that term. When I continued to stare up at him, Thurlow leaned down to kiss me. And then kissed me again. "I will get you through this," his words were soft against my lips. "I promise."

* * *

Le-Ath Veronis

Thurlow had to work to keep that promise—he and Kifirin both did when Thurlow returned me to Cheedas' kitchen. My body was still huddled on the floor, my arms wrapped around Cheedas' shoulders. Tony, Drake and Drew found us there.

"Lissa," Tony knelt beside me while Thurlow and Kifirin crowded close, "baby, you have to come."

I tried to keep everything Thurlow said to me fresh in my mind when Tony folded us to Rolfe's estate, but it was so terribly hard. There shouldn't have been tears left to cry. There were. Someone had gone to tell Giff that Rolfe was gone.

She'd taken the news calmly, they'd thought—her uncle Markoff had been the one to tell her. She'd gotten Yoff up and went to the kitchen to feed him. Or so she'd told her uncle.

Blood Redemption

She'd fed Yoff poisoned chicken, and then ate some herself before going to her bedroom to lie down. Giff and her tiny baby had died, poisoned with a plant poison that paralyzed the respiratory system.

It appeared at first that she and Yoff had fallen asleep. I stared at their lifeless bodies, curled up on the bed Giff had shared with Rolfe. Yoff was so tiny and now, he would never grow. Would never become a winged vampire someday, as his heritage promised. I wiped tears away as I listened numbly to the rest of the story.

Markoff hadn't suspected anything until Roff had arrived, and then he and his brother had been unable to rouse Giff. Had she known that Rolfe might be suicidal, and had taken her own measures? We might never have the answer to that question.

Now, I wanted to huddle on the floor and scream. Scream for little Yoff, who'd never had a chance to live. Scream for Rolfe, who thought he'd committed a crime when he hadn't. Scream for Giff—once innocent Giff, whose little brother had been taken away, pushing her down a path toward all of this.

Instead of huddling on the floor, however, I misted to the Green Fae village, Kifirin and Thurlow right behind me. They could find me—travel alongside me, even—whenever they wanted.

"What do you want?" Redbird snapped when she answered the door. She shrank back when she found Kifirin standing beside me.

"Not that it makes any difference now, since you've stolen his mind and heart, but Toff's sister and his tiny nephew died earlier. I don't suppose you'll ever tell him he had family that cared, will you?" I wiped tears away.

Chapter 13

"He is only a child himself," Redbird huffed.

"A child that should still be with his birth family, instead of you," Thurlow pointed out. "Someday, you will regret every action that brought you to this point. Someday this will bring pain to you that is unimaginable. Everything that you hold dear will be drained away."

I stared at Thurlow—he now had stars in his eyes as well.

"Who are you?" Redbird sounded insulting.

"I am a servant of the gods of light," he said. "Kifirin does not rule over the Fae houses, we do. You should learn to listen when it is prudent. Come, rhizha' sarroulis." Thurlow took my arm and folded me away.

* * *

"Roff, honey?" Roff was leaning against the glass inside my arboretum. I seldom had time to visit it anymore, although it was beautiful and a place of peace.

"Lissa." Roff's voice was soft—barely a whisper. I still heard my name when he said it. I was frightened that Roff would now blame me. Giff had.

What would I do without my winged vampire? Roff had supported me through so many things. Been the voice of reason, so many times. Would he now see this as my fault? My heart ached—both for Roff and for myself.

"Roff, if there was any way I could undo any of this, and make it turn out right for you, I would," I was weeping again. "If there was any way I could take this pain away from you, I would. If there was any way I could replace what was lost to you, I would."

"Lissa." Roff rustled his wings and drew them tighter around him. "Giff knew what was coming. She took matters into her own hands before the Council took away her freedom." He turned to me, then, his face filled with pain.

"But Yoff." I sobbed when I said his name.

"I know. I don't understand this either." Roff came to me. Put his arms around me and then wrapped his wings around me. We stood like that for a very long time, both of us leaning on the other, weeping for what we'd lost. What we couldn't replace. Upon becoming vampire, Roff could no longer birth children. Not as he had while comesula. All his children, taken away in one tragedy after another.

* * *

"I won't even try to provide platitudes—only the heart knows what pain is," Flavio told me two days later as we buried Giff, Yoff and Rolfe's few remains in the same grave.

All the Saa Thalarr had come, standing together to bid Rolfe farewell. Kiarra sang. It was the first time I'd ever heard her sing. Now I knew why they all begged her to—it was heart-wrenchingly beautiful.

Thurlow hovered, as did Karzac, Gavin and the others. Roff stood with me throughout the service. We both wiped tears away as Aurelius delivered the eulogy. Norian had been in and out—he and Lendill were still tracking Black Mist, but not much was happening.

The most surprising thing, I think, was that Shadow came to the funeral. I hadn't seen or heard from him since Cloudsong. With Roff's help, we'd decided to bury Rolfe, Giff and Yoff at what we termed *The Line* on Le-Ath Veronis—the spot where a vampire could go and look upon daylight to the north and still be in enough darkness to survive. Flowers had been planted there by vampire gardeners and they grew in profusion.

Chapter 13

Many vampires had known Rolfe, and they all came to the funeral to pay their last respects to the giant of a man. Wlodek gave some history on Rolfe before Aurelius delivered the final words, saying that Rolfe had come to him, already a vampire, from the wars that Alexander the Great waged against the Persian Empire.

Greek in origin, like Wlodek, they'd often spoken in Greek together when no one else was around. Called Deimos, back then, he was a warrior for Alexander, his height making him visible from a distance in any battle.

I'd never known those things about Rolfe and he'd never volunteered. It made me feel self-centered and selfish that I'd never asked him about his life.

"He would have steered you away from the subject of his life, even if you had asked him," Wlodek told me quietly afterward.

Everyone had come back to the palace by hoverbus later, where the vampires were served real blood that I'd had shipped in for the occasion. It wasn't something we did often, but it was done at times.

The kitchen served food for the others. When the guests left us, I misted to the top of my palace to gaze over the city named after me. That's where Griffin found me.

He didn't try to sit anywhere near—he knew that wouldn't be welcome. We remained silent for a very long time. Finally, he spoke. "Lissa, every selfish act comes with a price." I turned sharply to look at him.

"No," he held up a hand, "it wasn't your act of selfishness. It was mine. But the price wasn't mine to pay. You remember that old phrase; *the sins of the father are to be laid upon the children?*"

Blood Redemption

"From *The Merchant of Venice*? I didn't know you quoted Shakespeare." I was holding back most of my sarcasm.

"I don't normally quote anyone, I'm too old for that," Griffin muttered. "But I think I've finally lived long enough to learn my lesson."

"And what lesson would that be?" I hoped there was a point in this somewhere; otherwise, I was being subjected to this for no reason. I hugged my arms around my knees.

"That adversity can build or destroy. Sometimes it can do both. I thought I was mighty, Lissa. I could see into the future. Change things here and there, to make it turn out better. And then the Nameless Ones and The Powers That Be named me Oracle, because of what I could do. But that was before I came back in time and snatched up my daughter, whose birth I'd manipulated, to perform one last mighty act in an effort to save the worlds. She didn't fail us, my daughter. Handed over her life so those worlds could live. That was the day she surpassed her father. Became something that he holds no hope of ever being." Griffin shook his head.

"I should have left it at that and taken my lumps when the Green Fae decided to go against their teachings and snatch a child," he went on. "Who knows what Wyatt might become if they'd kept him? Perhaps Wylend would have destroyed them, turning from light to dark, as Karathians sometimes do."

Griffin breathed a ragged sigh. "I might have kept Wyatt away from the ball altogether, allowing a different child to be taken. All those possibilities stretched out before me, each one ending in a tragedy for someone else, never for me. I chose the one for you, thinking it was the least harmful. But

Chapter 13

as you most likely have guessed, I did not examine the minute ripples that were sent out from that single event. Did not look to see these three deaths, or the six-hundred-million others. These are on my conscience now, Lissa."

"It's so convenient for you to take responsibility for it now," I snapped. "When it's over and hasn't cost you a thing."

"Only those lives—and my daughter," he said before folding away.

* * *

"I know you wonder why I asked you here," I said. Thurlow and Aryn both sat inside my study. I was pacing behind my desk. I'd made a decision, now I'd see how it all turned out for the future.

Aryn, especially, looked quite surprised that I'd called for him. He'd expected me to be holed up with my mates somewhere, grieving for Rolfe, Giff and Yoff. I was grieving. I'd just come to the realization how things really were.

"I have something for you," I said. "While it might not mean anything immediately, it may mean something for the long term. It is up to you how you approach things after this." I pulled two small boxes from a desk drawer. Each one bore a name. I handed them across the desk to Aryn and Thurlow. "Don't betray me again," I said and misted away.

* * *

Thurlow opened his box first, finding the claw crown signet ring nestled on satin inside. Drawing in a breath, he lifted it out and settled it on his finger. It fit—Lissa had *Looked* to find his size. If she hadn't, he could have used power to do it himself.

She was telling him they had a future. He didn't expect to fall into her bed immediately—that would take time. But it was a promise that someday he would spend a night with her, followed by many other nights. Thurlow, once Thorsten, was satisfied with that.

Aryn was slower to open his box. He recognized the ring—she'd kept the old one he'd had before, when he'd been Gabron. Would it fit? He was taller and heavier since Kifirin had remade him.

"It will fit—do you think Lissa didn't notice?" Thurlow was smiling—a real smile that he hadn't experience in a long while.

Aryn tried the ring on—it did fit. "I'll have to court her," he sighed. "Make her trust me again."

"You've made a good start—you wouldn't have that if you hadn't," Thurlow pointed to Aryn's ring. "And we have to court the rest of her Inner Circle, too—make them trust us. We have a long road, friend," Thurlow slapped Aryn on the back.

* * *

"Lissa?" I'd gone hunting for Shadow. He was still wearing my ring; I saw that right away. He'd never taken it off. At least it meant he'd loved me the whole way through, even though he hadn't done much in the way of standing up for me or our love against his father and grandfather. That hurt more than anything, I think. Now, Shadow stood before a fireplace inside my huge library, thumbing through a book on ancient Refizani history.

"Learning anything new about Refizan?" I nodded at the book. "Karzac or Aryn can likely give you a better perspective on how things really were instead of reading that thing."

"Is that where Aryn is from?" Shadow still didn't know.

"Aryn used to be Gabron," I sighed. "Kifirin gave him a new face and a second chance. I just gave his ring back."

Chapter 13

"Lissa, you're not letting him back in your bed, when you won't even," Shadow couldn't finish his sentence, he looked so hurt.

"That's why I'm here, you difik wizard. I came to ask for my ring back. I'm not saying we're going to be perfect right here and now. You have an uphill climb, just like Aryn and Thurlow. I'm giving you the right to step back into the Inner Circle. And, if you don't piss me off too bad and if the surrogate thing works out with Erland and Gardevik, then in two years I'll consider doing the same thing with you. We'll find a surrogate and Grey House can stop getting their panties in a bunch over an heir from your loins or whatever." I sat wearily on a nearby sofa.

"Lissa, you make it sound so romantic." Shadow could do sarcasm as well as anyone.

"I'm not feeling particularly romantic at the moment—I just buried three people I love, my father decides to take responsibility after the fact and six-hundred-million people are dead because somebody aimed a Ranos Cannon, hoping to kill me instead. I'm not in the mood for flowers and violins right now."

"Lissa, I want us to be together. Like it used to be."

"Honey, that's not going to happen. Your father and grandfather saw to that, don't you think? Do I love you? I never stopped. Did you hurt me? Yes. When you didn't stand up to them. Didn't force them to look harder at what they were doing instead of jumping through the hoops that Marid of Belancour set up so he could get Cloudsong's noose from around his neck. Do I care if you take another mate? No. I just want it to be somebody you love if you do, not somebody coming in to provide broodmare services for a price. Erland has other mates—he loves them. I don't care." I flung out a hand. "Karzac has other mates. It doesn't bother me."

"But you held Karzac at arm's length, when Grace became pregnant with Kevis." Shadow pointed out.

"But Kevis needs to grow up with his father. Needs to know a father's love. That's something I never had and I feel it, Shadow. Right here." I thumped my chest with a fist. "I'm not about to take any child away from its father, or vice versa. Besides, Karzac and I worked things out. Somebody pointed out to me that one or two nights a month isn't going to take anything away from Kevis."

"Then come back with me to Grey House, and talk things over with Dad and Grampa Glendes."

"No, Shadow. I meant what I said—I'm not coming back to Grey House. Your father and grandfather could have talked to both of us about this, asking us how we felt instead of making an arbitrary decision that almost resulted in disaster for everyone. Yet they didn't. They didn't treat us as adults, Shadow, and I find that unconscionable. Maybe you can overlook it, but I won't."

"Lissa, I don't want to be caught in a feud between you and my family."

"I'm not feuding with them—I'm just not speaking to them. Sort of like I'm not speaking to my father. Maybe someday I'll get over it. I've noticed they haven't done much in the way of an apology. It's a little late now, don't you think? They almost bankrupt Le-Ath Veronis, and not a word?"

"They might not think you'd be willing to listen."

"No excuse for not doing the right thing," I snapped. "Or trying to do the right thing. We may share a child, one day, Shadow. At least I hope so. I'd like to see what a Quarter

Chapter 13

Karathian Witch and a Grey House Wizard might be able to produce. That doesn't even include what I got from the Elemaiya."

"I'll go talk to Dad and Grampa about it."

"Shadow, if you have to consult your parents, then you haven't grown up, yet. Grow up, then come see me if you want a child." I got up to walk away.

"I didn't mean for things to turn out like this." Shadow folded in front of me, holding out my ring.

"You think your father asked Glendes of Grey House if it was okay if he got your mother pregnant? Did he?" I knocked Shadow's hand aside, sending the ring flying.

"I see I've been too heavy-handed." Glendes showed up. Fucking nexus echo, no doubt. He'd been listening for me to call his name.

"No joke." I stalked away from Shadow again. "Fucking Grey House Wizards," I muttered.

"At least one of them isn't fucking," Shadow offered.

"And not likely to unless he finds somebody else," I whirled to face him.

"Lissa, I should have stayed out of this. I know that now. It's of little consolation to you, considering what you risked to get us all out of that mess." Glendes said.

"Yeah? Who told you that?"

"Griffin."

"Dear old Dad. He just can't pass up the opportunity to fuck with my life, can he?" I was close to tears, now.

"He said that if you'd interfered with the timeline in any way, they'd have stripped every bit of power away from you. You'd have given up everything, just to set things right."

"Yeah, I should have learned my lesson the first time, shouldn't I?" I wiped away tears.

Blood Redemption

"Lissa, I should have stayed out of this. I should have. I didn't. I hit you when you were weak; I know that now. My grandson was married to a goddess and I threw her out in favor of a two-faced bitch."

"A two-faced bitch who could have babies," I started walking again. "I'm still not coming back to Grey House."

"Will you have a baby with me? I don't give a fuck what Dad and Grampa think." Shadow begged. I turned one last time to look at him.

"I'll think about it," I said and disappeared.

* * *

Shadow used wizardry to *Pull* Lissa's ring to his hand. "What if she doesn't take it back, Grampa?" Shadow stared at the Tiralian crystal ring he'd crafted with love.

"Shadow, give it some time. I think she'll come around." Glendes almost crumbled at the look on Shadow's face.

"She once told me much the same thing she told you just now, and that was after I was almost ordered to kill her by the Vampire Council. You see where we are now." Gavin walked into the room.

"How long have you been here?" Shadow demanded.

"Long enough. If she wasn't willing to give you some time, she would have disappeared right away and you wouldn't have found her for months. She walked away and turned back several times. She loves you, Shadow. You, not so much," Gavin turned to Glendes.

"Then I'll work on that," Glendes said. "Shadow, see if you can find her. Tell her I went home with my tail between my legs." Glendes folded away.

"Where is she?" Shadow sounded hopelessly lost.

Chapter 13

"Probably on top of something, somewhere. She has absolutely no fear of heights." Gavin sounded positive about that.

"She has no reason to be," Shadow sighed. "I'll go look for her."

* * *

Kifirin

"I had to ask Garde if he knew where you were," Shadow landed beside me atop the royal palace in Veshtul. Glinda and Jayd knew I was there the moment I'd arrived. They hadn't bothered me.

"Remind me to kick his ass next time," I said.

"Lissa, listen to me. I promise none of this will happen again. I promise. I messed up. Didn't stand up well enough for us. All I can think about is how you feel in my arms. Don't turn me out or send me away again. I don't think I can stand it." He reached out for my hand.

I looked into his gray eyes—they seemed sincere enough. While he held my hand, he slipped his ring back on. I didn't try to stop him. He leaned in for a kiss—I didn't stop that either. I did have to fold us away before things got too out of hand—I didn't think Jayd would appreciate an amorous couple making love on top of his central dome.

Chapter 14

L *e-Ath Veronis*
     Lissa

     I stood and stared at Pearlina Rin for the longest time. She'd hissed at me when I'd first shown up, but had gone back to staring at the floor beneath her feet. Pearlina perched on the edge of her cot—it was bolted to the floor and held there tighter than that with wizardry Erland had provided. If we needed something stronger, I could always ask Connegar and Reemagar.

Pearlina's dark hair hung long about her face—she hid behind that curtain instead of glaring angrily at me, as others might have done. She was of medium height—taller than I by several inches, and pretty enough, with large, dark eyes.

That prettiness wouldn't save her from her fate— Vampire Councils everywhere were notorious for being ruthless.

Blood Redemption

"How does it feel," I finally said, "to be the one who murdered six-hundred-million people?"

"I've never killed anyone," Pearlina spat, handing me a nasty look.

"Yes you have. I can feel the taint about you," I said. "You've murdered by your own hand. The six-hundred-million, you murdered with a few words. The entire planet of Trell, blown to bits because of a few Alliance credits."

"Trell?" Well, somebody hadn't gotten the memo.

"Yes. All gone," I wave a hand. "I can give you the news-vids if you want—the journalists are still talking to the few people who were off-world at the time—they have no homes to go to now," I pointed out. "A few other worlds have offered assistance, but it won't ever be the same."

"But I was—my family—I," Pearlina was about to crumble. She was Trellian—I'd known it the moment I'd scented her.

"Dead now," I said. "Did you think Black Mist wouldn't hedge their bets when you handed information to them? If I hadn't been called away, I'd have been there too. Oh, you might have achieved your objective with my death, but honestly, after Kifirin got through with you, a teacup would be much too big to hold what was left of your remains."

"Kifirin," Pearlina snorted, turning her head away from me.

"I am allowed to protect my mate," Kifirin appeared, blowing heavy smoke. "I would kill you now, but my mate wishes to speak with you first."

"I've already told the others everything I can."

"But you haven't told me everything," I said. "Oh, I know somebody prevents you from saying where Black Mist is quartered. We'll move past that. When was the last time

Chapter 14

you saw him—the vampire who created Black Mist?" Pearlina's eyes went wide—I'd hit the mark.

"Eleven moon turns ago." The answer came grudgingly—I'd placed compulsion with the question. Now, all it took was asking the right questions to get around her other compulsion.

Somehow, the Black Mist asshole had locked her up, preventing Gavin and the others from getting information on him or his organization. It might be a combination of compulsion and wizardry, but more than likely it was le'meruh. I was doing my best to skirt around it.

Le'meruh was unbreakable compulsion—only the one who placed it could remove it. The only other way to kill it was to kill the one who held it.

"What kinds of foods did they serve there that you liked? Any kind of fruit you were partial to?" Every world had its ethnic foods. I was gambling on this, along with a few other clues Pearlina might give me.

"They serve a grassberry dessert, with cream. I liked that after getting the hind sandwiches from the cart outside." Well, it was one of the few planets that served deer as a regular meal.

"What color was the brick on the building nearest the cart?"

"Wasn't brick. Gray stone."

"Did you wear a coat?"

"Too hot."

Norian had shown up by this time, Lendill right behind him. Lendill pulled his comp-vid out and recorded Pearlina's responses as soon as he arrived.

Blood Redemption

"Does he feed from children or adults?" It was just a question. I wasn't really expecting an answer—most vampires hid this from those like Pearlina.

"He likes children." Pearlina actually shuddered.

"He kills them when he feeds?" I wanted to gag, but I kept going anyway.

"Usually. I saw him feed from a twelve-year-turn twice before she died. He likes to hear their screams. "

"Has he fed from you?"

"No—too old."

"You came here to get bitten by a vampire. Didn't you?" I had a feeling about her and I wasn't wrong, as it turned out.

"I volunteered after I found out that I'd get—you know—every time. The ones here don't withhold it, like *he* does." Norian lifted an eyebrow at Pearlina's admission.

Come on, Norian—vampires can give a climax with the bite, I sent.

And you never bit me?

Norian, I'm questioning the prisoner.

Sorry, breah-mul.

"Your favorite fruits or vegetables they grow there?" I went on.

"I love the coral fruit," Pearlina said. "Can I get some for my last meal?"

"If you tell me what you know about Solar Red," I promised.

"Those fools. They think they own Black Mist. Black Mist only uses them to clear the way for their own purposes."

"Where do they come from? Solar Red? Are they close to Black Mist?"

"In our laps, now," Pearlina laughed. "They bring the young ones for the meals."

Chapter 14

"How convenient," I snapped angrily.

"It is, isn't it?" Pearlina laughed again. "Like a buffet." That had me jerking my head toward Norian.

Norian—Black Mist is in the dungeon of Solar Red Headquarters!

But where? We have to know where!

Isn't Lendill working on this? We have deer sandwiches, coral fruit, grassberry dessert with cream. Come on, that has to give us something.

Seventeen worlds have that as a regular offering, Lendill sent to both of us.

Then we have seventeen worlds to look at. Before, we had nearly five hundred.

That narrows it down, Lissa, but even with one world, it's like looking for the pin in the hayfield. Norian wasn't budging a micrometer on this.

Come on, Nori. Missing children. Warlocks or wizards going in and out. Vampires, too—I'm sure he has more of them. Lion snake shapeshifters, possibly reptanoids with funny eyes—gotten any hits on where those we found traveled to and from?

Traced them to several worlds. Not one in particular, Norian was mentally grumpy.

Then the warlocks or wizards were transporting them, I returned. *Let's ask Pearlina.*

"Pearlina, for coral fruit and a grassberry dessert, were the vampire's warlocks taking the lion snakes far to send them out for assassinations?"

"I hated them; their eyes weren't natural," Pearlina snapped. "Zellar didn't like them either. He only took them two or three light-years distance. He said he couldn't stand taking them farther than that."

"How many snakes were there?"

"Only six that we sent out. The rest didn't have good speech, so we made them do other things. Clean up and such. Maybe fifteen or so when I left. Some of them died. The females all died."

Are you getting that? I sent to Lendill.

Got it, Lendill replied.

"What can you tell me about Zellar?" I asked.

"He did amazing things. The boss really liked him."

"What kind of amazing things?"

"He destroyed a starship once, when the boss asked him. Six light-years away and moving at light speed. That's amazing."

"That is amazing. Six light-years."

"Yeah. He's terrible in bed though." Lendill snickered at Pearlina's observation.

We didn't get much more from Pearlina. I didn't tell her, but the Council was scheduled to question her a final time the following morning. After that, they'd perform the execution. I was already asking Cheedas to prepare Pearlina's final meal for dinner as soon as we got above ground.

* * *

"This is getting us nowhere." Norian was so frustrated I thought he'd have a stroke. His hair was wild after he'd raked it with his hands too many times to count. We'd gone over the worlds that had the fruit, vegetables and other things Pearlina mentioned.

As Lendill said, there were seventeen of those. Then we overlaid a map of all the locations where Norian had found the reptanoids boarding ships to travel. We didn't have a good handle on comings and goings, so all of those were included. It didn't help.

Chapter 14

"Well, she did say that Zellar had a range of six light-years at least, if he hit a ship. Now, what if he hit that ship we were on that circulated Tykl?" I suggested. "Let me see if Erland can come." I sent out mindspeech. Erland was there in a blink, looking just as fresh and handsome as ever.

"Pearlina said that Zellar once hit a starship from six light-years away," I said. "Is that normal for a warlock?"

Erland stared at me. "It's not normal for any warlock. A few might do it. Not Zellar."

"But Pearlina said he did. Said he hit a moving starship from six light-years away," I insisted. "She believed it was the truth—I would have known if she were attempting a lie."

"Zellar doesn't have that kind of natural talent," Erland said.

"Even so, we have the ship that was hit while orbiting Tykl," I pointed out. "Let's pull up Tykl on a map and then draw a six light-year radius around that and see if it intersects with anything else we've gotten."

Lendill, deciding to humor me, pulled up the star map of Tykl on Norian's huge vidscreen. Then he asked the computer to make the radius drawing around it, highlighting any of the worlds we'd entered so far. There weren't any.

"Crap," I muttered. "And there isn't anything strange going on with any of the planets inside that radius?" Lendill went to take a closer look.

"Just that abnormality on Mazareal—those climate fluctuations I told you about, Norian." Lendill looked at us for a moment before wiping out the map.

"Wait. Did you say climate fluctuations?" Erland was frightened, and I'd never heard his voice sound that way. He was always smooth and confident. Not this time.

Blood Redemption

"They wanted us to check on it, but I told them to get with the Science and Technology Department," Lendill said. "We don't have time to research why their weather is hotter than it should be, or why the plants and trees are dying."

"Holy fuck," Erland borrowed one of my favorite phrases and dropped like a rock into my desk chair.

* * *

Wylend was in my office fretting, Norian was on the communicator with Ildevar Wyyld, Lendill was on the communicator with the RAA—Regular Alliance Army, and also speaking with the Governor of Mazareal. Things didn't look so good. If Erland and Wylend were correct, then Zellar had turned to the blackest of wizardry to do what he'd done for Black Mist—he'd tapped into the energy at the core of the planet and drained it to enhance his power.

According to Erland and Wylend, once the process started, the remaining energy would drain away from the planet at an accelerated rate with nothing to stop it. Mazareal was gasping its last.

That's why Black Mist had gone looking at Darthin—Zellar was about to run out of his power source. Wylend seemed to think that Mazareal might have ten years left—if that much. Then everything would die.

Unless the population could find another home, the swift death of Trell would look like a kindness by comparison. Zellar's draining of Mazareal's core also told me how Black Mist had blocked me from finding them when I *Looked*—so much power in a warlock's hands had accomplished that feat for them.

"But where could they be on Mazareal? Pearlina said a gray stone building, with a basement or dungeon, obviously—we've got vampires plus Solar Red, missing

Chapter 14

children, a sandwich cart outside, reptanoids and it was hot eleven moon turns ago." I wanted to rake my hands through my hair, but it would look so much worse than Norian's if I did that.

"We're looking, deah-mul," Norian muttered as he and Lendill went through city after city on Mazareal, trying to match everything up. "Why don't you go the kitchen and find something to drink? You look worn out."

"Fine." I walked out of Norian's office, heading for the kitchen. It was late—Norian had sent for sandwiches ages ago and we'd eaten those as we researched locations and argued. I was thirsty, that much was certainly true. I was digging around in the cold keeper and pulling out a bottle of fruit juice when he walked in.

He looked as if I could reach out and touch him, though I knew I couldn't. He smiled at me; something that I hadn't seen very often from him over the years. It twisted my heart.

"Lissa, they sent me back for only a little while," he said.

"I know." I looked up at Rolfe's square jaw and larger than life features.

"I didn't want you to suffer. Didn't think that you would, actually," he said.

"Honey, I love you. How could it be otherwise?"

"I didn't expect Giff to do what she did."

"I know that too."

"They tell me that Giff, well, it wasn't supposed to turn out like that, so they'll keep her for a while." Rolfe shrugged his wide shoulders. "And it won't be the same, ever again."

"Does that upset you?" I looked up at him.

"No, that's not a problem for me where I am."

"I understand," I nodded slightly. I was almost afraid to blink—afraid that he'd disappear.

Blood Redemption

"I brought something for you," Rolfe was smiling again. I didn't understand; he couldn't carry anything from where he'd come. In fact, I could see through him now; he was fading away from me already.

"What's that, honey?"

"Libadia." Rolfe vanished before my eyes.

* * *

While carrying my juice back to Norian's office, I went over and over what Rolfe had said. What did he mean? I had no idea. I had to go *Looking* eventually to see that the word he'd given me was Greek—it meant meadows.

When I walked inside my study, Norian and Lendill were still no closer to our goal than they'd been when I left. I sat and listened while they bounced ideas off one another, still going through lists and lists of cities, towns and villages on Mazareal.

Erland came to sit beside me as he yawned. It was likely we wouldn't puzzle this out before daybreak, the way things were going. Wylend had gone home while I'd been gone. I didn't blame him—if I weren't personally involved in this, I might go looking for my bed, too.

"I saw Rolfe," I leaned against Erland.

"What?" Erland woke at my words.

"Sorry, honey, forget I said anything," I mumbled. I was nearly asleep when Lendill's voice penetrated my brain.

"That's not it—that's in the middle of a poverty-stricken area. I don't know why they call it The Meadows, there's nothing green there for clicks."

* * *

Mazareal

Night had fallen on that portion of Mazareal as we prepared for our attack. "Lissa Beth, tell me you're not

296

Chapter 14

sending us on an imaginary duck hunt." Norian blew out a breath as I dressed in the black leathers Drake and Drew had gotten me for our stint on Falchan.

"Norian, you have permission to tease me unmercifully about this for the rest of our lives if I'm wrong," I said. "And we say wild goose chase where I come from. Do we need all these people?" He'd hauled in thirty ASD agents, some of whom I was sure weren't completely humanoid.

"We have to locate the building, Cheah-mul. We can't be everywhere."

"I can cover quite a bit of ground as mist," I grumped. "And take them too, if you want." Norian stopped dead in his tracks.

"How many can you take at once?" He looked at me speculatively.

"Honestly, Norian, those records you found were worthless," I snapped. "Didn't you get that information from Refizan?"

"No, I did not get that information from Refizan," he mimicked me while wiggling his hips.

"I don't wiggle my hips like that," I poked him in the chest.

"I'd like it better if you did."

"Norian, we're about to go looking for Black Mist and the head honcho for Solar Red, and you're joking around?"

"Yes. I want them dead. Orders are shoot to kill, except for Black Mist's leader. I want to question him personally."

"Honey, you're not going to take vampires out that easily. Or the warlocks. I can't imagine that the reptanoids or the shapeshifters are going to go down any faster."

"But we have these." Norian lifted a pistol from the holster he wore.

"Uh-huh." I gave him a skeptical look.

"Breah-mul, only the ASD is allowed these legally. Ranos pistols."

"Holy crap, Norian!"

"Now, tell me again how many troops you can carry."

"How many do you have?"

"Can you set us down where I say?"

"As long as you listen to what I have to say too, Norian Keef."

"I'll listen."

"Sure you will. Like every other male I know."

"Lissa Beth, are you going to argue with me for the next thirty years?"

"Norian Keef, how long do you plan to stay married to me?"

"Well, there is that," he shrugged slightly, mischief showing in his green eyes.

"Honey, do you always get this excited about things like this?"

"Most of the time."

"Great. Are you ready?"

"We all are."

Lifting thirty agents into my mist, in addition to Norian and Lendill, I went flying over the tops of buildings in what was referred to as The Meadows near Mazareal's capital city.

The area was large and overpopulated—more and more of Mazareal's residents were relocating there for various reasons, most of it having to do with failed crops, dying businesses and the economic instability that followed. The fate of the planet was affecting the fate of everything.

Chapter 14

My skin doesn't itch while I'm mist—but I feel a twitch of some kind, indicating the wrongness. I homed in on that—it was near the eastern edge of The Meadows.

Lissa Beth, are you getting something? I could feel the discomfort of Norian's thirty agents—they were ready to become corporeal again. Some of them were frightened out of their wits. I wasn't going to point that out to Norian.

On the northeast side, I sent back to Norian. Moving faster, streets and buildings blurred beneath us. Something was wrong. Something was very wrong. When I found the gray stone building Pearlina described to me, I hesitated, although Norian, who'd seen it too, was shouting at me to get inside.

If I'd been solid, my skin would have itched furiously. I rose higher, even as Norian's mental shout became louder. *Get us down there!* Norian's mindspeech hurt, it was so full of anger.

* * *

Black Mist Headquarters
"You're sure about this?" Viregruz trusted Zellar.

"Oh, yes. They're close. Very close." Zellar was smiling. He'd set up a perimeter spell around the gray stone building they'd previously occupied, and then ordered everyone moved to the warehouse across the street, leaving their former headquarters empty.

The warehouse across the street had become a temporary home and hasty preparations were made; the vampires had to have their underground accommodations built and light-sealed first. The warehouse's upper floors were currently under renovation; Viregruz planned to stay there until a new home on another world could be located.

Blood Redemption

"They've gone past the perimeter spell," Zellar nodded grimly, satisfied that the last of Mazareal's power could do this for him—that the last gasp of core power enabled his perimeter spell to detect anything that moved past it, including something obviously invisible. It worried him, though, that it *was* invisible. Until then, he'd imagined that only Viregruz held that talent. A shiver raced down Zellar's spine.

"Then set the time on the destruction spell—thirty ticks." Viregruz had a front row seat, watching through a wide window from a distance far enough that he wouldn't be affected, per Zellar's estimation. Zellar hadn't led him wrong yet. Viregruz was going to enjoy this.

Pearlina had been a true treasure. Too bad she was sentenced to die on Le-Ath Veronis. Zellar had set a spell so he'd know if particular questions were asked. Pearlina hadn't been instructed not to answer those questions—oh, no. She'd been allowed to give out the information freely, leading any enemies straight to the gray stone building and into a trap set by Zellar. Anyone who approached the former headquarters was destined to die.

Viregruz's two vampire Blood Captains stood at his back. They'd purposely not fed when they'd wakened—if there was any life left among attacking ASD agents, the vampires were set to drink and then kill.

Viregruz, too, had left orders that if the bitch queen came along, he would be allowed to kill her. He'd see how she stood against a King Vampire who had a powerful warlock at his side.

* * *

Lissa

300

Chapter 14

Lissa Beth, get us down there! Norian's mental scream had me cringing in pain. The verbal shout in my corporeal ear would have hurt less.

Norian's agents were even more restless now—they weren't used to this and most of them hadn't a clue what was going on. They could only see that they were floating somehow, with no control over anything and no idea if they'd ever be solid again.

Norian, please stop shouting; I can't hear myself think, I sent as calmly as I could.

Norian was cursing and shouting still, so I wasn't sure he'd even heard me. I didn't want to go into that building for some reason. Something was terribly, terribly wrong.

I did drop down a bit, though, to get a better look. There was no activity anywhere around it. Not even steam rose from the vents, as it did on the buildings surrounding it. I went cold. Norian was still shouting, and now Lendill was getting in on it.

* * *

Black Mist Headquarters

The enemy was so close—right on top of the gray stone building, if Zellar's estimation was correct. "You'll have your revenge in seven ticks Lord Viregruz," Zellar was as excited as he'd ever been. "Five. Four. Three. Two. One."

* * *

Lissa

Norian finally shut up the moment every window in the building below us blasted outward with a shattering of glass and a terrible boom, followed by billowing smoke and flames. I might never know if Zellar had spelled the blast well enough so the building would remain standing with the roof partially intact, but that's what happened.

301

Blood Redemption

Norian's agents would have been killed in that blast—no doubt about that—and I wasn't even sure I could have gathered Norian and Lendill up in time if I'd suspected it was coming.

Not if we'd gone down there, as Norian wanted us to. But this meant that Zellar, Solar Red and Black Mist had relocated. They'd set this up as a trap. No doubt, I'd been stupid enough to swallow everything Pearlina told me without questioning it or being suspicious over how easily it had come.

Lissa Beth? Norian's voice was small and quiet as I watched the building burn its contents below us.

Norian, they set a trap for us. It almost worked.

* * *

Black Mist Headquarters

"Zellar, you are a warlock among warlocks." Viregruz stood and nodded respectfully at his strongest wizard. "Please inform Tetsurna Prylvis that our adversary has been neutralized. Invite him up for a glass of wine while we watch our enemies burn." Viregruz was as gleeful as he might ever be.

Zellar wasn't about to go himself—he snapped a finger and a flunky came running. "You heard Lord Viregruz—what are you waiting for? Bring the Lord of Solar Red immediately, and several bottles of wine. We wish to celebrate the downfall of our common enemy," Zellar demanded, turning back to watch the fire through the broken windows across the street.

He had his doubts, however. All he could see was fire, and his talent had never been sufficient to allow him to see through flames. Other warlocks could do it, but when he'd

Chapter 14

been at his lessons more than two thousand years earlier, he'd never mastered the ability.

That, plus a few other failed lessons had kept him out of King Wylend's handpicked warlock elite. Zellar clenched his hands. He had an alternate strategy in mind, just in case things didn't go as planned. Perhaps it was time to put that plan into action.

* * *

Lissa

Settling everyone atop a tall building across the street from the burning structure, I sighed and stared at what could have been our deaths. Shaky breaths were drawn all around me as thirty agents checked their bodies over, making sure they were still intact. Their weapons and gear came next. Norian came to stand beside me.

"Lissa Beth, I want you to remind me next time that it's a damn good thing you don't listen to a single thing I say."

"Or yell," I muttered.

"Or yell," he echoed, turning to watch the black smoke across the street billow upward, blocking off any view of the night sky. I wasn't surprised that nobody had come to gawk, even—Zellar, Solar Red and Black Mist had likely made everyone afraid to come near.

"Well, where do you think they are?" Lendill came to stand on my other side.

"No idea," Norian replied. That's when I heard the noise.

* * *

Black Mist Headquarters

Zellar was clapped on the back—hard—by Tetsurna Prylvis, the exalted leader of Solar Red. Tetsurna Prylvis was well over six feet in height and his girth was enormous.

303

Blood Redemption

Zellar was repulsed by Prylvis' penchant for dining on humanoid flesh, but he hid his distaste well. Prylvis was laughing, too—a booming sound that Zellar imagined might rattle windows and shake buildings. Zellar didn't care. He had other things on his mind.

"Lord Viregruz, Lord Prylvis, I think I should order a celebration," Zellar said smoothly, bowing to Black Mist and Solar Red. "If you will excuse me, I shall go and ask for preparations to begin."

"Tell the cooks I want my favorite," Prylvis shouted. Prylvis knew not to slap Viregruz on the back; the Head of Black Mist would kill him swiftly for even the slightest of touches.

"I'll inform your cooks," Zellar bowed to Prylvis again and turned to go. He walked sedately across the floor of the upper room, opened the door to the fire escape and the bare steps leading downward, shutting the door quietly behind him. He walked carefully down until he was sure Viregruz could no longer hear. Then he began to run.

* * *

Lissa

"Lissa Beth?" Norian looked at me in concern.

"Norian, do you hear that?" I hissed. He didn't, but a werewolf ASD agent did.

"Someone's laughing," the agent came up beside Norian.

"Now why would someone be laughing?" Norian's forehead creased in a frown.

"Because they think we're dead," I whispered. "Norian, they're here. They wanted a front-row seat when they took us down. I know you're not ready to go back to mist," I turned and announced quietly to Norian's agents, "but this will be a shorter trip, I promise."

Chapter 14

Black Mist Headquarters

"Shall we take our old building back, my friend, or keep this one instead?" Prylvis turned toward Viregruz.

"I think we should leave Mazareal."

"But we haven't found anything suitable," Prylvis pointed out.

"Zellar thinks this is important," Viregruz countered. "I'm inclined to listen to my wizard."

"Our people are coming to join us, Lord." Prylvis was correct—Zellar had sent everyone in the building upstairs to, in his words, *view the victory.*

"I did not give permission," Viregruz snapped. One of his Blood Captains stepped forward, ready to take any order from Viregruz. He would send the rabble downstairs quickly if that were Viregruz's wish. Viregruz was prepared to issue the command when pandemonium erupted.

* * *

"Stupid, spelled locks," Zellar hadn't placed the spell on this lock; one of the others had and it could take ticks to sort it out and get it opened. Eight of Viregruz's lion snake shapeshifters were inside the spelled cage.

These weren't Viregruz's assassin snakes—those were upstairs now, most likely getting shouted at by Viregruz's Blood Captains. Zellar only needed a little more time. The lock fell to the floor with a thunk, bringing a surprised gasp of pleasure to Zellar.

"Farzi!" Zellar commanded, "Bring your people out. I have something for you to do."

A shapeshifter stood in the dim light. Farzi and his brothers had been caged in the warehouse basement and only allowed out if something needed to be cleaned or repaired. They were not happy with their situation, but then they'd not been happy all their lives. They were created to serve and that's what they did.

"We will come." Farzi nodded to his brothers. All of them were standing quickly. They had no desire to bear the lash of Zellar's anger. Farzi led his brothers from the cage.

Zellar motioned for them to gather closer—he needed them to be as near to him as he could get them. Zellar cringed when the noise of weapons fire sounded from the upper floors.

* * *

Lissa

If Norian wanted the enemy together in order to attack all of them at once, he was getting his wish. Norian didn't have any vampires in the ASD, except for me. If we lived over this, I might have to rectify that.

The two werewolves he had were trying to do battle with older, stronger vampires. Six of them. Two wizards were hurling blasts at us. I was thankful they didn't have better aim—wherever those blasts hit, holes were knocked into thick stone walls.

The noise was debilitating, too. Shouting and cursing echoed through the building—even as I watched a vampire run past me screaming, flames consuming him as he ran.

I misted toward one of the older vampires, removing his head with a sweeping slash of my claws. Norian and Lendill were killing with their ranos pistols—those things were splattering anything they hit.

Some of Norian's agents had gone down—two of the vampires were killing them as quickly as they could. The floor was slippery with blood already and others were losing their footing.

Chapter 14

I went after the vampires as mist, taking heads swiftly. A large man who had many others surrounding him was hit in the head by one of Lendill's shots—the man was taller than his guards. His head exploded, sending his guards scattering like pigeons.

"Norian!" I shouted—four lion snake shapeshifters had appeared and they were viciously biting anything that came near—friend and enemy alike.

Norian turned in my direction when I shouted, barely avoiding decapitation by another vampire who had appeared out of nothing—Black Mist's misters had arrived. I went after them as mist.

The blackest of purple-blacks—that's how they appeared to me. Using a small amount of power, I forced them back to corporeality. The moment they were solid, they died.

Norian was firing at lion snakes. Lendill, too, had started firing at the shapeshifters. A large window in the side of the building was blown out by gunfire and three of Norian's agents were hurled through the opening. I had less than a second to react. Should I save them or keep fighting?

* * *

Dungeon, Black Mist Headquarters

"I not have my tools," one of Farzi's brothers whimpered as he followed Zellar and his brothers.

"Shut up or I'll kill you," Zellar snarled. The shapeshifter hushed quickly. Zellar was leading them toward a side door that led to the street between buildings. The noise was loud enough from the upper floor that Zellar knew all the building's inhabitants were engaged.

He needed to get as far away as he could—he didn't want to risk Viregruz's wrath or allow any remaining warlocks to feel his power signature when he folded the shapeshifters away. Zellar had plans, and they no longer included Black Mist or Solar Red.

* * *

Lissa

My geometry classes always taught me that the shortest distance between two points is a straight line. Misting in a straight line would have taken too much time and Norian's agents would have died.

Instead, I folded space, disappearing from point A and reappearing at point B, with barely enough time to keep three operatives from splattering against the brick streets six stories below. Capturing them as mist, I settled them onto the street.

"We're all right," one nodded, nervously lifting his weapon. I knew what that weapon was—Norian had equipped three of his people with the same. Flame throwers. They were the weapon of choice to combat vampires, and probably the reason this man had survived. Many of Norian's people had gotten decapitated before I could get to all the vampires.

"Good," I nodded at the agent's words. "Ready to go back?" I was ready to fold them back anyway when movement caught my eye. In the darkness of the smoke-filled night, most humanoids would have missed it. I was vampire and could see more than well enough in the dark.

"Get down," I hissed, pulling the man down. His two companions dropped beside us. I watched—more movement. The three agents didn't see what I did. I pulled the flamethrower away from Norian's agent. If it were vampire, it was about to be hit. What appeared instead shocked me.

A man stole through the shadows, followed by eight others. While my eyesight is good, I'm not sure I would have

Chapter 14

suspected if Norian hadn't shown me the vid-photos. These men were all shorter than the man they followed; Just as the reptanoids on Norian's vid-recordings had been. Someone was leading reptanoids away from the battle. I wondered who it might be.

"Stop there!" I shouted, rising and pointing the flamethrower. I barely had time to fire the thing before all nine disappeared before my eyes.

Shouting and cursing, I folded all three agents back to the battle. Tossing the flamethrower to the agent I'd borrowed it from, I went back to work, removing heads. Thankfully, Norian and Lendill were still alive, although there were only six of the thirty ASD agents remaining. Three of those were the ones I'd saved. I kicked things into a higher gear.

Chapter 15

Mazareal

Lissa

"Is that all of them?" Norian had called in extra people from somewhere. Honestly, the man has more resources than anyone I'd ever seen before. Bodies were quickly separated into different areas, friends on one side, enemies on the other.

"Yes," I said aloud. *No*, I sent mentally.

What is it? Norian returned. Aloud he said, "Well, let's get them loaded up, then. Lendill, can you take care of that for me?" Lendill nodded at Norian's question and went to issue orders.

There's one left, I informed Norian as I toed a head toward a body. The body belonged to an enemy—I wouldn't have treated any of Norian's people that way.

Blood Redemption

The floors beneath out feet were slick with blood, gore and vampire ash. Wizard blasts had knocked out an entire wall—the one surrounding the windows. The wizards had died too.

I made a mental note to contact Erland—just to see if any of them were on Wylend's list of wanted warlocks.

Where? Norian's question filtered into my mind.

Rafters, I replied. *Shapeshifter*, I added. What I didn't say after that was that it was also vampire. Amid all the scents inside the room, there was only one that bore the signature of Dark Elemaiya.

I figured this was how Black Mist had survived for so long—it was headed by a shapeshifting vampire who could likely mist as well—that's where the Black Mist name had originated.

They say that every person has an opposite. I'd found mine. There was a good chance that this one was a King Vampire, a thought I found frightening. And he held le'meruh—something I didn't have.

What are you going to do, Lissa Beth? Norian signed off on an assistant's comp-vid.

"Nori, I want to wash my hands. Do you think there's a bathroom here somewhere?" I spoke aloud. Norian would know what I was about.

"Has to be. Try downstairs." Norian nodded toward the fire escape stairway.

"I'll be back," I said and walked through the door.

* * *

Le-Ath Veronis

Cheedas smacked a bowl of popcorn down in front of Drake and Drew. "My little girl off doing things like that? You should not be enjoying this," Cheedas muttered, moving

Chapter 15

things around on the island while Drake, Drew, Gavin, Tony and nearly all of Lissa's mates watched the news-vid from Mazareal.

A reporter was standing in front of a burned-out building, saying it was the former headquarters for Black Mist and Solar Red. Images of bagged bodies being hauled from a building across the street were shown in an inset.

"Rumor has it that at least sixty ASD agents were killed while taking down the enemy," the female reporter continued.

"Just like always—exaggerate and then apologize later," Tony tossed a popcorn kernel toward the screen.

"You'd know about that," Drake nodded to the former Director of the Joint NSA and Homeland Security Department.

"They'll have to apologize quickly, Mazareal is dying." Karzac sat down heavily to watch the vid. "Have we seen anything of Lissa yet?"

"Not yet," Gavin growled. He was angry. Garde was also angry, as evidenced by the curls of smoke drifting from his nostrils.

"Wait, look!" Rigo had caught sight of something. All of them focused where Rigo's finger pointed.

* * *

Mazareal

Lissa

My advantage over my opponent was that I could see him while he was mist, but he couldn't see me. Not while he was still a falcon, anyway. It was genius, actually. Who might suspect a bird sitting in the rafters of assassination sites from one end of the universes to the other?

313

Blood Redemption

Even if anyone had seen the bird, they'd have thought nothing of it, more than likely. Now, all I had to do was decide what to do with my quarry when I grabbed him and he turned back to vampire and started fighting.

Mist always works. It had never failed me—not even once. When I gathered our homicidal falcon into my mist, he was held there in a sort of stasis, just as anyone else would be.

Oh, he could still see and experience emotions—fear being the most important one—but he couldn't act on that fear until I let him go again. A power bubble is what I formed on the streets of The Meadows, the poverty-stricken portion of a city that could no longer boast a sandwich cart outside Black Mist headquarters.

The founder of Black Mist was left a prisoner inside the power bubble while I misted through its edges, coming back to myself just outside its perimeter.

The falcon turned, just as I imagined he might, hitting the inner wall of the bubble with vampiric force. The bubble held. He was shouting at me while I stared at him, my arms crossed tightly over my chest. Norian and Lendill came to flank me.

"Who do we have here?" Norian asked.

"Unless I miss my guess, he's the one who created Black Mist," I replied casually. Our prisoner, whose hearing was just as sharp as any vampire's, heard clearly.

"I'll kill you!" he shouted. "You have no cage, no cell, no dungeon that can hold me!" He pounded again on the wall of the bubble. Well, at least the bubble was holding him. For the moment.

"What's your name?" I asked. Well, we still didn't know that. Did we?

Chapter 15

"I won't tell you, you fucking bitch. I'll kill you. I'll shred your skin and feed your blood to dogs!"

"He looks like a teenager," Lendill muttered.

"Oh, he's older than that," I said. "Around thirty-six hundred, unless I miss my guess."

I saw the media trying to get close to us, their cameras trained in our direction, but Norian's people and the local constabulary were holding them back. It didn't keep zoom lenses from invading the space, however, or spy-mics from hearing everything that was said. Norian might have to confiscate those recordings later, but this was going out live to the Alliance.

"What made you create Black Mist?" Norian asked. "I have to admit, it was a work of genius. I've never met anyone who could even come close to this." Norian was playing on this guy's vanity.

"I am powerful," the vampire said instead. "You have no idea what you're fucking with, here."

I had an answer ready for that, but Norian gripped my wrist in his hand. I held my words back. "After all," Norian continued, "we've been chasing you for a very long time. You've stayed out of reach every time. Offered us false trails, phony leads and bogus information. I was beginning to think you might be a god or something, you'd become so powerful. Every Alliance citizen lives in fear of Black Mist. No King, Queen, Governor or politician feels safe if you target them. Honestly, that's quite a resume you've built for yourself. Still don't want to tell us your name?"

The vampire continued to ignore Norian. Instead, he came to stand right in front of me, pressing his nose against the inside wall of the bubble. "I will drink you dry," he hissed. "When I escape, and I assure you that I will, I will make your final moments terrifying and painful. You will wish you'd never heard of me, little pretender. You think you're a Queen Vampire? My sire told me they were weak. That any male could make them do their bidding, just by giving them sex with the bite."

"You fucked up, short-sighted, pea-brained, tiny-dicked, poor excuse for a worm," I pressed my nose against the opposite side of the bubble. "If I wanted to kill you swiftly, I would have done it already. Who do you think is holding this bubble around you, shit for brains? If I want to know your name, all I have to do is pull it out of your head, *Viregruz*," I snapped. "You think I can't smell Dark Elemaiya from a mile away, you pathetic moron?"

Viregruz's head snapped back when I said his name. It didn't mean anything to Norian, but then the ASD didn't have any information at all on Black Mist's founder.

"Go ahead," Viregruz taunted, turning his back on us. "Lock me up. See how long you can keep me. I promise to kill all of you slowly, very soon."

"Gee, that's too bad," I retorted. "Too bad you'll never get the chance." Viregruz's back was still turned to us. Too bad *he* didn't see the first fingers of sunlight reaching through The Meadows as a result.

* * *

Le-Ath Veronis

Karzac was the only one still eating popcorn while watching the vampire who created Black Mist fry on live Alliance television. Viregruz's shrieks could be heard clearly as he screamed and fell, his skin blackening and melting in the early morning light on Mazareal.

Gavin, Tony, Rigo, Aryn and Roff all stared in horror as they watched a vampire die in sunlight.

Chapter 15

Mazareal

Lissa

"Lissa Beth, tell me you didn't know how close the dawn was," Norian hissed as he gripped my arm and hauled me toward a waiting hovercar.

"Norian, there are two things every vampire knows," I said, trotting alongside him and then climbing into the vehicle ahead of him. Norian shut the door and barked for the driver to take us away.

"One," I continued, "is that we will always know when night falls." I settled myself against the padded seat, attempting to get comfortable after an extremely long night. "The other thing," I added, "is that unless it is blocked with power somehow, a vampire will always know when dawn approaches."

I'd answered Norian's second, unvoiced question with my first answer. He'd wanted to question Viregruz. I wanted him dead. Norian might have thought the ASD could keep the Black Mist creator locked up—I knew better.

Viregruz could mist through walls, just as I could. His mistake had been in never trying. If I hadn't created the bubble out of the power I now held as Kifirin's equal, I wouldn't have been able to hold him, either.

Viregruz wanted to stay to watch what we did and identify targets for the new army of Black Mist assassins he intended to build. I'd fooled him temporarily and grabbed him unaware.

I'd also blocked his senses with my shield and he hadn't suspected that dawn was so close. His death in the sun was final and irrevocable. The entire Alliance, more than likely, had just watched him die via live news-vids.

Blood Redemption

* * *

Le-Ath Veronis
Lissa

Norian hasn't spoken to me for six months. I feel a tiny hole in my heart as a result. Even if I'd told him what I knew about Viregruz, he wouldn't have listened. It will take time for Norian to come back to me, but he will. Even now, I watch him when he comes to dinner. He watches me when he thinks I don't know.

The other thing that happened after Black Mist and Solar Red died is this—one spring day, when the weather was warm and the comesuli farmers were out planting their early crops, Poradina went into labor.

I felt inadequate, somehow; another woman was experiencing pain for me, so I might have a child. Five hours later, Rylend Davan Morphis came into the world, shaking his tiny fists and crying out his displeasure to the world.

Six days later, Evaline's labor commenced and Torevik Rolfe Rath joined my growing family. I often wept when I held my babies, even as Erland and Garde looked on. This is a gift beyond price for me, and they are growing so quickly.

Shadow arrived a day after Tory's birth, going to his knees before me while I fed Ry by bottle. "Lissa, tell me you will do what you said before—that we can have a child together like this." His dark head rested against my knee. I reached out and touched his face.

"Shadow," I brushed black hair away from his forehead, "I will gladly have a child with you. I've asked the Larentii. The Wise Ones have seen our daughter already, my love."

* * *

Larentii Archives
"I have something for you."

318

Chapter 15

Nefrigar, Chief of the Larentii Archivists, hid his surprise. Only a handful might approach the Larentii homeworld who weren't Larentii. The planet was heavily shielded and protected against invasion by other races. Only a handful of non-Larentii knew its location.

Nefrigar, standing at a cubicle table inside the Larentii Archives, had been poring over newly acquired records from a long-dead world. The ancient Larentii now blinked at his unexpected visitor.

"Ah, I should have known," Nefrigar smiled as recognition dawned. "Welcome to the Larentii Archives, Mighty Hand." Nefrigar bowed respectfully.

"I've brought copies of Lissa's diaries," The Mighty Hand offered a box of records to Nefrigar. "I've added to them somewhat—a few paragraphs here and there, just to explain what was going on with others around her and to complete the history."

"We do not mind that here," Nefrigar nodded. "Information is welcome in every form."

"That's why I've brought it to you—she has considered destroying these at one time or another. Much of the story is painful to her."

"I understand that; Connegar and Reemagar have supplied parts of her history already. It is a sad tale, at times."

"Yes, it is certainly that," The Mighty Hand agreed. "I will bring you more in the future, on one who is not yet born." He smiled at Nefrigar and disappeared.

Blood Redemption

Epilogue

Campiaa

"No, I already have enough warlocks on my payroll, although I appreciate the offer," Arvil San Gerxon held back a grimace as he gazed at Zellar.

The left side of the warlock's face was severely burned, leaving one eye closed forever. It was a wound received during Zellar's escape from Mazareal, Arvil realized.

Arvil could have used another warlock, but Zellar was actively hunted by the ASD for his association with Black Mist. Arvil didn't need that target painted on his own back.

"I have what I need with these," Arvil jerked his head toward the eight shapeshifters Zellar had offered the gambling magnate and crime kingpin from Campiaa. "But I hear Cloudsong is looking to hire."

Farzi and his brothers stood helplessly by as money changed hands.

The End

* * *

Lissa's story, as well as that of Toff and Lissa's children, will continue in
Blood Reunion (Blood Destiny #10)